Mile Marker 312
Purgatory 3 Miles

by

W.E. Ramber

Library of Congress Control Number: 2026911882

ISBN:
eBook: 979-8-90224-289-5
Paperback: 979-8-90224-290-1
Hardback: 979-8-90224-291-8

Published by:
Authors Publishing House
1178 Broadway, 3rd Floor
New York, NY 10001, USA
Main Line: (855) 624-0155
Email: support@authorspublishinghouse.com

Table of Contents

It's Out There

"For now, we see through a glass, darkly; but then face to face: now I know in part; but then shall I know even as also I am known..."
1 Corinthians 12, KJV.

The Californian sun was slowly sinking into the sea. He never grew tired of watching a good sunset, whether it was here or in the Arizona desert; they never failed to make his day, another end to a beautiful day in southern California. There was that old feeling, that this had all been done before. He could not quite shake it. It was turning into one of those dreadful feelings he would get as a kid before something happened. Usually, it was something bad that would happen, so he was not enjoying the feeling right now. It had been a long time since he felt this way; he better be careful. He was thinking about a day gone by, not so long ago. A day that stands still in his mind, Anna sat in the morning sunlight out on the deck, looking at the Dragoon mountains east of Tombstone. The day was crisp and cool on that spring morning. They lived in an old house near Fremont Street. It had been built with care and skill back in 1955, but by the time they bought it, the house was just another casualty of the current economy. In need of repair and an overhaul, the house sold cheap, but the real work was yet to come. A labor of love for the next two years until all the blood, sweat, and tears paid off in what was to be their new home. Rumor had it that the house had been made from the old barracks that the Buffalo Soldiers occupied at Fort Huachuca, located in Sierra Vista. It was made entirely out of old-growth redwood and put together with love. Nobody knew if this was true, but it made for a good story, and redwood was sold from the base back in 1955 when the new barracks were constructed.

What was it she said? Oh yeah, "It's out there," as he looked off in the distance to the area where Cochise and his people held so long ago. "What's out there?" He thought, "What are you talking about? Is it out there, and what is it?" he said as he looked at her and took in the moment for what it was, another great morning living in the most famous western town in the world. "It's not out there where I'm looking, but speaking in a figurative manner, it is waiting out there. It's what is waiting out there someday." Still not sure of what she meant, he inquired again, "Someday when?" he replied, not sure where this was leading. She explained. "We all have our fate or destiny to face in this world, and it's out there, that's all I'm saying. You have yours, and I have mine. We may rush to it blindly or take our sweet time, but either way, we will be there the day the Lord has determined. It's out there…" Anna always had a different take on life than John; she would be the one to point out the good in things before the bad. He was at once reminded of the old proverb "Death in the marketplace." It goes like this: "A wealthy merchant in Baghdad sends his servant to the marketplace for provisions. Shortly, the servant comes home white and trembling and tells him that in the marketplace he was jostled by a woman, whom he recognized as Death, and she made a threatening gesture. Borrowing the merchant's horse, he flees at top speed to Samarra, a distance of about 75 miles, where he believes Death will not find him. The merchant then goes to the marketplace and finds Death and asks why she made the threatening gesture. She replies, "That was not a threatening gesture, it was only a start of surprise. I was astonished to see him in Baghdad, for I had an appointment with him tonight in Samarra." The moral of the story is you cannot outrun Death. It's out there.

So why was he thinking of this now as the waves rolled in along the Santa Monica coastline? The man looked out into the sea as the waves rolled in, just another Sunday at the beach. The people on the shoreline were having fun going about their day in Southern California. He looked down the beach toward the Venice Beach area and imagined how it looked back in 1948 when his Grandparents lived in an old, run-down house on Grand Avenue, and his dad roamed these very shores as a teenager while they built their home. That was so long ago, and most of those people are no longer here, but some memories of that time remain. Looking now at the current Santa Monica beach, he saw an ordinary day, but there seemed to be an undercurrent of events happening here.

He always saw what others couldn't or wouldn't see. He saw beyond the frail existence of humanity and into the great beyond; he had always had this talent for better or worse. He had been born here, but it was far from home. Having traveled the world and moved so many times, he loved this place and the memories that it held, but those were different times. Most of the people he grew up with in this place were either dead or gone to some other place. His family, whom he loved to be around, and friends he would never see again. Time could be so cruel when you only have memories to guide you through old haunts and childhood moments. It was late July, and the beach was packed with all the people coming and going; some were tourists, others were locals. He would be considered neither. He needed to get back on the road to Arizona soon. The place he called home for the last 20 years. The sea called him home again, if only for the weekend. He had lived in Arizona for 20 years, but he still got the same old feeling when he sat on the shore and looked at the ocean. It was in him, like his DNA, the old call of the wild back to the sea. Whenever he could see or smell the ocean, a weird, wild feeling overtook him, like a sense of freedom and abandonment of normality. He did his best to suppress these thoughts and feelings, but old ways die hard.

The pier looked inviting, and it was full of people having a great time. He had grown up here from a young boy playing on the merry-go-round to a teenager with his friends at night in the penny arcade. So many times, on the weekend, they would spend hours in that place. The pier was different back then, less crowded and fewer tourists. It was like he had it to himself when he was young. The games have changed, but it was still there, full of kids.

As a young boy, he would go to Pacific Ocean Park, a huge amusement park that sat south of the Santa Monica pier. They would go on the rides and walk around and look at the people, then go home to the old house in Venice that his dad called "The Fort". That was the house his Grandparents and everyone related to them built for three long years. Dad always told him that the Fort took his youth away. Pacific Ocean Park was later torn down in the early 70's to make way for condos and yuppie shops. The coast looked empty without it, but the memory remained. He walked over to the pier to check out Bubba Gump's store; Anna always wanted a T-shirt from here, so he got her a nice one that she would later modify and make into a woman's riding shirt when she was out on her Harley. They rode many miles together on the back roads of Arizona. You never know a place until you see it on a motorcycle with the wind in your face and the smell of the country around you.

The long drive ahead of him weighed heavily on his mind. Looking into the storefront window, he saw his own reflection but barely recognized the man he had become, with dark hair and tints of gray running through it. He had a trimmed beard and blue jeans on, a Laughlin Rally Tee shirt on that had a picture of the grim reaper with aces and eights, the proverbial "Dead Man's hand" that Wild Bill Hickok was dealt when he got shot in the back of the head in Deadwood, South Dakota. The years had been gracious on him, but they still took their toll. He thought to himself, "If only I were home now, I would be sitting on my deck talking to Anna right at this moment instead of driving back all night. We would be having a cold ice tea watching the desert grow dark under a summer sky." He didn't like to drive at night; his doctor told him he had spatial driving disorientation. It just meant he didn't do well at night. He was ok until about 3 am, then the feeling of fatigue and weariness would overtake him. Tonight, he would drink a bunch of Redbull's. He had come to Los Angeles for a US Naval ship reunion in Long Beach at the Convention Center. He had been stationed there a couple of times while in the service, so it was time to see some old friends. Man, how we have all aged; he didn't think he had grown that old until he was around his old shipmates. Time waits for no man.

Kind of ironic to live in Tombstone after living in all of those big cities, he was a country boy at heart. Grandpa taught him how to drive the old John Deere tractor and plant orchards. Grandma taught him how to kill a chicken and pluck it properly, something that he has not needed to do since that day. Everybody should listen to some Waylon and Willie now and then just to clear out the voices in their heads. It's always good to know stuff. They were simple, honest people who taught him a lot about life and then some. How did he get so far away? Venice Beach was his old stomping ground, as well as Long Beach, San Diego, and parts in between, throw Hawaii in there, and that's pretty much his upbringing. How does one end up in a desert 571 miles away from his childhood place of birth? He thought he would always live by the beach, but Tombstone is not the beach, and there is a whole lot of nothing in between here and there.

The man's name was John Pezdel. He was 49 years old and dreaded becoming 50. Arizona had been his home for the last 20 years, and he knew of no other place he would like to be. He was born under a bad sign, the sign of Scorpio, which was the sign of death. All Saints' Day was when he was born, just missing Halloween by 10 minutes. He didn't think his birthday was special, just another day after trick or treat. He got to have two good days in a row. Sometimes he would get so much candy that the next day the birthday cake didn't taste so sweet. Mom used to tell him, "John, I was trying to have you on Halloween, but you weren't having any of it, you waited until after midnight, then you just came out all of a sudden like you were in some kind of hurry." With five kids to raise and John being the middle child, there wasn't a lot of time to spend with each one, and work outside the home also. She did her best, given the circumstances.

The clock ticked away the minutes as the sun was gone from the sky. John left the pier and walked along the sand to his parked pickup truck. Time to go. Getting out of LA was easy on a Sunday night, not much traffic on the I-10, so he made good time. He always loved leaving LA; it was nice to visit, but it wasn't home anymore. Watching the city disappear in his rearview mirror was a welcome relief. Too much time in LA made him kind of crazy. He loved California, but what had been done to it made him sick at times. Suppose the people who ruined it loved it like him, then the state would be doing well. He drove across the desert, into the night, as the air temperature grew warmer and the memories of the past disappeared. Twenty miles past Quartzsite, the monsoons were acting up. The desert sky flashed with lightning, and the washes began to flow with rainwater. "I love the monsoons," he thought. They brought the water and cooler temperatures to the hot, dry desert. Anna would tell him, "I hate the late summers in Arizona because the monsoons always cut the summer short." He disagreed, but didn't make a big deal about it. She was a true fair-weather person; she loved the sun and heat of the summer, but hated the weather that it brought to this region. She also hated the snow and any cold climate. They had lived in a cold country before, but not for long. Anna just couldn't take the temperature drop. Southern Arizona was the best place for weather if you love the desert, and they loved the desert. People have been dwelling in the deserts for thousands of years, and it comes down to this: you either love the desert, or you don't. There is no room for middle ground; everything in the desert was intended to bite, hurt, eat, or kill you. Why wouldn't you love that?

Company of the Dead

"A man who strays from the path of understanding comes to rest in the company of the Dead."
Proverbs 21:16, NIV

He awoke as if having a bad dream, looking around, trying to get his bearings. "Where am I?" he asked himself as the surrounding landscape looked so strange. Then he remembered he had stopped at the truck stop near Picacho Peak State Park. He must have been asleep for a couple of hours because it was already 2:00 am; John started up the truck and headed for Tucson. It was only about 35 miles away, and then the drive to Tombstone was another 75 miles. He drove on, thinking about his life and Anna; they had been married forever, it seemed, but it never got old. She was good for him, and she was the only woman he ever loved. With blonde hair and blue eyes, she had stunning features and an inner beauty that left you wondering what she was about. She had a few tattoos, but who didn't nowadays? They only made her that much prettier. John never thought he would end up with such a fine person, but we all get what we deserve. He got off the I-10 in Tucson for some gas at Park Ave., just a quick stop, then he would be on his way. Sometimes in life, a moment can seem like an eternity. Time just sort of hangs in that place as it does, and all movement stops. This was one of those moments. John didn't really see it coming, just a large dark shape forming beyond his peripheral vision. Like a huge leviathan coming up from the murky depths of the ocean, the form grew larger and larger until it engulfed his left side with light and dark all at once, then the moment when time stands still.

They say that your life flashes before your eyes the moment before you die. Nobody has truly returned from the dead to confirm this theory. There have just been a lot of near-death experiences that don't really qualify. Because if you're near dead, then you really didn't die at all, you just got close. John never really saw what was coming from the side. If he did, he would have seen a large City of Tucson front-end loader garbage truck, making its early pickup throughout the greater Tucson area, that failed to stop at the intersection of Park and Ajo due to an inattentive driver. He also didn't see the Construction company truck that was waiting for the light to change in the other lane. Sandwiched between the two vehicles, he didn't have a chance. Time stands still. What is it like, you might wonder? It was almost like being in Iraq or Afghanistan when an IED goes off under your truck. The moment of impact hurls you around as if you're on a ride at Disneyland, the teacup ride or Space Mountain, then sends you rolling in another direction until you come to rest with the force and destruction that can only end life. So much twisted metal and broken glass, plastic and blood, Time stands still. The clock on the dashboard read 3:13 am.

In war, it is often stated that you never hear the bullet that gets you. Possibly because it happens so fast that by the time the sound reaches you, you are already dead. John didn't hear or see the one that got him on that early morning. A sensation that time stood still, and then a moment of sadness, the kind of sadness you have when you just lost your best friend or loved one. It's a deep-seated feeling that comes from your soul, the kind of feeling that you know is already too late. It's a feeling of knowing that everything you were going to do and all the things you were going to see were never going to happen. He didn't see his life flash before his eyes, just the sound of thunder and the sound of silence.

The monsoon had let up this morning, but cool desert rain drizzled down throughout the carnage. It carried a smell of far-off lands and places never to be traveled to. You could smell it in the air like the smell of electricity and burnt rubber. A smell of twisted metal and bloody, torn flesh permeated the scene. John had his eyes open and looked out into the night from the broken glass. The rain fell slowly in drops you could catch with your hand. The light from the street signal, frozen in a red glow, made it look like blood around the wreck. He knew something had happened, but not really. He just felt it. His once-new Nissan pickup lay wasted and crumpled all around him. It only had 1245 miles on it; this couldn't be real. In the passenger seat, he saw what looked like a figure of a person sitting there. He didn't remember having a rider with him. He didn't remember anything. He stared for a long time at the unknown stranger in his truck and asked him his name. "Who are you and what are you doing here? Are you a hitchhiker? Do I know you?" he asked, but the stranger just sat there as if in another time or place. John tried to move but could not; he tried to reach over to the strange visitor but could do nothing but stare.

Where is Johnny?

"It is a pity that, as one gradually gains experience, one loses one's youth."
Vincent Van Gogh

The big old Plymouth station wagon rolled slowly down the block. It was a 1955 Plymouth Belvedere Suburban model painted a faded two-tone blue and white top. The woman seemed preoccupied as she drove to the grocery store with four young children in tow and one on the way. Little Johnny loved to look out the window. The world would just roll by as he stared at all of the wonderful people and scenery that graced his view. This was a mysterious world that held excitement and a small degree of fear to his young mind. At four years old, he was old enough to sit by the back door, even if his older sister thought otherwise. The world went by so fast while traveling at 30 miles per hour. "This was like those rocket ships that go to the moon," he thought. Always a dreamer, he often thought of distant worlds and other galaxies. At such a young age, this was not encouraged or condoned. The beast of a car rolled down Alameda Street with the greatest of ease, like an ocean liner on its maiden voyage, or the fish that ate Jonah. Either way, it was a monster. A creature built for navigating the streets of Long Beach. This 3329-pound metal behemoth was made for the road. Equipped with a speedometer that topped out at 120 miles per hour, this baby could get up and go.

But not today, today was just another run to the grocery store for the Pezdel family. Mrs. Pezdel hated to buy groceries. She also hated to cook. She also hated most everything that dealt with the mundane task of raising a family. She should have been an actress like Marilyn, or at least another Raquel Welch. She could have been anything but a wretched housewife living in Long Beach, California. Mr. Pezdel was off on one of his business trips to Nevada. There was a lot of business going on in Nevada these days. She knew he was up to no good, but she could never really catch him with any evidence; she had a few things going on that Mr. Pezdel didn't have to know about. Johnny looked out the window and dreamed of Mars, Jupiter, or the Moon. She still looked good even after having four brats, but time was ticking, and she often dreamed of leaving someday and going to a far-off land. Hawaii would be nice, or even New York, right now, Bakersfield would do. The door was always locked, it was always locked, and no need to worry since the door was always locked. Today was different, today the car door seemed locked, it felt locked, and by all practical purposes it was locked. But today was different.

She had to turn left since the store was down the block off Long Beach Blvd. Just the slightest of a bump was all it took as the blue beast slowly made its left-hand turn. Johnny was leaning a little too much, but that's how you lean when you're looking at all of the stuff. The big old station wagon took the corner with grace and poise. It had done this a million times, and today was no different. Johnny went rolling out of the moving car at 25 miles per hour onto the intersection of Alameda

Street and Long Beach Blvd. He was taken by surprise since the door was locked and he knew that this must be a dream. He flew through the air like an astronaut in space, about to land on the moon or a distant star. Slow motion took over as he tumbled to the hard pavement, hitting his head with a terrible thud. The next thing he knew was the oncoming truck coming toward his head. "This seems so real, but I know it's just a dream," he thought as the darkness overtook the light. Where do you go when the lights go out? When darkness and nothing fill your once conscious mind, and all you have left is the black and the silence.

"Mommy, you lost Johnny," cried Rebecca, his older sister. Mrs. Pezdel said, "Quit fooling around, we're almost at the store". But she turned around to count her young children anyway, just to be sure, one, two, three, and four. All accounted for. "Mommy, stop for Johnny, he fell out of the car," they all yelled now. Count again, one two three, four, or no wait, a minute, that's a stuffed Raccoon that looks like a kid. Mrs. Pezdel slammed on the brakes and turned the huge beast around in search of her lost child. By now, she had traveled over 1 ½ miles from where little Johnny had catapulted out of the Plymouth. Her heart rate jumped as her once drifting mind filled with one thought, finding her lost boy. She might have been in a dead-end relationship, but she always loved her children. Whatever the future held, she prayed to the Lord above not let anything happen to Johnny. He was an innocent boy with hopes and dreams who deserved a chance in this wretched world. That day, the Lord above heard the prayers of a desperate Mother. Nothing in this world is as strong as a mother's love for her children.

A crowd had gathered around the boy as he lay unconscious on the ground. "Where did he come from, and whose kid is it?

"Somebody please call an ambulance, hurry," a woman yelled from the crowd. Several people asked him what his name was, but the boy would not answer. The big old Plymouth came roaring up minutes later as Mrs. Pezdel jumped out to pick up her lifeless son. "Don't die, please, Johnny, don't leave us like this, please…" she cried to the boy. The driver of the truck that nearly crushed the young boy's head was sitting on the curb, shaking with fear and dread. Another second and the boy would have been flattened under his rig. He barely had time to stop if it wasn't for the voice in his head that yelled "STOP" from nowhere in particular. Was it his voice or the voice of God? He didn't know. He still remembers looking up ahead and seeing a small shape in the road, but that didn't make him stop as much as the huge shape of a heavenly Angel of about 10 feet high standing over the boy; now that made him stop. Shaking and weak from adrenaline, he waited until the police and ambulance arrived, then he was let loose. He got in his truck and drove slowly away. The man knew what he saw was real and never forgot that day for the rest of his life. The ambulance departed and took Johnny to Saint Mary's for treatment. He was awake now and not really sure what had happened. He remembered leaning into the turn and flying through space than nothing. He saw a strange man following him a few feet from his mother. He did not look to be of this world since he looked rather tall and had a face that looked like an angel, and then he was gone, just like that, vanished into thin air.

The Messenger

"Behold, I send my messenger before your face, who will prepare your way before you."

Matthew 11-10 NJK

The rain fell slowly on the disaster that was strewn over the intersection. In the desert, the rain always smelled different, not like the coastal towns where it was so common and full of saltiness; in the desert, it was more precious than gold. The windshield was shattered, which allowed the rain to fall into the truck as John sat motionless with his eyes closed. John opened his eyes and looked at the figure next to him in his passenger seat. "Who are you and what has happened?" he said with a weak voice. The darkness concealed the features of the man, but a faint light from the traffic light revealed a look of angelic peace upon his face. "Do not be troubled, my friend, for I am with you even unto death. I shall hold back the hand of the death angel and the evil one at bay until your time has come." The visitor said. John tried to place the voice and the words, but both slipped from his mind's eye. John asked the man again, "Who are you and where did you come from?" The figure replied, "I am a messenger from our Lord Almighty, and I have come to prepare you for your journey. My name is Abiel, and I have been with you since your first day on this earth. In fact, even before that, when you were in your mother's womb. I have been with you since you left our heavenly realm and came here on earth to become a child."

John thought on this and replied, "Some kind of Guardian Angel sent from the heavens above to protect me? Why am I here in this wreck, dying and not home with Anna? Why did I just dream about that day I almost got run over in Long Beach? I just saw you in my dream as they wheeled me down the hallway at St Mary's Hospital. If you're such an angel, then take me home to my wife and dog. Please get me out of here." The Angelic visitor just stared at John, choosing the right words for this moment in time. His body features were shrouded in the night, but his face was clearly visible and not of this world. He had a peaceful, joyful look that John could not comprehend in his dying state. In his mind, he heard Led Zeppelin's "Kashmir" playing as the angel sat silently. "Oh let the sun beat down upon my face, stars to fill my dream I am a traveler of both time and space, to be where I have been..." John loved Led Zeppelin, but even now, they couldn't help with his current predicament. He just kept thinking, "Where are your wings?"

The angel finally spoke, "John, you are dying; this will be your last few moments on this earth. You have come to the end of yourself, and what awaits you I must prepare you for. The visions you are seeing are not dreams or distant memories. I have brought you to these moments in the past as they are actually occurring. You are thinking that time travel is impossible and you are just having hallucinations, but I can only tell the truth, and you are there as these events unfold. You will feel as though you are actually there, and in reality, you will be there, but you exist in their time like a spirit or a wisp of the wind. You can see, hear, and feel the moment and even smell the event's surroundings, but due to the Law of causality, you cannot change or interfere with that timeline. We do not want a paradox or worse to happen here. So, if you're thinking about going back ten minutes ago before this wreck, I cannot help you because you are where you are supposed to be. I can go to any place in time I wish if it pertains to a client, but remember, you are there, but only as a spirit.

It was I who stopped the driver of that truck while you lay passed out in the street that day in Long Beach so long ago. This is evidence of when I have been with you while God has directed your steps. These are not visions of sorrow or disaster, but a testament to God's ever-present love for you and his joy in your life. You think you can just get up and walk away from this. You are wrong; most of your bones are crushed, and even as we speak, the blood flows freely from your veins. You will not survive; in fact, in earthly minutes, you have only a few. I have held back the pain from your injuries, but for a moment, I will let you feel the extent of the damage. I fear that is the only way you will believe what I am telling you is the truth. I do have wings, and I will show them to you when the time has come."

Just then, the Angel of God removed the pain barrier he had placed upon John. John felt a rush of pain and suffering that he had never felt in his entire life. He wanted to pass out from the intensity of it all. The bones in his legs were crushed along with his left arm. His neck was twisted at an unnatural angle and sent sharp waves of pain to his head and neck. His blood was seeping slowly from a severed carotid artery onto his shirt and truck seat. He almost passed out again from the sheer power of all that he felt, and he couldn't move his limbs. He glanced outside, and the people were moving as if they were drugged and in slow motion. The pain was immediately stopped before he lost consciousness. The angel spoke, "What you are sensing is not real; the world around you has infinitely slowed to a snail's pace. You are not really moving or looking around. You only think you are. I have slowed the passage of time down for you; everyone else is moving as they would and experiencing the tragedy as humans often will. This has been done because you don't have much time left, and I need to get you ready. All that you knew and all that you ever did has come down to this moment in time. We usually just let them pass to the other side, but you are given a degree of preparedness not afforded to all. A minute for God could measure half of eternity, right now you get mere seconds, and you must heed what is spoken between us because you will not get another chance."

This was too much to figure out all at once, but if the angel told the truth, then he didn't have long to live. Also, the pain that he had felt was all too real, and he didn't want to feel that again. Minutes or seconds were all he had left; who knew but it would come for sure. Like a condemned man awaiting execution at midnight was how he felt. So he would die here tonight, on the streets of Tucson, in the rain, in the twisted wreckage. There were worse places to be. "Who do you need? Who do you love? When you come undone…" Duran Duran was stuck in his mind now as he thought back to Anna in Tombstone and of how she would have to hear the news of his passing; she would regret it for the rest of her life that she couldn't be with him in his final moments, but if she were here, she would have to die also. Great sorrow filled his heart for his wife and children and grandchildren and the ones who loved him. She would think that he was alone, but in reality, God sent his angel to comfort him in his final moments. To John, it didn't feel like comfort, and the angel beside him didn't seem like a friend.

Waimea Bay

"Most of us, I suppose, are a little nervous of the sea. No matter what its smiles may be, we doubt its friendship."
H.M. Tomlinson

Waimea Bay is located in Haleiwa on the North Shore of Oahu in the Hawaiian Islands at the mouth of the Waimea River. Waimea Valley extends behind Waimea Bay. Waimea means "Red Water" in Hawaiian. Some days, the surf would roll in with a lazy motion slow enough to fool the casual visitor into thinking that this is a really nice beach. Then there are those days when the true spirit of the sea would rise up between 10 and 30 feet, then crash itself upon the beach. Eddie was a lifeguard at Waimea Bay on this very beach. Eddie was the first lifeguard hired by the City and County of Honolulu to work the North Shore. While Eddie was a lifeguard, not one person lost their life. Eddie braved surf that often reached 20 feet high or more to make a rescue. He became very famous for surfing the big Hawaiian surf and won several surfing awards, including First Place at the prestigious 1977 Duke Kahanamoku Invitational Surfing Championship. Eddie lost his life on March 17, 1978, while attempting to swim to the island of Lanai during a storm. In true Eddie form, he was trying to save his crewmates on the capsized voyaging canoe "Hokule'a". Eddie was never seen again.

John was visiting his cousin Marty Burrows, who lived near Pearl Harbor in the Naval housing near the Navy-Marine golf course. His Uncle Ryan was a Chief in the Navy and worked on an old destroyer, the USS Nichols. He was always called "the Chief." he was related by his dad's sister, Aunt Alice. Today was Saturday, and it was a day for the beach. Waimea Bay was calm this morning, so they all jumped into the wagon for the trip to the north shore. Johnny had never been anywhere like Hawaii before. He only knew the Californian coast; this was paradise for sure. The drive was only 28 miles or so, but it was one of the most beautiful drives Johnny had ever seen. You start off leaving base housing, then you pass Pearl Harbor on your left. The Arizona Memorial was a beautiful white tomb sitting in the bay. Next, you pass through Pearl City, where the local shops and a big shopping mall are located. Upon leaving Pearl City, you notice a wonderful, sweet smell in the air. The sugar cane plantation in Waipahu still makes sugar after 100 years. The smell is something you want to keep for someday in the future when a smell like that could lift your spirits and give you hope.

The freeway opens up to miles and miles of pineapple fields. They really don't look that great, but the smell of processed pineapples fills your nose and replaces the sugary smell. This is even better than before, and now you have a new memory. The town of Haleiwa lies sprawled before you, and you love the look and feel of the place. Sugar cane fields surround the town, and the sun is filtered through cloudy skies. This is truly paradise on earth, Johnny thought. The station wagon stopped at Matsumoto's grocery store on the left. Inside it doesn't look like much but they serve the best shave ice in the entire world. Today just keeps getting better. Johnny sat in the back of the wagon looking out over Haleiwa as the passed over the rainbow bridge. "I want to live here someday." He thought as they passed Waialua Bay and drove along Kamehameha highway. The beach looked so inviting and surreal as they drove the coastline into Waimea Bay.

It was about 10 o'clock in the morning when they drove into the parking lot. Not too many people for a Saturday, that was good. The waves were crashing right on the beach and the life guard warned of possible undertows. Johnny put down his bag on the beach blanket and ran to the surf with his cousin Marty. The water felt warm and invigorating on the skin. The smell of salt and sand filled his senses. California beaches weren't like this. Even on the hottest days the water in southern California was a frigid 68 degrees or so. He swam out a little and tried to do some belly surfing. For about 2 hours he played in the water with his Marty and his family until lunch was served. The whole family was here today except uncle Bob who had duty on the ship at Pearl Harbor.

The beach has a way of lulling you into another place. Johnny lay on his beach towel with his eyes closed. The sound of children splashing in the surf and people running along the sand filled his ears. The waves crashing on the beach had a hypnotic effect. He could hear his little brother crying for more ice cream and Mom saying no. She fell in love with Hawaii and wished they could live here but San Diego was their new home. The sun beating on Johnny's back and a full stomach took him to that place we sometimes go to. A place between here and there, sleep and awake. That place we love to be in right before we drop into the abyss of our own mind then sleep. Johnny was there now and it felt so good. There was a seagull making noise, a dog barking down the beach, the sound of a baby crying. These and more filled his dreams as the waves of Waimea Bay sang a lullaby.

Startled awake by the warm sand being thrown on his back Johnny chased his cousin into the water. It felt so good and right, he started to swim out a way into the surf. Little did he know that the surf had grown quite a bit since he last went the water? Eight-to-ten-foot waves were crashing on the shore with a terrible undertow that was forming. Johnny hadn't noticed the big waves until it was too late. He was pulled out faster than his arms could swim he fought the tide and the large surf. Finally, he could fight no more and was swept out about 200 feet into the waves. His mom and family were on the shore trying to get to him but it happened too fast. Johnny tried to swim one last time for shore and was caught up in a huge wave of enormous stature. It picked him up then thrust him to the bottom sea floor in the blink of an eye.

Time stands still. "I can't breathe any more, I'm going to die, and I'm only 10 years old, too young..." he thought as the weight of the crashing wave pulled him deeper into the sea. Right before he succumbed to his death, a hand pulled him from the surf. A Hawaiian lifeguard had seen the boy and saved him from drowning. He pulled Johnny onto the shore and pumped his stomach to release the salt water. Johnny looked up, astonished and coughing up salt water, but he was still alive thanks to this stranger. "You all right now, little brudda, be mo careful next time, eh, the kine surf eat you up, spit you out if you no careful, see ya." The man started to walk away, then Johnny asked, "What's your name, sir?"

"My name is Eddie, and you watch yourself today." He said as he walked to his lifeguard jeep and drove away. Johnny thanked God and Eddie for saving his life that day.

The ride home wasn't as fun as the ride there. Johnny remembered the sand and water being swallowed and the roar of the ocean when he was pulled free. Marty asked him "You don't look to good Jonny is everything alright?" Hell no, everything wasn't all right; he just about met his maker. His lungs hurt from drinking in the ocean water, and his eyes were full of sand. He had a fun day, except for the near-drowning part. Thank God for Eddie and his quick timing; it could have ended badly for Johnny. Next time, he would keep an eye on the waves. He still loved Hawaii and its beaches, but today brought with it the reality of how frail life could be. He was almost taken in the wink of an eye from this life; next time, he would have to be more careful, Johnny thought, there shouldn't be a next time if he could help it.

Retribution

"An angel can illuminate the thought and mind of man by strengthening the power of vision."
St Thomas Aquinas

John could smell the salt water, sugar cane, and pineapple as he looked into the rain. The vision or past visit he just saw hung with him in his mind as he slowly realized he was in his truck in Tucson, waiting to die. "You were there, weren't you? I know now that you were there. If I were going to die today, then why save me back then? It's all the same in the end; the outcome is always the same, we all know how the story ends. My life hasn't been a game-changer since that day, and I haven't made a big difference in this life on humanity or the big picture, so why save me?" John looked at Abiel as the rain hung in the air in a weird, trippy way. It was like being on acid or eating too many mushrooms. John knew a lot about that stuff, another life, and another time long ago. Abiel reflected on the moment and tried to make John see the answer. "I was there that day; I didn't save you because that's not how it works. The man who saved you was prompted to save you by my urging and guidance. We can never physically touch or harm a human life. It is done with the help of other people or the manipulation of the moment. Much like this moment that seems frozen in time, it is very much real and alive for you just as much as it is for those around us. You see, John, time is a manmade occurrence that people on this earth use throughout their lives to manage and control it. What will seem like mere minutes to those around us outside your vehicle will seem like hours to you. This is how it must be to complete our mission."

"What mission are you talking about? You're the Angel, not me, I'm not on a mission, I'm dying, remember?" he told Abiel.

John stared at Abiel as he spoke, but didn't speak. John did not see his lips move, but he heard his voice in his mind. "There are many types of Angels, and we all have different tasks according to our abilities. Some are counselors or spirit guides; others act as messengers to the living, while others must fill the void between heaven and earth so that none may perish. But people do perish, and their lives once lived remain but a memory and a dream. They are the ones who fan the flames of hell. They wish that if only they could have changed their path, then things would have been different, but they have an eternity to think about it. The souls of the lost and broken are many. They could fill the cosmos between here and the sun, or they could all fit within a thimble. Such is the perspective of things unknown."

"I am here now to reveal to you what you already know, it is all within you, and you will remember, but only if we go that path to see what is hidden within your soul. The events of your life unfold before you. You now remember the day at the beach and the day in Long Beach? These moments are relived as though you are living them again. This is how it must be." Abiel told him as John listened in awe; he could do nothing else at the moment. "Eddie saved me that day. I remember his face. Why did he go missing at sea, and why didn't he get saved? I have thought of that day often with no answer to my question." John asked. "Eddie did save you, but his fate and yours were only entwined for a moment. He did what was his to do. The day he was lost at sea, we were there with him until the end. He did not die in vain. He died as he lived in life, always helping others and doing what he loved to do." Abiel replied. John thought about what Abiel had said, more like thought it into his mind. The past was forgotten sometimes or twisted around in his memory to fill some longing for a better yesterday. This Angel had shown him moments of his life that were all but forgotten in his 49 years on earth. It was what it was. Where would this messenger from beyond take him next? He didn't want to know but could do nothing to heed the voyage. He was a captive to what lies ahead.

Psychosis

"When we remember we are all mad, the mysteries disappear, and life stands explained."
Mark Twain

The coast was deserted today, mostly because it was dinner time and cold as hell. The houses had their lights shining bright on this November night. John could see the people at their kitchen tables talking about what a wonderful day little Joey or Janie was having, school was so grand, and they learned so much. He didn't eat at the supper table with mommy or daddy much these days. Times were complicated, and in the course of the two of them screwing up their lives, others got caught in the wake. It was November 1974, and this was Ventura, California. He was going to Weston's house, two blocks down the beach. They always had the best parties, lots of booze, and lots of weed. Tonight was a particularly cold evening, even for this time of year. A big fire on the beach would have been great, but that would attract the cops; we don't need any cops tonight. Sometimes he would sit on the beach at night and watch the waves crash on the shore with the moon illuminating them as they fell. His mom was asleep at home, but mostly his dad was on a business trip to wherever. Mom was in her own little world; they had gotten divorced, but living here was another futile attempt to save what had been lost long ago. Old habits die hard, they say.

The beach was dark except for the light of the houses seen from the shoreline. John walked along the shore until he reached Kingston Lane.

Down the stairs and 8 houses on his right, the party was in full swing. Loud music rang out from the garage as young people milled around a keg of Miller beer. Weston was a little bastard who would have been picked on in school except he was mean as hell and would bite your arm or leg off if you messed with him. He was also the kind of kid who would burn your house down with you in it. It was best to be friends with Weston. John liked him, and they had a little gang of thugs who roamed the streets at night and stirred up trouble every chance they could. This was a rocking party as David Bowie sang on the ghetto blaster, "You've got your mother in a whirl, She's not sure if you're a boy or a girl, hey babe your hair's alright…" This was going to be a good night. There were the usual suspects, Donnie, Mike, Bobby, Matt, and Ricky, Debbie, and Susan, and a lot of strange but familiar faces. Some of the kids were from the Avenue, and they were a little worse than his lot, so it was best to stay away from that crowd. Parties brought about strange people. The ones who liked to rule the night and sleep late in the morning. You know the type of people who didn't really have jobs or money, just what they could scrounge up by bumming at the beach or cashing in Coke bottles. Some sold drugs; others stole from whomever they could, not the sort of people you took home to Mother. These were his people, and he didn't want to hang with anyone else. Weston's Mother was working right now; she was a stripper working at one of the dives on the Avenue, trying to make ends meet. Weston didn't know his dad and really didn't care. Mom would work until 3 in the morning and sometimes not come home at all, but there was always a pot of pinto beans cooking on the stove, and the kids could eat whatever commodities she would collect at the welfare office. There was no end to the Government cheese that sat abundantly in the refrigerator.

All the coastal towns in California were somehow basically the same in terms of who lived there. The tourist came and went, but the locals were in control. You hung around with your people or group and despised all of the rest. There were the surfers with their blonde, stringy hair and the girls with their unshaved legs. The jocks didn't hang out at night, too busy playing sports or trying to get laid. The nerds and brain heads weren't allowed outside after dark, but then there were the stoners. They ruled the night with all of its danger and enticements. They were slow at best during the day, but the night brought out their inner beasts and keen senses of the moment. They lived to party and partied to live, every day was another chance to get higher than before, and there was never enough night to last for any of them. They sought a higher purpose that normal people would never understand. They had brothers and sisters who were part of the hippy movement, but the stoners saw through all of the peace and love BS. The free love and brotherhood movement was all but lost on this bunch; the party was all they had.

Weston gave John a glass of beer and yelled for Bruno. "Bruno, you dipshit, get your ass over here or you're dead," Weston yelled into the night. From the shadows came a pure black Labrador retriever. He was the most beautiful dog John had ever seen. Weston grabbed Bruno by the back of the neck and pulled him up on his hind legs to hug him. Best damn dog in the world. John secretly wanted that dog for himself, but Bruno kept Weston sane for the most part. It was 11 o'clock already, and the night was young. John had met someone who gave him some 4-way window pane, a form of LSD currently being used in vast numbers. You were supposed to cut it four ways and only eat one hit. John didn't want to do that, so he ate it all. That was enough to make four grown people trip for 12 hours straight and then some. He was feeling the effects within 20 minutes that stuff worked fast. After an hour he was in a full-blown hallucinogenic experience. John watched the people at the party having fun and carrying on with the moment. They all looked like huge praying mantises to him; this was too intense for him so he split from the house and went to the beach. The ocean always had a calming effect on him. It had to do with the pull of the tides and the sound of the waves, all that ebb and flow stuff that made the world go round. Away from the music and the crowded house John sought solace sitting on the sand.

The moon was full that night and John could make out ships on the horizon. Going to wherever they went. The effects of the acid were tremendous. He saw things that were not of this world, saw worlds he shouldn't have seen and came to the brink of his own sanity. Some people hit acid to get closer to God; John took it to get away. Some people went to sleep to dream away their troubles; John liked acid once in a while to get away from his life. He had some bad trips but tonight it was all good. He wasn't what you would call an acid head of any sorts, more like an acid enthusiast who took it now and then to keep his mind tuned up. So many times, he had tripped away his life, always looking for that which could not be seen with the naked eye. There was a world that existed between the seen and the unseen. It lies just beyond the consciousness waiting for whoever went in that direction. John could see that world now and make out shapes of people from the past or future as they walked along the shore oblivious of his being there. He loved and hated it all at once like riding a roller coaster but on acid you didn't know where the ride would end.

At one point in the night, he was about to go into the surf and swim away to Hawaii or at least Catalina Island when an old man came walking down the beach. "What is that which troubles you son this late at night?" the old man said. John looked into his face and saw the face of father time. His eyes were black and pulled him in; His face was worn from years of living on the beach. He had a crazy look from too many nights sleeping in a blanket under the sand. He said he used to be a doctor and healed many people. That was another life time ago. So, John told him "I have seen too much and I want to swim to Hawaii so my mind would empty out and my sight would become clear again, this would be a good night." The Doctor looked at him and said "True you have seen too much, but you are young and you will see much more beyond your dreams. You will swim in Hawaii again just be patient my son. Tonight is not a good night to swim to Hawaii; it's the rainy season over there. Not a good time for a young man like yourself. Drink some of this tea and you will feel better son." So, John drank the tea, a kind of bitter sweet mixture with a touch of honey. After that he fell fast asleep. The Doctor faded into the night along with his dreams and magical potions, never to be seen by John again.

John awoke to the feeling of water soaking his leg. The sun was not up yet but the tide was rising and John was sleeping in its way. Up he went and staggered back to his house 2 blocks away. The beach lay deserted except for a man on the rock jetty fishing in the early dawn. Sunday morning and the world was still asleep. John went up the stairs into his bedroom. Real quiet like, so as to not wake up Mom. Dad was off on business in San Diego and won't be home for a week. John felt like crap and wondered what happened last night. He remembered the party a little then some guy named the Doctor, then nothing. Maybe today will be a good day. Why did he keep thinking about Hawaii?

The Long Way Home

"Seeing his days are determined, the number of his months are with thee, thou hast appointed his bounds that he cannot pass;"

Job 14:5

"What was so important about that day? I didn't die or even come close. I remember some of it and I know that you weren't there." John said to Abiel. "Also, I do remember that nothing happened so why did I have to go there?" Abiel responded with this "I was there and you were in peril. The drugs you took diminished your sense of danger or reality. You were planning on swimming to Hawaii and you would not have gotten far. The man who helped you was sent from the Lord to get you on the path you had strayed from. He was a local vagrant that you had met before but couldn't remember when you were on the drugs that night, God can use anybody anytime to get his word through and the good Doctor was happy to oblige he just couldn't remember it either. It only worked that night because you drank from the tea of knowledge and truth. Had you not drunk the tea your life would have ended at the age of 15 on that night instead of this night. All you have done and all of the people you have helped would never have happened. You may not know all the good that has been done because of you but the Lord knows and the balance between good and evil has been shifted because of that. A man never gets to know how he made a difference in this world, like ripples in a pond his life touches so many but he may never see the results." Abiel stared into the night and watched the rain as it didn't hit the ground. The rain fell suspended in a frozen dance until it will be released to fall to the earth. Soon enough he thought.

John had thoughts of his own. "Why me and what did I do to deserve this?" The pain he felt a few minutes ago was real. It was the worst thing he ever felt in his 49 years of living. That part was real so the rest must be real. When he was brought back to his past it was like he was living it in a detached sort of way, kind of in it but watching from the side lines. To what purpose will it lead? The outcome would surely end in his own demise, "It's out there" he thought but not really, "It was already here. No longer out there but staring me in the face. Where was the grim reaper? Was Abiel the grim reaper disguised as an angel of light? What am I supposed to learn in such a short time? I had my whole life to learn these things why now in the final moments, is this a cruel joke from God or am I just damned?"

"You know I can hear your thoughts and everything you just asked your self is perfectly normal in your situation." Abiel told him in his mind. "I'm not the grim reaper or the angel of death that you are looking for, but look out beyond the wreckage, past the trucks and broken glass. Over there in the shadows across the street, do you see him?" John looked past the wreckage and the trucks and broken glass into the night, at first there was nothing but then he saw it. In the shadows beneath a large Palo Verde tree was a shape taking form. At first it just seemed like the night. But slowly it was formed into a man standing beyond his sight. He could see the huge wings upon his back, another Angel waiting for him to die. John asked "What is he waiting for?"

"He is waiting for you; His job is to ferry you to the other side when your eyes have been opened and your heart lifted." Abiel said, "Also I cannot show or teach you anything that you don't already know. That would be against my Lords will. I am merely a messenger who brings good tidings from our Lord. You have all of the answers inside; you just need to find them. The angel of death is not to be feared, all men and women on this earth will someday meet him, someday if their path is straight. Otherwise, they meet the grim reaper; he is the one that people fear. He will take you where you don't want to go. Look outside you cannot see him yet but out beyond the angel of death, another dark angel awaits, he is a high-ranking minion of Lucifer who waits just in case. Your time draws near. You only need to wake up." John asked him "Why is that demon out there he has no power over this situation, does he think my soul is in peril?"

"No John, he sees us both and knows he has no business here, he's like one of those people who stops at a horrendous wreck like this and just have to watch and stare, also they feel better that they are not you. But he is more or less observing for his master. His master will be glad to know that you are leaving his world soon and not doing any more good things to cause chaos to his mission in this place." John knew what the devil's mission was; to steal kill and destroy, he hated the devil and all he stood for. Yes, his passing would be glad tidings to that ancient beast.

John asked "Why would the Devil care if I lived or died? I'm just another man leaving this world, who would care in the grand scheme of things?"

"Well John in a sense you are right and the Devil cares little about most people who live or die on a daily basis, He just really hates it when a good soul gets away that was otherwise coming his way. Now your soul was never in question as far as the heavenly realm is concerned but Lucifer didn't know that. He always thought that you would be serving him for an eternity. What he didn't count on was your love and servitude to our Lord almighty up above, He failed to see that the times he was most close to you were the times that drew you most close to God until you had enough and turned your life around for him." Abiel said.

John thought back to the days of his youth and being a young man, how close he was at times to be lost way back then and never having this conversation with an angel. It's funny how it's the little things in life that become so big in the end. He always thought that life was just one long day and you were born then you died and everything in between was just gravy. He now realized it was a little more complex than that, the balance of life and death are also a balance of good and evil, John knew the bible and how the story ends but his story was ending also and the devil still had to ruin it for him. Just a little peace and rest was what he wanted. This was way too much to think about at this moment in time.

Wake Up

"And the angel that talked with me came again, and waked me, as a man that is wakened out of his sleep."
Zechariah 4:1

The San Joaquin Valley lay sprawled before him. A vast agricultural land that supplies up to 25% of Americas produce is comprised of nearly 27,280 square miles of farm land and agricultural industry. It is home to 5 of the 10 most agriculturally productive counties in the United States, as measured by value of total annual sales. It is a diverse land with many nationalities and cultures living together to form a common goal. It was also the home of John and his family since moving from Ventura in July 1975.

It was late that night and the moon was not in sight. November 1977 had come already and Thanksgiving was not too far away. College would be out for break and John would get to work full time at the shop instead of just 4 hours a day. God he so tired. The long days of school then work then school then this 18-mile drive home thru the orchards and dairy lands. Why was he here? The thought would surface now and then. Born in the big city of Santa Monica, John never wanted to move out to the country. That was his parent's idea. Now that high school was over and he was enrolled in the local community college it wasn't so bad. Once again, his parents decided to try another shot at marital redemption at the cost of what? John was old enough to know that marriage was the last thing he wanted in his young life but that was for fools and dreamers who searched in vain for a thing called love.

Life takes on new meaning once you're out of high school. This was his third semester in school, after this, one more to go then Cal Poly would be next. It was all so drawn out in black and white. Do two more years of under graduate studies then get his Engineering degree? After that the world is his oyster. He didn't really like oysters though. Clams were more of his style. He remembered last summer going to Pismo beach at the coast, it was a three-hour drive but the closer he got the better it felt. The Valley weather was terrible in the summer. He and some friends stayed at the beach all day then slept in the pickup truck and a tent. In the morning people were digging clams out of the sand so they went to this restaurant on the pier and ate a bowl of clam chowder, man it was good. He snapped out of it and paid attention to the dark road up ahead.

This drive was always so long at night. It was November 10; a Thursday and tomorrow would be Friday. John only had to go to class then work until 5 o'clock. Then party on Friday night. His mind was busy with the events of the day. Get up at 4:30 am, eat get dressed and drive to school to get there by 7:45. Go to three classes and get out at 12:05 pm. Drive to the sheet metal shop and bend tin for 5 hours until 5:30. Take a break then go to his last two classes from 6 to 10:00 pm. Then get in his car and drive home. This was his schedule every day except Fridays, excluding the weekends of course. Friday would be an early day only 9 hours. He was used to it by now but it sure did make him tired some times. They say that youth can conquer most things but sleep deprivation catches up to all men.

He only had 3 miles to go to get to the bridge by his Grandparents house, then home. He would sleep like the dead tonight. It was highly known around the Trucking culture that Benzedrine and other forms of amphetamines would likely help in sleep deprivation situations. White crosses or bennies were widely available to those who drove our nation's highways long hours into the night. This was the 70's so relax. That might have helped John right now but he didn't take speed or any kind of amphetamine product. He rarely drank coffee. He didn't like that anxious weird sweaty kind of feeling you get when you do it. Tonight, would have been a good time to start. The road was a long straight stretch that went from Visalia Ca. to his house in the country. About 18 miles as the crow flies with not many obstacles. John was slowly being lulled to sleep with the heater on the 75' pinto blasting against the chill of the November night. The music of Bob Seger singing out of the radio earlier trying to keep him awake "Out past the cornfields where the woods got heavy, out in the back seat of my '60 Chevy, Working on mysteries without any clues, Working on our night moves …" Fade to Black.

Sometimes in a person's life a second could mean everything. Sometimes if you miss a second and trip or run a red light you could come out of it fine. Sometimes a missed second could just be that, a missed second, don't worry there will be more. But not this time, a second was all it took for John to close his eyes and fall asleep. This should have been the end of the story. The story should have rightfully ended and John should never have met Abiel. John should have been dead that night so long ago. With all the school and work and school and living, he just got caught up. Everybody falls asleep at the wheel once or twice. Tonight, would be different. In the time it took to close his eyes, one second, the car had veered from the right lane over to the left side of the road into an oncoming bridge abutment. This was all it took to end a life. Nobody would have driven by for hours and John would have been long gone. While this second was happening John was out, the kind of place you go to when you're lying on your couch on a Saturday afternoon and you close your eyes watching TV. Just a quick little nap or snooze to ease the mind. This is great if you're not traveling 70 miles per hour to your death. That night John slept the sleep of the damned oblivious about his upcoming demise, an angel intervened. "On a dark desert highway, cool wind in my hair, warm smell of colitis, rising up through the air, Up ahead in the distance I saw a shimmering light, My head grew heavy and my sight grew dim, I had to stop for the night..." the Eagles blasted out Hotel California on the radio while John fell out into oblivion.

Abiel was there that night with John. He was the co-pilot on that long country road. Abiel was not tired; he didn't need any sleep. He wasn't an earthly creature governed by our laws or practices. He was a heavenly host assigned to guide and guard John thru his walk on this earth. This was not in the plans. Most things are set before you like a storybook. An angel has certain knowledge of the length and worth of a person's life. This was not in that story. The rules state "Angels shall guide and guard their human counterparts, no direct involvement by the said angel shall transpire for any reason except to maintain the path and direction that the human must take. The fabric of time and space could be altered if these rules are not adhered to. Do not alter the fabric of time and place, it is far above your pay grade" In other words, angels just kind of help in small ways, sometimes big things are done for mankind but that's more biblical. Those are rare and far between. You could say on a small scale they are being done daily and that equates to Biblical proportions. But this was big. This was a deviation from protocol and could look really bad for Abiel, not to mention John. John wasn't supposed to fall asleep, period.

One second missed could catapult a person from this world into eternity. It happens every day. You see and hear about it on the nightly news. A person doesn't see the oncoming train or a truck that hits them. A person didn't know the gun was loaded as they shot their brains out. And the old adage, he fell asleep at the wheel. It happens every day. The difference between them and John is that they were supposed to die that way. It happens every day. But not today, Abiel saw the oncoming bridge on the left coming up so quickly. He only had a second to do what he had to do. A second for Abiel could be like a year. Time and its constraints had no effect on him. Remember, he wasn't human and did not comply with our earthly laws and discoveries. So, the problem wasn't time; it was how to save John without his knowledge. The angels' rule book also states, "If an intervention must be made by a heavenly host upon a human, the human shall have no knowledge of its occurrence." That was a simple yet very complex rule. How do you save a man without their knowledge of being saved? He looked out of the window into the night. The dark shapes of cattle could be seen a way off, grazing or just walking. The moon could be seen rising in the east above the mountain range. The stars looked so beautiful tonight. It was too nice a night to die on. Abiel took action; he decided to just wake him up. Abiel leaned over and yelled into John's right ear…" WAKE UP!" was what he yelled, only that.

"WAKE UP!" was all John heard as he opened his eyes and looked ahead. The irrigation ditch bridge abutment was almost in his front bumper, so he swerved the 75 Pinto hard to the right to avoid the collision. It was almost too much because he barely missed the other side by inches. He swerved back to the lane he was in, crossed over the bridge, and pulled over to the side of the road. Shaking and full of adrenaline, he sat for a moment to figure out what had happened. He heard a voice yell Wake up, yes, he did. There was no one in the car. He got out and looked around the vehicle. No one was around. The night was cold and dark. He could make out the shape of nearby cows grazing in some farmer's field. The moon was almost up in the east by the Sierra Nevada. It felt good to be on his feet. He felt sick from the adrenaline rush but grateful to be alive. He thought he heard a voice in his head to wake up, but he must have subconsciously heard his own voice. It could happen.

That was just too weird. He now knew that he had dozed off and his car was on a dead course for that concrete bridge railing. He looked at the bridge and studied its sheer mass of concrete and design. No one would have survived that head-on. Also, he wasn't wearing his seatbelt, so that would have ended his life. He couldn't find anybody who yelled; he might have been just waking up from a dream and had dreamt it? That's got to be it. No one would believe a story of an unseen voice yelling in his ear. It could have been the voice of God for all he knew. Thank you, whoever you are. John got back in the car and slowly drove on the road. Still shaking but a little better than before, he drove the 3 miles home and went to bed. His mind was still trying to make sense of the night's events, but nothing seemed to fit. Maybe he had a guardian angel or something. Abiel sat in the front seat next to John, awaiting the wrath and fury from above for breaking protocol, but no wrath or fury came as they drove home. He thought to himself how lucky they both were that night, and he even looked in the back seat for his guardian angel, but it was empty as it should have been.

Discovery

"The real voyage of discovery consists not in seeking new landscapes,
but in having new eyes. "
Marcel Proust

"I knew it, I knew it." He yelled, "I knew you were there with me that night. I have thought about those few moments so many times, and I know I heard a voice, and I now recognize it as you. You saved me that night; I knew it, but what about now, angel? I'm dying here with nobody but you for company." John spoke to Abiel in a rush of words. Abiel saw the wonder and disappointment in John's face and told him, "Yes, I was there that night with you as always, the Holy Spirit was there also, that little pinto was tight because another Angel was sitting in the backseat also. The angel of death was waiting with us that night. You were not supposed to perish in that Pinto on that lonely highway; it wasn't in the script, but the angel of death takes no chances. He was waiting then as he is now." John looked out into the night by the Palo Verde tree for the death angel. He did not see him by the tree; he was about ten feet closer to the tree than John's truck. John knew then that time was really short, even though Abiel had slowed it down.

John was still perplexed as to why he couldn't have just died. What was the big deal? It happens every day, he asked Abiel that question, "Why did you step in that night? I should have died. It was a natural occurrence and not intentional." Abiel thought for a moment before answering. John was very vulnerable right now, and he needed to understand what effect his life had on this world. "True, I could have let you die, and today wouldn't have been, but I saw the book on your life, and all of the other times from birth until now were all in there. I just had to be there to not let that happen to you on that lonely highway so close to home. That night was different; something changed in your world, and that moment was a surprise to me also. True, we had you no matter what, and your soul was saved, but it was very strange, and I've seen it all. Your death on that night would have sent me to an unwanted duty of a dreadful nature. I would have been forced to search the planet for lost souls and try to send them on their way to redemption, which is not an easy task, and I don't want to do that. Anyway, I've always been a guardian angel, so you're stuck with me for a little longer. I have thought of that day often with no rest or answer. I guess some things are only known to God." He told John.

Into the Darkness

"Deep into that darkness peering, long I stood there, wondering, fearing, doubting, dreaming dreams no mortal ever dared to dream before."

Edger Allen Poe

They were sitting at the kitchen table of the old mobile home, smoking the last of their stash. Nobody was around tonight or even most nights; that was just the way it was. John and his friend wanted to get high, but all they had was an old pipe and some roaches. They smoked it all, but to no avail; they needed more. In the cupboard was a can of spray paint; it would do in a pinch. They both started huffing it in an old brown bag. Henry, John's friend, said, "Man, this paint ain't getting it. I need some more smoke, bro." John was about to agree when it hit him. The aerosol paint and lack of oxygen to his brain kicked in, and John passed out. Henry didn't know what to do, thinking John had just died, and he didn't know how to bring him back. "Wake up, John, wake up, bro, come out of it," he yelled at John's lifeless body. Trying to shake him back to life did no good. John, on the other hand, was seeing a different sight.

He knew he had done wrong. He knew that he was not coming back. He was at the kitchen table, then the next moment, he was looking at another world. He had the strangest feeling of sorrow and dread as he had just lost his best friend, a feeling so strong he knew that where he was wasn't of the earthly realm. He looked out into a vast emptiness and saw what looked like a bride to nowhere with someone or something standing at the end of it. It wasn't a good feeling, but he knew he was heading that way no matter what he tried to do to avoid it. Walking across the bridge, John was thinking of his life up to this moment; he hadn't really lived much, and someday he wanted a wife and maybe some kids. He knew that this was the end, and all of his tomorrows were gone. He would be just another teenage death who killed himself so senselessly, while the papers portrayed him as a troubled youth who didn't have much to live for. This might all be true, but John didn't want to die. Not now, like this, on a one-way trip to eternity. He didn't know anything else except that he had no more answers.

Halfway across the bridge and into an eternity, he heard a voice from beyond this place talking to him. "There is still time…" was all the voice said as a vision was shown into his mind. It was of a horrendous wreck sometime in the future where the vehicle was demolished, and the driver didn't make it out alive. The wreck occurred at night in a city he had never been to on a street he had never seen. He could see a man, all broken and crumpled, slumped across the driver's seat, bleeding out as he stared into the night. Then he woke up on the floor of his house about 20 feet from where he started. Henry was kneeling over him, and the room stood still. He heard the voice one more time say, "There is still time…" Just then, everything began to move in slow motion, and he could see Henry start to talk and cry at the same time. He could hear the ticking of the old wind-up alarm clock, tick tock, tick tock, slowly at first, then back to regular speed. "Bro, I thought you had died, don't do that shit anymore, ok?"

"I'm good, Henry. I don't think I will be huffing any more paint." He got up and went outside into the summer night. Far off, he could see the cars on the highway, and he heard a coyote howling in the distance. It felt so good to be breathing and alive. The vision he saw was meant for him to see. Maybe he wouldn't die this night, but the future would wait for no one, so he would know some day if that was his fate. Maybe what he saw that night was someone else dying in a wreck. Hopefully, he would be an old man with a terminal illness. He wished that were true.

"I had forgotten that moment in time when I saw someone or maybe me die, maybe I blocked it out for a reason, but to no avail, it has come to pass," John said as he stared out the window for once realizing this is what he saw so long ago in a moment in time stuck between this world and the next. So many times, he had lived his life so recklessly, knowing deep down that the hand of death may have been close in his life, but it never laid its fingers on him. He wasn't immortal; he just knew his time of dying wasn't going to be the way people thought it would be. "So that's the price we pay for knowing the unknown." He told Abiel as the angel sat silent. Abiel asked, "What price is it you speak of, John? The price for doing things in this world that could lead you to another one by pure accident? I can't tell you how many times those clients of mine have cut short their otherwise long lives from ignorance or stupidity. The freewill that our Father gave you humans is not always free; it comes with a cost that you alone must pay. The sad part, John, is the ones you leave behind who have no idea why a young man would do such a thing to end his life; they are the ones who suffer in silence and cry away the night."

"But what about our destiny and the days of our lives written in the Lamb's book of life, what about you being there all of those times, making sure that I was here today to die in this truck in Tucson, Arizona? What does it matter if I had died that day?" He asked the angel of the Lord. "It matters; it always matters. The life you would have lost back then would not have allowed the people and circumstances of your life to have manifested. Your kids, their kids, and your interactions that have changed the world would not have been accomplished. You would not have been remembered by the people who you knew for long or of much consequence. I don't know the outcome of that day if you had died then, instead of now; they only tell us so much. I do know that today is the day written in the Lamb's book of life for you, and all who knew you will remember you with joy and love. I do know that. In life, there is an unseen balance or scale, so to speak, of good and evil. The two sides are always at war with each other, and in your life, you have shifted that balance a little more for the good side, and God is grateful." Abiel told him as he watched the angel that death had moved closer ever so slightly.

"I have seen enough, I get it. Just take me now to wherever I am going. This place is done with me in this life. Whatever else is up your sleeve, you can forget it because I'm ready to be dead. Let's go." He practically yelled to the angel. "You are forgetting one thing, John, and that the time has not yet come, and the angel of death has not yet gotten hold of you. Once he gets his hands on you, then it will be over, not now but then. You seem to forget that I am a mere messenger of the Lord and the events of your life are for you, not me. I've been there the whole time, and I do not forget a thing. You will finish this task, for it will be your last in this world." Abiel spoke with authority and encouragement to John as he lay there slumped across the seat.

Battle of the Bands

"The ideal man bears the accidents of life with dignity and grace,

making the best of circumstances."

Aristotle

The night was cool and clear. John and his brother Joe had arrived at the pasture at about 8:30 that night. Joe was about four years older than John, but that didn't matter much since they always found the time to get together and party, like right now in this cow pasture. You could hear the band playing nearby, a small stage was erected, and the partygoers were surrounding it, listening to the music. This was just a cow field during the day, but some enterprising farmer's son staged a local "Battle of the Bands" for $5.00 a head. That included all the beer you could drink. "Hey, bro, let's grab a couple of beers from the keg before we see the show," Joe said as they climbed over the barbed wire fence. A young man was there to take their money, then off they went to the beer kegs. A bonfire blazed high into the night as youths stood around it, talking loudly and drinking beer.

John was an observant sort, and he noticed something wasn't right with this scene. Around the fire was a group of low-rider Mexican kids getting drunk and smoking their Mota. On the other side of the flames were a group of redneck cowboys who most likely lived on the nearby farms. During the day, most times these two groups avoided each other, and all was well, but not tonight, with a full moon and with beer in their bellies and weed in their lungs, things would get out of hand. It was like something out of a bad movie as John watched the events unfold. John told Joe, "Keep an eye on those guys; something isn't right about it, I can feel it."

"You and your feelings, you're worse than Grandma Pezdel with all of your intuitions and spooky talk, let it rest, Bro, tonight we get wasted," Joe told his little brother as they grabbed some plastic cups and started to drink some beer. The stars looked so close tonight, and a hint of winter was in the air. John looked off to the crowd gathering around the musicians on the small stage; the sound carried itself off to unknown lands. He looked over to the fire and watched the odd group exchange harsh words, and then he saw a cowboy grab a huge burning branch and hit a young Chollo over the head. Sparks and fire flew into the night as the young man fell over the fire onto the ground. Time stands still…

John was more or less casually looking at the fight erupting before him. He knew what was going to happen next as a young Chollo gangster pulled out a 38 revolver from his belt and started shooting at the crowd. The bullets flew into the night, one cowboy got shot in the arm, and then the gun was pointed at John. Like a slow-motion movie, he saw the flash and heard the bullet race by his ear. "This is not happening tonight; I just wanted to party and hear some tunes." He thought to himself. He saw a flash again and knew it would hit him in the face, but he stumbled backward as the bullet flew into the night. Lying on the ground with his brother Joe beside him, he yelled into his face, "We have to leave now, Bro before he reloads.", he looked around to see what he had tripped over, but the earth was flat with no obstacles, so they jumped up and ran to the Pinto hatchback to escape more pandemonium.

In the car racing down the country road, John's heart was pumping way too fast. He had to breathe before he would pass out. The night was still young but they just wanted to get home. "John, are you all right? You didn't get shot, did you?" Joe asked in a panicky voice. "No, I'm good I was really close though, and I told you I had a bad feeling about tonight, next time listen to me," John replied as he watched the dark shapes of cattle in the pasture eating away on a full moon. He could hear the sound of the rock and roll music fading away into the night. They decided it would be a great night to go home and party out back in the shack behind the outhouse, no bullets there.

One Day

"One day, your life will flash before your eyes. Make sure it's worth watching."
"Unknown"

John could see the Angel of Death in front of his truck, just moving ever so slightly but steadily in his direction. Beyond the death angel were multitudes of bright orb-shaped glowing balls floating in the air. He was amazed at the sheer number of the orbs as they floated slowly before him. Moving at a different speed, he knows that they would not be visible to the naked eye. The orbs were not of this world, possibly the lost souls of wandering spirits, but Abiel would have to tell him that.

"Abiel, why was that moment so important? I missed getting shot by tripping over a log or something. What's the big deal? I didn't die or come close that night?" he asked the heavenly being beside him. "You just saw the moment, and you even saw yourself looking around on the ground. Did you find a log, a branch, a hole, or anything besides dirt? No, you didn't because I tripped you that night. I know it's bad protocol, but it was a little trip, and I didn't even touch you much. The angel's handbook forbids the interaction if at all possible, but sometimes I have to bend the rule book like that night." He told John. "So, without your bending of the angel rules, then I would have died that night? That's what you're saying?" he asked Abiel. "Yes, John, that's what I'm saying, but you didn't, so we still have tonight, do you remember the moment you saw when you died in your living room breathing that paint?" John said, "I remember it like it was yesterday, and the moment I saw has already come to pass. This is exactly how I saw myself dying. For years, I knew this day would come, but you try to rationalize it and say it was the paint or lack of oxygen. But deep down, the truth is in me all of my days. I always had no fear of death because death had me in its hands, but threw me back.

I figured someday he would get me. It was just a matter of time. The old grim reaper would catch up with me someday; I only wish it wasn't today. Like a thief in the night, he creeps up on you slowly and suddenly when you least expect him. I just never thought I would see an angel like you at the end." Abiel said, "I know John, that things don't always turn out the way you want, but you were blessed to have knowledge of your own demise. Few people are shown how they will die, and fewer still are shown when. The manner and moment of death in a human life are counterproductive to the laws of nature. Most people stumble through this world, hoping there is an afterlife, but too afraid to go to it. Those orbs you see are other people from other times, "Absent from the body, present with the lord." That is true, but man misconstrues its true meaning. What really happens is they are present with the Lord, and they are welcomed into his kingdom, but some things in life can hold you even after death, so they are returned in a different form to work out the reason they can't leave. You knew how you were meant to die, but not when. I think that knowledge helped you on your journey through this life. It stops here, though, and your future is already written; you will be a part of the heavens and in the presence of the Lord. You will know then, as you have never known, and all of the mysteries of life and death will be clear to you. Hang on for a little while."

"Why are they out there now? Are they waiting for me?" John asked Abiel while thinking of the orbs. "Those orbs of light are drawn to this place of death. They await your passing, and you are like an orb to them; they see you as you see them. They only stay back because I am with you, and they cannot cross over to us. They are more curious than not, because they want to see if you will depart from this world in your true form; if you don't, they will gladly welcome you into their fold. You don't know it, but part of you is already gone, and what's left here now is who you were on earth. That too will fade like the morning dew on grass. You will no longer need this part where you're going; the orbs were like you once, earthly beings that lived just like you. They have a glimmer of their former lives since they are still confined to an earthly home, but they are wandering spirits that never rest." Abiel told John. "Why don't they just go to heaven or hell like the rest of us?" asked John as he stared at the glowing circles of light. Abiel replied, "They don't leave because they can't; some aspect of the life they once lived keeps them anchored to this world. They are like ghosts, but not. Very rarely do they have the energy to manifest into their former selves, so they band together and feed off each other's energy to sustain their existence. They can leave at any time, but they have been here so long that they don't know the way out."

"That is so sad, to think of staying here waiting and watching for an eternity. I'm glad you're taking me away," John told him. Abiel explained to John. "Don't be misled, I cannot leave this earth either until my work has been finished. You are not the first or last soul I have had the pleasure to protect and serve. My job will go on until my Lord brings me home, also. I will not accompany you from this place. The death Angel has that task, I'm more like the conductor who helps you on your train, but I never board it myself. I have been here for a very long time, but time is just an earthly thing. I don't age, and the passage of time has no effect upon me. I only see the ones I knew grow old and die, some die young, and some die later, but they all die just the same. If I knew sadness, then I don't think I could do these things for you and those who have passed. I can feel what you feel, but it's not the same; it's more like having leftovers the next day from a great meal. It tastes good and all, but never as good as the first time it was made. Do you understand?"

John looked at Abiel and was getting a different feel from him; he didn't view him as some mysterious heavenly being that just dropped in; he saw Abiel and God's hand in all of those dreadful times in his life. He remembered John 8:32, "and you will know the truth and the truth shall set you free." It rang inside his mind like a loud bell, ringing the truth of his life lived and lost. "I can hear your thoughts: I told you that already, it is very flattering what you are thinking, but I'm only doing the Lord's work, but thank you just the same," Abiel told him.

"Will those orbs ever make it home, or is this just what they have left?" John asked. Abiel replied, "They will all come home eventually when this all passes away, and a new world has been made. Did you think this was the only planet like this in all of the cosmos? This is just the one you and I live on for now. There will be other places like this with other people like you in them. Planets don't last forever, either, John. Their time may seem greater than yours, but a housefly's time may seem like yours when compared to a human's. It's all relative to your point of view or station in life. A condemned man sits in his cell, looking at the clock tick away his last moments on earth. It's no different than you right now, except you're not condemned. The time ticks away for both of you, but you have a purpose and place beyond this life. The condemned man can only hope. If he knows the Lord, then he will die with peace and dignity. If not, then the Grim Reaper will be waiting in the room when he passes. That is something you will never see, so be thankful."

Intrigued, John asked Abiel about the Grim Reaper. "What does he look like, and is he really an evil presence? I have always thought of him as a bad thing. Is that true?" Abiel knew what the Grim Reaper was, but he didn't like to talk about him but John didn't have much time, "He can be scary and evil and mean and nasty, but he can also masquerade as an old grandfather or an angel of light to lure his victims to their doom, they are already going to hell, the reaper just has to get them there. He does make a stop in front of the Lord to show the poor soul who the real master of this universe is, then off to Hades to do the Devil's bidding. It's easier sometimes to fool his clients and take them peacefully to the gates of Hell; after that, there isn't any peace at all. He is not evil like you think; he just has a bad job, and somebody has to round up all of the lost souls in this world. He was put here for a purpose, and imagine how crowded the world would be if he didn't round up those lost souls? Also, I'm glad it's not me. I have been on this earth longer than you would like to know. I've seen it all, man's humanity and inhumanity. It never fails to amaze me how certain people you would think are going straight to Hades end up on the other side. The good Lord only knows the final outcome. We just do as we are told and hope for the best." Abiel told John as he sat there staring at him.

The Sailor

"I must go down the seas again, to the lonely sea and the sky, and all I ask is a tall ship and a star to steer her by."
John Masefield

The Great Lakes, Illinois, were a long way from the Pacific Ocean. John enlisted in the US Navy about 9 months ago, went to Boot Camp in San Diego, and ended up here. He was supposed to be on some ship somewhere in the South Pacific or Indian Ocean, but those orders never came; instead, he was stuck here in Boiler Technician Basic "A" school. It was May 25, 1979, and he had made a reservation on Monday to fly out to California to see an old friend. Today was that day, only one problem, the Chief of the Boiler training Module had caught John sleeping in class and told him that this weekend coming up was John's time to swab the barracks. John had other thoughts as he was getting ready that Friday morning to catch a bus to O'Hare International. There was another problem, that sick, aching feeling that he was about to do something wrong. He had it before, and most times heeded the warning because bad shit does happen, but today, he just wanted to ignore the feeling and go to L.A.

The thought of going AWOL was not sitting well with John; he knew that if he left for this weekend, the chief would tear him a new one and take a stripe. Being an E-3, he couldn't afford it, but this place was too much for him right now. Walking back to the barracks, he went into the lobby and ran right into Chief Brown, who was sitting in an easy chair. "I hope you're not thinking of going anywhere, shipmate. Your ass is mine at 0800 tomorrow morning, sailor. You understand me, Boy?" the chief yelled at John, "Yes, I do, loud and clear, Chief 0800 I will be there." John told him as he vaulted up the stairs to his room. He only needed a few things for the trip; he was flying back on Sunday night, and it was only being AWOL for a weekend. He knew guys who did way worse and survived the wrath of the US Navy judicial system. The feeling in his gut was worse than before, and he almost said hell with it, but not today, today he would make the rules. He grabbed his overnight bag and went down the fire escape to avoid Chief Brown, who was the biggest ass hole he knew, besides most of the other Chiefs were too.

Outside the base on the strip, he sat waiting for the bus; he had a minute, so he drank a quick beer at the Keg Bar. It was dark and smelled of urine; most bars outside the base were like this. Sailors don't care. All they wanted was a cold beer, a cool bar, and maybe some time away from the base or ship. The life of a sailor was simple: do your job, follow orders, and always say yes, sir, to an officer. The bus pulled up as he was just walking outside. He got on and checked his watch; it read 1105, and he still had time to catch the plane. Boarding should start around 1400 hours, so he had time to call Los Angeles and make sure someone would pick him up. They were about 2 miles out of town, ready to hit the freeway, when a semi tractor-trailer jack-knifed in front of the bus and flipped over on its side. The bus driver barely had time to stop, but the car behind him didn't, so they were stuck in traffic until the police and ambulance arrived. It was 1230 by the time a new bus arrived, and John was able to get out of there and still had enough time to get on the plane. He arrived at the airport and then went to the bathroom quickly. An old man was standing by the urinal, clutching his chest.

"Son, I'm having a heart attack right now. Could you help me?" This was not happening, John thought to himself as he went to help the old man. "I will go and get someone for you, ok?" he told him as he started to leave. "No, don't go. I just need my nitro if you could get it out of my luggage, I should be alright." He said to John, so John searched the luggage for about 10 minutes until the old man said, "Wait a minute, Son, I have it right here in my pocket, and just fish me out a pill, please." So, John grabbed the pill bottle and was trying to get out a small nitroglycerin tablet when the bottle just seemed to fly out of his hand onto the floor, spilling out all the pills. "I'm not going to eat those pills, Son, not off of this floor. I would rather die." He yelled at John, who almost walked out on him, but he didn't want the man's death on his conscience, so he asked if he had more pills. The man said, "Yes, I do in my other coat pocket, Son." So, John grabbed the other bottle and gave the old man a pill. He ate it and asked John to wait for a minute so he could regain his composure. John looked at his watch and noticed the time was 1445, so he knew he had to go. "You look pretty good now. I have to go." John said as he ran to the gate to catch his plane, looking back at the old man, he had a weird grin on his face, not doing too badly for a near heart attack.

The gate was empty except for a couple of counter people talking, "Where is the airplane to L.A., I have to get on it now?" he said to both of them, then one woman said, "Sir the plane is ready to roll down the tarmac awaiting take off, we could get you on the next flight, would that work?" John looked outside as the American Airlines jet sat about 100 yards from where he stood. If only he had gotten here a couple of minutes sooner, he would be on that flight. "When is the next flight out?" he asked the woman. We have another flight leaving in 3 hours if you would like to take that, sir." He stood there looking outside then realized the feeling had gotten worse in his gut and now he was shaking. "I don't know, let me sit here for a minute I don't feel too great." He told her as he watched the plane slowly roll away from the area onto the tarmac.

John watched as the American Airlines flight 209 taxied down the runway ready for takeoff. He watched as it slowly turned then waited for a moment before throttling up for takeoff. He watched as the airplane lifted off the runway then sort of hang there for a second as it took a roll to the left then it plummeted to the ground. He saw the flames and explosion from where he stood; He felt the building shake from the crash. He then realized he was just spared from being on that plane. The sickening feeling he had vanished like the wind as that thought raced thru his mind. Inside the terminal people were running around and a lot of screaming could be heard. He just calmly walked away and caught the first bus back to Great Lakes.

While on the bus his mind raced from the events he witnessed. Thoughts of death and dying filled his head as he watched the scenery go by. He was staring at his boarding pass as his mind reeled. He then realized he wasn't supposed to get on that plane and God and his angels prevented from doing just that. "Tell me how does all of this work and why me? What is so special about my life that someone else would have to take my place?" He thought as he got closer to the Naval Base. He wondered if some other poor soul died in his place. He just kept seeing that plane hit the ground near a trailer park and everyone on it vanish into smoke and flames. He thanked God for this day and for saving him for whatever the rest of his life would be.

Rest

"Come to me, all you who are weary and burdened, and I will give you rest."

Matthew 11:28

John looked at the dashboard clock as it read 3:18. Only 5 minutes had gone by, but it seemed like hours because his sense of time had slowed down to a snail's crawl. Looking over the bench seat at Abiel, he knew that he had been there at the airport that day, but to what extent was unknown. "You are wondering what I did or didn't do to make you miss that plane? Also, you are feeling bad for the person who took your place. Don't worry, John, I was there, and I did affect the outcome, but not in the way you think. I didn't cause the truck to crash, and I didn't give the old man a heart attack; my only role was to make you want that beer before you left Great Lakes. You didn't need it, and had you not drunk it, then you would not have gone to the restroom to relieve your bladder. You would have made it to the plane and boarded with the rest, a little late, but still, your fate would have been sealed. The person who took your place was destined to die that day anyway. He just went a different way, but still in the same time frame." Abiel told John as he sat still, caught between then and now.

"So, you can alter my thoughts to change my freewill, I don't understand? I thought freewill was the basis of being human, so how do I know that my thoughts were not always being influenced by angels or demons? Are we just cattle being led to our eventual slaughter, or is there something else? Tell me, angel." He spoke this to Abiel. Abiel told him, "You don't understand the logistics and probable outcomes of this world. So many like you are following their own path, and so many like me have to keep them on that path. I have lost more souls than you want to know over stupid, careless moments in time. They should have gone to the light, but ended up in darkness just the same. We, as angels, have no power over your thoughts or minds. The thought I introduced was just like all of the other million or so that you have daily to ponder on. You don't act on 99% of them, but once in a while, the one that seems most appealing or logical gets through. You were going to have a beer sooner or later, so that was what I presented to you. I knew the old man was in the bathroom, but he wasn't really having a heart attack; he just thought he was, and the time it took for you to help him was what I needed to get you away from checking in and also checking out. Would you have gone to the dark side that day? I know you would have because your heart and soul were not aligned with the heavenly realm."

"Do not be upset for missing that plane or the outcome of that day. The soul who took your place was meant to be there as well as the other passengers. It's a mathematical impossibility to get that many people in one place at the right moment so they could all go to their eternity. I do not delve into such matters, but there are those that do, and that's all they do day and night as your world slowly turns. Why have you not gotten past this day after all of these years? I have taken you too many such days, and there are more to see, but this one holds you back; you must release it so you may go also. This is how the orbs and spirits of the lost stay here. Don't be like that." Abiel pleaded with John about that day.

"I know that what you say is the truth, and I have always held that day close inside because it had upset me so much. Looking back, I now see that by holding on to it, I was not getting past it. I know that my life had great meaning and added balance to the good side of the scales, but I have seen many wrong and bad things, and those are hard to look away from in this world. The love of God and all of his wonders are apparent in everything that is good and pure. I also know that we have many things to see before I leave this place, so I can let that day go now." John told Abiel that as the weight of that day slipped from John's body, he felt a little more at peace with it all. He felt cleansed and purified as if awaiting a final renewal of his soul. The memory of that day actually ceased to exist in John's mind as he looked out of the window at the angel of death. He was closer now than before, but not quite close enough to make out his features. Just a dark winged creature getting larger each moment. Not sure how much time he had left, John looked over at Abiel and asked, "Are we good here, or do we go off again? I don't remember much death and destruction after that day; I could be wrong, partner."

Wrong

"But the thought of being a lunatic did not greatly trouble him; his horror was that he might be wrong."
George Orwell

How wrong could a man be when the final moments are upon him? You would like to think he would get it right with so little time to spare. John sat looking out into the boiler room of #2 fire room on the USS Hoeltstein DDG- 33. They were on Westpac from Pearl Harbor for about two months now, somewhere between the Straits of Malacca and the Indian Ocean. They were heading toward Diego Garcia for repairs with a submarine tender down there. It was 0315 am on a Sunday night, and all was well in the #2 boiler room. The men standing watch were alert yet settled into that time frame of not knowing where in the world they were and not giving a rat's ass. The boilers were steady as the main engines held 15 knots. He could feel the power of the main engines pushing the small ship towards its destination. The boiler room held a hypnotic effect on those who steamed in it. The sound of the loud machinery and the forced draft blowers feeding the furnace made one think that they were in some form of hell. John was thinking about home and how he could be doing anything else in the world besides this.

The North Shore really looked great right now, and Anna was an Angel sent from above. How she kept it all together while he was gone, only the good Lord knew. They had an agreement, as most military couples have, about who will pay the bills and buy the food while the other is away. There's more to it than that, but someone has to keep the lights on and the children fed. Anna was not a typical Navy wife, and she knew it. If you called her a Navy wife, you would get a dirty look or worse. She took her marriage seriously and loved her life, but John was the one who signed up, not her. She would not hesitate to tell you either. She had friends that she knew from John's coworkers on board his ship, but she really was close to her family, and that's all that mattered.

Being a Boiler Technician was one of the most dangerous jobs to perform in the Navy; only a fool would do this type of job day in and day out. It only took 8 seconds to turn a man's body to mush when a major steam leak broke out. It's best to stay frosty and not drift off. "2 Fire main Control, this is the Eng Officer of the watch, we have a report of rough seas coming our way, secure for rough seas." The order came out on the intercom between the main spaces. "Rough weather, that's going to suck," John thought as he told the watch team to tie down everything loose in the boiler room. Anything could become a projectile in rough seas, a wrench left out, or a mop bucket rolling around; it didn't matter. John hated rough seas and how they tore the little ship apart. Best to go around such weather events, but not tonight, they were going right through it. Like Jonah in the great beast, John held onto the control board as the waves picked up. The little destroyer heaved up and down while it rocked back and forth as the storm raged upon them. The seas got worse as the waves pounded the ship, and the crew wished they were someplace else. John and his watch team became alert as one. John had been in rougher seas before; he had once gone through a typhoon that took about a week to get to the other side of it. The only thing to do when you're going through hell is to go through it. The sun will shine again someday.

The law of unintended consequences was alive and well daily on a ship. This night was really such a night. Two years ago, while the ship was undergoing a 6-month dry dock repair, the boilers were opened and inspected. This should have caught the small crack in one of the welds developing on the large 8-inch down comer located in the front part of the boiler. The shipyard inspector that day was having a bad allergic reaction to some type of foliage on the island, which in turn caused his eyes to water badly that morning. With watery eyes and severe sneezing, he failed to catch the crack right before his eyes and signed off on the inspection. The boilers were buttoned up and put back in commission when the ship was launched again. Now, to the present day, the small crack became bigger and bigger until this night at this time when the storm hit and caused undue stress upon the boiler's foundation and frame. At 0420, the 8-inch downcomer welds let loose from the stress and cracking. The steam pressure in the boiler was at 1275 psi that night, so when the downcomer came rushing loose, and all that water flashed to steam, the watch team didn't have a chance.

John was down on the lower level, looking out at the firing alley and checking the control console when it happened. The whole front of the 2-alpha boiler ripped open, and the main space was filled with superheated steam. He then sounded the alarm to evacuate the boiler room. He couldn't breathe, he couldn't see, and he couldn't hear. He knew this was it, and he knew he would die in this hole if he didn't think fast. Crawling on his hands and knees, he was slowly making his way to the escape trunk before he passed out from the intense heat.

The air temperature was over 185 degrees and rising as the high-pressure steam and water filled the main space so fast that it felt like being boiled alive. In the pandemonium, John felt calm in that moment. Like being in a snowstorm back in the Great Lakes, John followed the person in front of him slowly to the escape trunk. He could make out the shape of a man in dark coveralls and knew it had to be the lower-level man, Tom. Time seemed to stand still, and he could not really make out the person he was following, but it was a man who knew where he was going, so he kept going until he finally opened the door to the escape trunk. Full of steam and hot to the touch, John ran up the 24 rungs it took to reach the main deck. He then fell on the dark main deck, surrounded by some shipmates helping out. "Get him inside fast; this storm will take us all over the side if we don't leave now." Someone yelled into the night.

They took him into the ship's corpsman's office, and he was soaked down with ice water until he came around. "How are you feeling, Petty Officer Pezdel?" the Corpsman asked him as he lay in a pool of sweat. "I am ok, what about the guy in front of me? It was Tom Hansen, wasn't it? Is he ok?" John asked him. "I don't know of anyone else making it out of there except you. You lost 3 of your watch team down there. I'm sorry, but no one else is alive. Tom Hanson and the other two, Jones and

Dalton, didn't make it." The Corpsman told John as he sat in disbelief. Trying to figure out who the shape of a man was in front of him was confusing, to say the least. No one else made it out that night. The boiler failed with the downcomer separating, causing a major steam leak in fire room #2. Three of his friends died that night in just a few moments. The sedative that the Corpsman gave John kicked in as he slowly slipped into unconsciousness, thinking about the shadowy figure. Maybe it was an angel or something else as the room went black.

Heroes

'Where does it go, the good Lord only knows, it seems like it was just the other day."
Honkey Tonk Heroes, Waylon Jennings

John remembered it like yesterday, and he knew that Abiel was the one he saw that night. "I know it was you, now that I think about it. Why me and why not my friends? Was it their time that night, or did they get caught up in an accident like the Navy claimed it was?" he asked Abiel. That was over 20 years ago, but it still seemed like yesterday. John was sweating now, thinking about that night. They called him a hero for making it out, but his watch team perished from the heat and steam. He never felt like a hero, just lucky sometimes. "I don't think luck played a role that night, John. All things created by man will fail someday, and that was the day the boiler let loose. You did what you were trained to do, and you survived. I just did what I was supposed to do, and I am the one you saw that night. Your friends passed quickly with no pain or suffering, and you only received minor burns on your right arm. I hoped it would have been different, but it rarely is when dealing with these things. The accidents in this world are really never that at all. Behind the scenes, a lot of actions and circumstances are created for the smallest of accidents to happen. It's not God's idea of a cruel joke, just a way of keeping up the flow down here." Abiel said to John. "Flow, that's it, flow, we are just a steady stream of human events designed to keep the flow going down here? And does the great one sit back and watch in amusement while his flock of angels creates a perfect flow? Just another number or name on a tombstone. A week after I'm gone, only a close few will ever know that I existed at all. Is that the worth of a life lived? King Solomon was right in Ecclesiastes about everything being the vanity of vanities. We think we matter or make a difference in this life, but it's all just sand castles on the beach. I don't think that I can make it to the end; this is too much for any man to bear."

John was sinking into a place where a man will go when all hope is lost; he had been there a few times before, but always came through it unscathed. Today would be different, and the end was near. A great sadness overtook him as he saw his lifeblood slipping away, and the few moments he had on this wretched planet would be gone in a few minutes. Only the solace of an Angel to comfort him, "How I wish I could see Anna's face one last time before I'm done."

He imagined her in the morning with the sunlight filtering through her hair as she sat on the back porch watching squirrels. The sound of birds and wild things fills the air on the cool summer morning. The great sadness would not evade him so easily. Whenever he was in a bad way, he would go to a happy place, but right now, all the happy places were gone. The summer rain came down in motionless drops as the Angel of Death slowly came closer, the minion of Satan standing just outside of his view with burning red eyes of fire, awaiting his demise. A guardian angel was taking him slowly down memory lane to places he didn't want to go. He wanted to climb out of the wreckage and choke the evil life out of the minion of Satan, and that would have made him feel better.

These were not happy times, and then he saw it in his mind's eye, a happy place. It was true about Disneyland; it was the happiest place on earth. He was a small boy of about 5 years old, and his parents took the whole family to Disneyland for the day. They didn't have much money back then, but he remembered having so much fun. His mind had taken pictures of that moment as he ran by the French Quarter with the Tom Sawyer steamboat behind him. It was a perfect moment trapped in time, just for this moment now. He felt better about what was to befall him. It's funny how stuff like that stays with you after all of these years. Kind of like an oasis in the middle of a desert just for times like these.

John said to Abiel as his spirit sank lower into a dark place, "You have every right to feel that way, but the things in your life that you have done for the Lord can never be forgotten or erased. I told you before that it's like ripples in a pond, and you may never see the true impact of all you have done, but it is not in vain, and you will be remembered by each and every person you have helped in God's name. They may not see it like you in the final moments, but you will be remembered by more than you will ever know. Trust in the Lord and lean not on your own understanding. Also, I do hear your thoughts, so please refrain from the negative ones about your guardian angel. I have been with you before birth, and although I will miss you, I will see you again, John. That demon outside has no life for you to choke away; only hate and evil courses through its veins. It is just a spiritual being with one purpose to report to its master these events taking place. Don't waste your time thinking of that." Abiel reassured him. John looked out into the night, absorbing all that Abiel had just said. He was right, and John knew it, but in the end, with the promise of another day, the night looked so dark. He stared at the nearly frozen raindrops and looked over to where the angel of death stood in the shadows. He was patiently making his way toward John ever so slowly as if he had all the time in the world. He probably did, but with so many people dying to get into heaven, there had to be someone like him. That's why he never believed in Santa Claus either, but some things in life and death have to be seen with your own eyes to understand the greater picture.

He looked over at Abiel and asked, "So, how does he do it? How does the angel of death ferry so many to heaven in so little time? I know there are a lot more people dying at this moment who are going there also. How does he get around so quickly? I want to know." Abiel looked at John and was a bit surprised because no one had ever asked him that question, and he knew the answer, but it was difficult for a mortal to comprehend. "Well, I'm going to make it simple; he just can. He has the hand of God upon him, and he does the impossible very well. What you see is really not him exactly. He is at this moment taking others' souls up as they depart. He is here in spirit, more like a reservation, because your time has come, but he still has time to take up the other 150,000 to 180,000 people each day. It comes out to about 1 or 2 a second, depending on the amount that is leaving. Sometimes he takes a whole bunch if they went at the same time and are not going to the other place. But he is good at what he does. It doesn't take long to get to heaven once you don't have a body. You don't know the exact time of your departure, but I do, and he does, and also that demon beyond the angel of death who waits also knows you are not long for this world; he doesn't have knowledge of the exact moment, but he knows that when the angel of death is near someone always goes with him. They have been keeping their eyes on you for a long time, John, and after tonight, those demons will sleep a little easier when you have passed.

John looked beyond the trees and saw the glowing red eyes of the evil one as he awaited John's departure. He would remain near until the last breath is drawn and John has left this place. "I see him standing out there waiting. He can wait all he wants and go tell his boss after I'm gone that I went home and not to his Hell." John said to Abiel. Time waits for no man, and John looked at the clock on the dash. It read 0315; only two minutes had gone by in earthly realms, but it seemed so much longer to John, who had the time slowed down by the good Lord for this moment. Where would the angel take him now? He was sure that the worst was over, and he would leave this lonely place. He often thought that when his time came, he didn't want to die alone. He now knew that he wasn't alone and it would be all right. The more they talked, the more he knew that Abiel and the Lord had been there all of the days of his life. It was a bittersweet thought just the same. If he only knew all of this before, would his life be any different?

Awake

"Why does the eye see a thing more clearly in dreams than the
imagination when awake?"
Leonardo da Vinci

She awoke with a jolt in the night. The house was so quiet and
almost like a tomb in the long dark bedroom, funny that the town would
be called Tombstone when at times like these she thought that's where
she was. The Clock read 0315, and Anna just kept thinking of John as
her mind wandered. He was on his way home right now somewhere
close by, she hoped, and maybe he would be walking through the door
in a little while to tell her about the trip. He had gone to California for a
ship reunion and to see some old friends. He didn't talk much about that
night on board the Hoeltstein, but she knew that some scars ran deep.
She always remembered the story of the guy who helped John out to
safety, but he was always vague and confused about who it was.

Anna was a beautiful woman, born in Newport Beach and raised by
the ocean. She wondered often why she loved the desert so much. The
coast is overrated, and there is always so much noise. She wanted less
noise in her life these days. Why the weird feeling inside right now?
John was the one who always had those things, not her. She could not
shake the feeling of dread that had awakened her from a not-so-sound
sleep. "What was I dreaming?" she thought as she recalled the
disturbing dream. She started to remember the dream, they were out
hiking on a sunny morning near the Whetstone mountains, John was

walking some ways ahead of her with his back turned, she couldn't see his face. Anna would try to reach him, but he kept walking away from her. Every time she reached the spot he was at, she saw him further away from her. Beyond John was a very steep hill that was dark and ominous-looking. He was walking up the hill at a fast pace, and Anna could not keep up. She knew that once he reached the top and went over the other side, he would be gone.

She was feeling a great sense of loss and sadness. It was only a dream, but it seemed so real. "Life is but a dream…" kept going through her head. That stupid song would not leave her mind. She got up and went to the living room to look outside; it was still quite dark, but she could make out the mountains in the distance. All the creatures of the desert were in their holes and sleeping away. Only the night creatures were out on the hunt, looking for their next meal. She loved to sit on the porch and watch all of the animals playing in the yard. Tombstone was a great place to live. The old history was here, and the new history was being made daily. What did the strange dream mean anyway? John would be home soon, and she would go back to sleep after he told her of his trip and the reunion. She sure missed him when he was gone. The days were not the same, with his funny stories and just being around the house together was enough for Anna. Some women wanted it all, whatever that meant, but Anna just wanted what she had already, not too much to ask for. It wasn't always this way.

John was in the Navy for a while, and the separation was intense. She raised the children, but at night, she would lie awake sometimes and wonder where he was on the huge blue ocean so far away. It wasn't like it is today; there wasn't any internet or Skype. Just good ole paper and pen. The letter would sometimes take three weeks to get home to her, but she loved to read them anyway. Anna went back to bed and tried to go to sleep, but the nagging feeling of dread continued, so she just closed her eyes while sleep overtook her thoughts.

Subtleties

"Knowledge of the self is the mother of all knowledge. So, it is incumbent on me to know myself, to know it completely, to know its minutiae, its characteristics, its subtleties, and its very atoms."
Khalil Gibran

It was 0230 am, and they waited outside the business watching for signs of occupancy. John saw that the other two guys were waiting for the night watchman to come around to the back of the jewelry shop. He made his rounds on the half hour, and he should be here soon. John had gotten out of the Navy 6 months ago, and times were hard. He and Anna did not have much money, and the kids needed food and diapers. He had a job at the refinery down the road, but the economy was bad, and jobs were scarce. He worked 40 hours a week at the lowest pay scale, trying to keep up. His boys were both sick with the flu, and they had no medical insurance; times were hard. These two guys that John was with were local friends from the Irisher bar over in Seal Beach. They had told John about a job they were going to pull off at this jewelry store in Hawthorne. It was full of gems and jewels, and the owner would take the bank deposit out in the morning. All he had to do was hit the guard over the head to knock him out, and then get the stuff.

It was a simple plan, but even the simplest plans of mice and men sometimes go astray. Tonight was one of those times. They waited behind a smelly trash dumpster for the guy to walk by. 0235 came, and no watchman yet, the boys were getting antsy. This was supposed to be an easy job; he would just hit the guy and knock him out, and the boys would grab the keys to the shop and turn off the alarm with the watchman's alarm key, easy and simple. John sat there looking down the alley at nothing, only thinking that the Navy wasn't so bad after all. He didn't have to hit anyone in the head, and he didn't have to steal from others to support his family. He knew this was wrong, and the old feeling inside was back again. That nagging gut-wrenching feeling he got when something bad was about to transpire, it was a slow-moving tremor in his gut that would eventually render him sick and shaking. No time for that now, he had some business to contend with. Too late, the watchman was coming toward them. He was getting closer to almost 10 feet when he stopped, turned away, and went down the alley as if getting a call somewhere else. John didn't need any more than that to change his mind; he got up and ran down the alley away from the boys and away from the situation. They didn't know where he was staying or even who he was, for that matter, but John would take a chance, so he got back to the motel and told Anna to grab the kids and everything they owned because it wasn't safe. Just like that, he decided he would go back in the service for another tour; it wasn't as bad as this. They stayed at Anna's sister's house until John got back in the Navy. Anna asked him about that night for years, but he just told her it was a drug deal gone wrong. She figured it was the truth since they were doing a lot of stuff back then. Times weren't right, but at least they were not right together. Years later, John knew that the secret to their blessed union was love and understanding of what once was and what would be.

Life

"Only a life lived for others is a life worthwhile."
Albert Einstein

Just like that, it was all gone, leaving a dark, rainy night at an intersection in Tucson, Arizona instead. John knew what he had just seen and remembered all of it. Times were bad back then, but he had forgotten how bad they could be until now. He was going to help rob a jewelry store by knocking out an old guy and stealing money. "So, Abiel, why did we go there? Of all the times you saved me in the past, why did we go that night? I didn't see any reason or life-threatening situation arise. It was just some thugs robbing a store." John asked as the rain fell slowly upon his face, drop by drop, in slow motion. "You were there because that was a pivotal time in your life. I was there also, but the need for me to intervene did not present itself. You chose to leave that place before you harmed the guard. Had you stayed, it would not have ended well, my Friend. The man you were about to strike would have died from his injuries. The thieves that you were with were going to shoot you after the job was completed. You would have lived from the injuries, but the police would find you at the scene and charge you with the crimes. As a young man, you would have spent the best years of your life in prison until you were 49 years old. Anna would be gone; your kids would be gone, and you would have no one and nothing. Then, like now, you would have died anyway in a like manner on some lonely road far away from your home. I would have still been there on that day as I am now, but things would not have bided so well for you, and even then, your soul would have been suspect. We spend a lot of time in the past and present, but the future is not for your eyes to see. I have seen both sides of the road that you have walked upon. I would have been with you either way, but it was not God's will for you to rot in a prison cell. You have lived a wonderful life reflecting the image of your maker, and he is pleased. So, tell me, John, do you see what could have been?" he asked John carefully. "I see now as if my eyes were clear like Saul who became Paul on the road to Damascus, I now know why God has saved me all those times, is this it now? Am I going home?" he asked with sadness inside.

Abiel thought for a moment before answering. How many times in how many places had this same scene unfolded? He was a heavenly being, but all this time on earth has softened his angel heart. He wasn't supposed to get close to his subjects, Angel rule # 27, but it was too late for some people; you cannot help it. John was just a man living his life; he could not see the big picture that he was part of. When you are on the ground looking up at heaven, it is a long way off. At this moment in time, John is just a breath away from eternity. He wanted to tell him to let it all go because he was going to his inheritance. Humans sometimes get stuck in this place, always afraid of dying and seeing what's beyond. If they only had the faith of a mustard seed, they would know what he knows.

"Yes, in due time you will be home, not much longer, my friend, we have only been in this wreck for a few minutes of this earthly time, but for you it has been hours, and you still have as much further to go." Abiel told John, "But Abiel, is there any way I could get a message back to Anna? What would she do when she hears the word of my death? I would give anything to be in our bedroom right now as she sleeps." "John, I can see her now. She was awakened from a strange dream, but now she sleeps. I promise that no matter who my next client is or how long, I will look in on her from time to time. She will never forget you, John." Abiel knew that he spoke the truth as John worried about his wife. Abiel was never surprised at the love between the people he watched over had for one another. If they only knew how it would be someday, they would not mourn their passing.

Surprise

"Which death is preferable to every other? The unexpected.
"Julius Caesar

The night was warm and smelled like the islands. This time of year, the trade winds blew through, bringing smells from distant islands and places far away. Hawaii was a great place to be stationed if you were in the military. The Aloha Stadium swap meet was extra crowded since it was Friday night. John took Anna and the boys there on weekends to get out of the house and get some good deals. They walked thru the crowds of people with the kids in tow looking for a bargain. You could find anything here if you just looked hard enough. Further ahead Anna was waking past the fortune teller tent.

The woman was trying to get inside to tell her the future. Anna did not want to know her fortune since that was not favorable to God, so she kept walking. John soon walking up to that spot when the woman turned around to ask him if he wanted a reading but stopped in mid-sentence. She was staring into John's face but it looked like she saw the grim reaper. Her face was drained of all color and she turned around running and got lost in the crowd. "That was strange," John thought as he kept walking. He wondered what had made her so afraid; he looked in a nearby mirror at a sunglass vendor and he still looked the same. Later as they were all getting in the car a man walked up and demanded all of their money and jewelry. He had a gun pointed at John's face but John was so upset at being robbed by the thug that he grabbed his hand and they got into a scuffle. A moment later the man pointed the gun at John and pulled the trigger, nothing happened. The startled man dropped the weapon and ran off into the night. John picked it up and pointed it into the air and pulled the trigger. A loud shot rand out as he waiting with ringing ears for security to show up and take a statement.

Chance

*"Two roads diverged in a wood, and I... I took the one less traveled
by, and that has made all the difference."*
Robert Frost

"I know I was lucky that night, Abiel; it is no mystery. The guy's
gun misfired, but what was it that the women saw that made her run
away so frightened?" he asked. "You were just a reflection to her that
night; she saw into the depths of her own soul mirrored in your eyes.
What frightened her most was what she saw of how she would end up
after so much dabbling in the occult and witchcraft. She saw the end of
her days and the Grim Reaper taking her to her final destination. She
thought you were the reaper, but it was only a visual of what is to be.
The man with the gun is a different story. The gun did not misfire; I had
my hand between the hammer and the firing pin. You would not have
liked a 38-caliber bullet to your face, would you? He ran off but was
later caught that night trying to sneak into someone's house. The
homeowner did have a gun that did not misfire, and the man was shot
dead." Abiel said to John. John asked him, "If I wasn't there that night,
would the man still have lost his life?"

"Yes, he would have because he would have broken into that house
to rob it anyway. His days were numbered, as are yours. At the heart of
the matter is not the time spent but the work done in that time, and how
you live it. The greatest tragedy in life is not the number of moments
that you are given but what is done with them. You have always had a

sense of urgency in your life; you have always eaten a little too fast, moved a little too quickly, and lived a little too much for the average person. In your mind, you have rationalized it with terms like, "I have ADHD, or I'm just hyper," but in reality, you have always known that your days were numbered, also. You have always burned the candle at both ends, and some would argue that you would have spent your moments carelessly and without regard, but the truth is, the candle burning at both ends is the brightest candle in the room. It is not always the victor that wins the race first, but the one who enjoys the race that really wins.

In answering your question, the woman had always known she was walking a thin line between this World and the other. She was raised in a catholic home, and had known the presence of the Lord in her life often. It was only when she lost her dear loved one that she cursed God and turned to the dark world. It was in that world that she thought she had some form of power and gifts of prophecy, only to realize that the face she saw that night, the grim reaper, was just a prophecy of things to come in her own life. She was trying to bring the spirit of her dearly departed back from the grave to communicate with him. She failed and only managed to open the door for other spirits to come through. The ones that go bump in the night and the ones who pass themselves off as your ancestor, but they are working for the evil one. They are familiar spirits who have been in this world so long that they know everything about you and your ancestors; it's not rocket science, as you say.

Very few people have been given the gift of foresight and knowledge of things yet to come. You have it now since you know you will not leave this truck alive. It will be all right in the end. Does this answer your question, John?" Abiel asked. "In a way, it does, but I remember my own Grandmother talking to the dead. How do you explain that? Was she a witch or a medium or just an old woman who talked to dead people?" He asked. Abiel replied, "She was neither, she was just a woman who had the ability to see and hear things that were not of this earth, you have it too in a lesser degree, but I think in some ways you see and hear more than you would like to. Your Grandmother was incapable of not talking to those spirits; they came to her constantly, and she did tune them out, but occasionally one would come through and reveal itself. They were not from a bad place, just lost souls waiting for the day of reckoning." John knew now that the woman was seeing her own reflection that night. John looked outside into the darkness. The strange red glow was still enveloping his vehicle as he tried to find the angel of darkness, and there he was, just coming out of a tree line of Palo Verdes. John could now make out some features, broad shoulders, and huge wings of power and might; he could also see a hint of his face. He was an angelic being with a sense of purpose and determination. John felt better at seeing him out there, but it was bittersweet because the more of the angel of death he saw, the less time on earth he had left.

John could also see the demonic creature hidden in the shadows. The truck lights illuminated the angel of death, while the demon crept back in the shadows; only his red, fiery eyes could be seen. The dashboard clock read 0316; only 3 minutes had passed since he had gotten into the wreck. He should have bled out by now. Maybe the wounds were not so bad, and there might be hope. Just then, a slow-motion flickering of red and then blue could be seen coming down Park Ave. John's heart leaped for a moment at the thought of rescue, but he remembered what Abiel had said when he first talked to him about this being a one-way ticket out of here. There was so much sadness to endure before he left. He wondered how other people felt before him as they drew their last breath and went away from this world. Did they go kicking and screaming or just whimpering? John would do neither since he had his angel right here to be with him until the end. He thought of a song that just popped into his head, "Life is but a dream…" then it passed into nothing. Would he remember any of this on the other side? Or will he just be a big ball of energy floating through the cosmos forever? There were so many questions but so little time. He sure was hungry right now, no last meal for him. If he were on death row instead of in death's truck, he would have a last meal. What would he have? "I guess a pastrami sandwich with a side of fries would be best, also a chocolate malt and some pecan pie," John said to Abiel. "That would be your last meal from all the meals that could have been picked on this planet? I do not eat, but I have eaten before, you know, for appearance's sake. The angel handbook makes an exception in such instances. We can eat just like you, but we don't need to. Food provided nothing for us except a momentary taste of what it is. Aside from the nutritional value, it does the same for you, too. For my last meal, I would have lobster, a New York Steak, mashed potatoes with some brown gravy, French fries, clam chowder, a pepperoni pizza, and some cold beer. After that, a plate of flapjacks smothered in maple syrup." Abiel told John. "Why would you eat so much even though you don't eat?" John asked him. Abiel replied, "I just love the taste of food, and those are my favorites. Also, if it were my last meal on earth, I would like to make it special. You won't get a last meal, but we will make it special just the same. Not all you see is what you get, and vice versa. Sometimes, what you see isn't always the way things are. We will explore this in time, my friend."

Consequences

"The Wrong we have Done, Thought, or Intended will wreak its
Vengeance on Our SOULS."
C.G. Jung

As the hope abandoned John, he remembered he had once read that anyone who saw the Death Angel would surely lose their life. No escape route here, just the cold realization that his time on this earth was numbered, as with everyone. John was thinking about how he learned a friend of his in high school had just passed away last week. How distant that all seemed now that he thought about it. They just had the funeral yesterday while John was in Santa Monica. It was all so surreal when he thought back and felt the remorse, then astonishment that someone he had known back then was gone. They weren't that close, but he would see Tommy now and then when he was back visiting the folks. Some small talk and pleasantries, but that was all. He now knew what it would be like for those who knew him after he was gone. The ones he loved and those who loved him back would grieve and feel sadness in their hearts, that is the nature of things, but others would say the old "did you hear what happened to John?" routine with a somber look as they tell the grisly details. Even in life, we mock and avoid death like an uninvited dinner guest who has overstayed their welcome and won't leave without wanting some leftovers. You know the one who drank a little too much and ate way too much. It's the loud, obnoxious one who just will not shut up, and when that moment finally comes when you escort him to the door, he turns around and grabs hold of your coat and says, "It's Time" as he takes you to eternity.

Through the broken windshield, John could make out the features of the Death Angel. He knew now that the moments on this earth should not have been wasted in vain. Abiel was trying to prepare him for this with all his talk of past deeds and work for the Lord. John was just a simple man who enjoyed life and the people who meant so much to him. He would miss so many things in the world, not the bad or evil nature of man, but all the good things in life. His mind started drifting to moments lost in time, when he was a younger, more ambitious man. He would miss his wife and children, His grandchildren, and those that are yet to be born. Would he meet them on the other side? He also missed sitting by a warm fire on a cold night and watching the full moon, seeing the waves break early in the morning on the North shore of Oahu. Like smelling the fresh-cut hay in the San Joaquin Valley in summer. Telling a joke to his granddaughter and hearing her laugh. He loved staring into the beautiful eyes of Anna as she laughed at one of his jokes, which she had heard too many times, and the many things that would be missed. He knew that he would never see another sunrise or sunset. We only have the moment, and then it passes. He now felt the words of King Solomon when he wrote in Ecclesiastes 12:6 that "the silver cord would be loosed, that the golden bowl is broken, or the pitcher is broken at the fountain, or the wheel is broken at the cistern," and he would pass from this life to another. There was so much brokenness to end a life; whatever happened to him dying in his sleep?

John thought back to a guy he knew in Prescott who had cut open his femoral artery by accident with a skill saw. His buddy was working with him and drove him to the hospital while he held his leg tight to prevent it from swelling. He said that while pulling into the hospital parking lot, he almost blacked out and would have died right then. It didn't matter much in the long run because he died 10 years later from lung cancer; ten years was better than nothing. John grabbed his neck and tried to slow the blood loss for a chance at life. Abiel spoke up just then, "It will do no good, John; you will only restrict what flow is going to your head and pass out sooner. All you have is this moment in time, and we have places to go and people to see, so stay with me, ok?" John looked at Abiel and saw a look of urgency that had not been there before. The Angel was serious, and important matters were at hand.

Darkest Before the Dawn

"In the time of darkest defeat, victory may be nearest."
William McKinley

The day was beautiful in the land north of Prescott off of Highway 89 as John made his way to the Drake Road turn-off in the National Forest. There was a chill in the air as he drove the pickup down the bumpy dirt road. His trusty dog, Nathaniel, was by his side to ward off any predators, plus the 45 caliber. Colt helped. It was early, and he told Anna he would be back by noon to go cut some firewood. This was something he liked to do, and it was more therapeutic than work. Big Nate stared out of the window, looking for something to chase. He was an AKC Rottweiler bred from good stock and looked the part. All in all, he was just a good dog. It was about 36 degrees outside, and John had brought a thermos full of coffee. A couple of doughnuts would have been good, but Anna packed a Bagel for breakfast. She always thought more of him than herself. The health kick she had him on wasn't bad, but a doughnut would have been great. I guess she thought he would live forever if he just ate the right things, but John knew better, and the end was always near. Like Jim Morrison used to say.

This was northern Arizona, much different than the lower half. The summers were mild and the winters a little cold but bearable. Today, he was hoping to cut at least half a cord of Juniper, so that was the plan. They found an area about a half mile off Drake Road that hadn't been cut up too badly. "This looks like a great spot, Nate," John said to his eager pet. He opened the truck door and watched Nathan jump out and chase some unseen creature down the trail. He was a good dog and wouldn't venture far. John went to work on cutting firewood. It was hard, laborious work, but good exercise, and it would heat the house for about a month. It was getting to be about noon when Nate wandered off the trail to check on something. John followed him down a stream that disappeared into the ground. That was odd because most streams went south somehow or another. Next to the stream were the tailings of an old gold mine dug over a hundred years ago. Behind a stand of juniper, John could make out the entrance to a mine shaft. It had not been disturbed for years, and John was the first to venture into it for decades.

Nate was outside chasing rabbits as John took out a Minnie Mag light to see into the darkness. It was warmer in here as the light from outside faded and the silence crept in. He knew this mine was near here, but forgot about it. They called it "The Juniper Load" since it produced a fair amount of gold back in the 1860s. John was about to turn around and walk out when the ground gave way, and he fell down a dark hole into nothing. He hit the ground with a hard thud and felt his ankle snap. Pain shot up as he lay crumpled in the darkness, his flashlight dimly showing the great distance he had fallen. It would have been a chore if he had not had a broken ankle, but now it was just impossible. His cheap cell phone wouldn't work down here, and Anna knew kind of where he was, but he was not supposed to be down here. He knew they would come looking for him when he didn't make it home that night, but right now, he had to remain calm. Nathan could be heard high above him, looking for his master. John yelled out, "Nathan, go get Anna, get Anna, boy." Nathan heard his master and ran outside in search of Anna. He made it to the truck and waited for her to show up. That was about 10:30 am.

John lay in the cold, dark mining tunnel. He couldn't see much since the darkness ate up the entire flashlight, so he only saw a dim light above his head. After a couple of hours, even that was lost to total darkness. The feeling of dread and despair settled over John; he knew he would be found sometime, but he didn't know if he would be alive. This was the last time he cut wood alone. John's watch said 7:22 pm, and he would be missing by now. All he could hear was silence and the occasional coyote out on the prowl. Right now, he had to cover up with an old flannel shirt. He tried to stay awake as the pain shot up his leg into his brain. John got his cell phone out and took a picture of himself as he lay in the dirt; he wanted Anna to have one last photo so she would know he was thinking about her.

When all you have is time, then thinking is all you can do. He was reminded of the days and months spent out on the ocean while serving in the Navy. How he hated those days, and the separation was unbearable at times. There were around 385 men on board, but in the scheme of things, they were all alone. John would lie in his bunk after watch at 4:00 in the morning, trying to figure out the time difference and wonder what Anna was doing right then. Mail took forever, and whatever was written happened so long ago that it didn't matter. John wasn't meant to be a sailor, but he was good at it, so that's what he did for a while. He could hear the rustling of something above him in the darkness, so he shone his flashlight to the cave's ceiling and saw several hundred bats waking up for their evening flight. At first, John was freaked out, but he told himself to remain calm, and they would not bother him. That was partially true until they all took off as one, and the cave became congested with what seemed like thousands of bats flying around until they found a hole above and escaped. This would make a great story if he survived, but inside, John knew that this was not how the story ended. He had seen the vision of his demise and knew that today was not that day. All that vision stuff kind of falls away in times like these. His faith in God and his trust in the Lord were all he had in the world that kept him going. Oh yes, he had Anna.

He could see her that day as they sat in some tavern in Seal Beach, drinking a cold beer and listening to Bob Seger on the juke box. Bob sang "And I remember what she said to me, How she swore that it never would end, I remember how she held me oh so tight Wish I didn't know now what I didn't know then" Anna had a glow and beauty that transcended time and space but she didn't see it that way "Why do you keep staring at me like that John, like you have never seen me before?" she asked him. He replied, "I have seen you always long before we met, and right now, I really see you for the first time." They had only known each other for about a month, but he knew she would be his wife someday, and this day would be just a memory. He snapped out of it as he heard a coyote howling in the distance, then silence. Nate wasn't even around. John felt truly alone again.

The blackness engulfed him and lulled him into a restless sleep. In his dreams, he was lost at sea in a small raft; the sea was dark and restless as it pushed him further from the shore. He could see the lights of a distant town as the rain fell and the raft shook violently. He was utterly alone with no one to help him. Just then, he remembered the story of Jesus and the disciples in the storm. They were frightened, but Jesus told them not to be alarmed; he would be with them always, even unto death. John awoke with a start and realized he was not in a raft but stuck in some hole in the ground, awaiting help. He felt a calm sense of peace as he lay here thinking about his life and how he had made it this far. With the newfound sense of calmness, he knew that he would be found alive and all would be well. A noise in the distance could be heard; John stared into the void and listened for the source. At first, nothing but the night and the silent tomb he was in, but then he heard it, far off, the sound of a rescue search helicopter and several search dogs barking. They were getting closer as John lay there in the damp cave. After a few minutes, he could hear voices calling his name and the sound of Nate barking above, telling the rescuers where he was. Then he heard Anna's voice above it all, and this made him yell her name repeatedly until a flashlight could be seen above from the rescuers. He was pulled up out of the abyss into the night; Anna was standing by the rescue truck, crying for joy. He tried to walk but couldn't, so they put him on a stretcher and let Anna see him. "Don't ever go cutting wood by yourself again, John. I was scared half to death, promise?" she said in a trembling voice. He told her, "Next time, we just buy a few cords from the neighbors."

Peace

"Nobody can bring you peace but yourself."
Ralph Waldo Emerson

"I remember that day and even that night not so long ago. You were there with me in that dark tomb. I can see it all so clearly, and I remember getting rescued and seeing Anna outside. She never looked so good as that night when she was crying and thrilled that I was still alive. We go through life oblivious of tomorrow, always thinking it will be there like money in the bank. We never really see it all until it is in the rear-view mirror, but by then it's all too late. If only we had just one more hour or one more day, what difference would it make, and how would we use it?" John said to himself. "Abiel, what part did you play? If I was going to be rescued anyway, I wasn't in any immediate danger, and it all worked out fine," he asked Abiel. "John, I was with you that day, and I stayed with Nate until the rescuers saw him and he guided them to you. You and every other human on this planet are a witness to the Lord Almighty, whether you know it or not. What you do and say is reported to our Lord through my eyes and every other angel in this world. That's a lot of angels, but then again, we were made for this purpose, also the Lord sees the just and the unjust, so nothing is a surprise to him." Abiel told him.

"So, what are the other Angels for? There is only one Angel of Death, and I see him now in front of my truck." John said to Abiel as he stared into the night with his headlights shining now on the Angel of

Death, not 30 feet from his truck. He knew that when the Angel reached him, his time would be over. 30 feet was not a lot of time to spend in this world; he didn't know how much time it was, but a sudden feeling of hopelessness filled his soul as he knew that the time was at hand. The death Angel looked awesome and full of purpose; never in John's life had he seen a look of determination as he saw now on the angel's face. From that last episode or vision, John knew that the end was near; he only fell into that dark pit and broke his ankle about 11 years ago. Funny how time flies when you are dying.

"Why is he not moving faster like we are in real time? Does he have to obey the same law of time as those on earth?" John asked, confused by the slow motion of it all. "No, he has his own time agenda, but right now he is walking in the moment as anyone on earth would do. If time were not frozen to a snail's crawl like it is, he would have snatched you away long ago, and we would never have met in this crumpled-up truck. I am sure I would have seen you again, my friend, maybe not in this world but in the heavenly realm. The angels who occupy this time and space are called to earth because that is their divine purpose, and that would not be taken away. Many are called, but few are chosen. The purpose that we are devoted to is of the greatest importance to mankind and heaven.

There are others like me, but they have different tasks and purposes. Just as the minions of the evil one never rest until a soul is in their control, we too have the purpose of keeping them out of his grasp. The bible says that someday the serpent will be cast into the lake of fire for eternal torment, but that day is not today, and even the angels do not know when it will happen. Only the almighty knows the end to come, so we just do our duty to save all the souls we can before the judgment day." Abiel said to John as he stared out the windshield at his coming fate. He now felt a sense of peace that he once heard of in Sunday school when Anna taught the little children, and John would act as the bouncer or doorman. Those were the days, and he learned so much from those simple lessons taught to children. Everyone was a child once upon a time. The problem was that we forgot all of it and became adults in an ever-changing world. The sense of peace was like a drug, but better; all was well within his soul as he welcomed the death angel to take him home again. "You can feel it now, can't you? It's like your already gone but just one foot is planted upon this earthly realm and that's all that is holding you here, wait a minute John you are not finished yet, we still have a few more steps down memory lane that you have forgotten, I'm sorry to burst your moment but it must be finished before you can start again." Abiel said to John. John knew this to be true, but he was weary of this game, and if death must come, then let us get it done with. He was always a man of purpose and decision in all that he did. His life was not rigid, but it was the meaning that had meant something to him; he was always a little on the ADHD side of things, but he still managed to make sense of it all, even if others could not understand his motives. All in all, he just hated to waste time; everything else in life that was of the material nature could be replaced, but time was a precious commodity that he did not waste. It must have stemmed from the vision he saw so long ago that has come to pass in these moments, who could deny the existence of God when he sent his Son and angels to comfort him now?

Understanding

John stepped into the doorway of the house in Tombstone, a fixer-upper that was being sold as is, but needed so much work. A strange feeling overtook him as he walked through the house from room to room, thinking he had been here before. It was impossible since they rarely came down to Tombstone, and if they did, they just stayed in a motel. Last time it was at the Sagebrush Inn, and they stayed in the John Wayne room, which was awesome. This was different, and John knew it. He had a sense of vertigo and fear, like he was going to die, but not really. He had this feeling before on several occasions, but this was much stronger. How could he know the layout of this place if he had never seen it before? He also knew about the basement and the little room off the basement. Right now, it was calling him down there, but he took his time checking out the upstairs. Anna had a bad look on her face as she stood behind the realtor with the universal wife signal of no and hell no on her face; yes, he knew it well and could read her mind right now. The house did stink of old dog and old food, and the overpowering smell of mold permeated the air. What a diamond in the rough, but his dear wife would not see it that way.

They walked from room to room as the smell and sight of soiled carpets and garbage assailed them at every step. John knew it was a pipe dream, and there were other homes in Tombstone much better than this, but he could not shake the feeling of familiarity and homecoming that he now felt. He saw past the old house in decline and envisioned what it could be, a place to live out his days with Anna and become a member of this community. They walked down some narrow stairs into an old, unfinished basement made from cinderblock and concrete. It was cooler down here even though it was mid-June in southern Arizona with temps in the 100's. John could sense a weird feeling down here, as though bad people had lived here but had since moved on. No bad spirits, just bad people. He went outside into the little room next door that served as a furnace room with dirt floors. An add-on he could see since upstairs held a large master bedroom,

This room was a little creepy but much colder and smaller than the basement. John felt a shiver run down his spine as he could sense that something still occupied the space, but not of a bad nature. He just had the feeling of being watched and observed. Outside, it was 102 degrees, but in here, it was not even 50 degrees. It felt nice, but whatever was in here was not leaving, so he took some pictures and then left with Anna. John could sense that the things that occupied this room had been down here for a very long time. He did not know what or who they were, but that they only wished to be left in the darkness, he could do that. The look on Anna's face remained, so they told the realtor they would think about it and call her back. That always meant no, but John really didn't mind since the place needed a lot of work. They left and drove out of town on Route 80 for about a mile, then Anna said to John, "I really don't like the looks of that place, but I have this overwhelming feeling that we are supposed to get that house, let's go see the agent and make an offer." They turned the car around and headed to their destiny.

That was 10 years ago, and time does fly when you're having fun or just dying. John longed for those days back then, when they worked for hours and days on the house. There were no really bad things living there, but sometimes John would wake up and see his world the way that Anna saw it; she held a different view on the world than the average person. She knew, and John knew, that the afterlife was just another step to take. The years spent as a children's pastor and her belief in the Lord kept them sustained even in the bad times, which were few. The house became a type of home base as they traveled the country and went off to travel the USA for a while. It always was there to greet them and welcome them home. One morning, Anna asked John if he had passed before her, and what she should do. He said, "Just cremate me and spread my ashes on Allen Street when it gets dark, preferably on a Saturday night when the town is in its best form." Tombstone on a Saturday night was like stepping back in time. You could sit outside the Crystal Palace and listen to the sounds of the night. Too many tourists during the day, at night, only the locals and the few souls who rented motels for the night came out. Not quite Disneyland, but close enough.

John realized he was having the last thoughts of a home that he would never see again. Those were the best times he could remember in a long time. He looked over at Abiel and wanted to know something from him, so he asked him, "Why do you do this? Do you have a choice, and if you refused, would you cease to exist in any dimension?" Abiel looked at John and said, "Sure, we all have a choice in this world and the next. I do this because this is all I have ever done. I was created to be a guardian, and I can do nothing else. Some positions are noble and ranked high among my kind, and then again, there are the not-so-noble jobs that must be done. The job of being here on earth every day and being involved in a person's life, no matter what the cost, that is my job, and I take it seriously."

"So, Abiel, what you're telling me is you just stay here on earth and hang around one person until they die, then you move on to the next, don't you ever get tired or bored or maybe need a vacation? Also, do you ever get attached and have favorites?" John asked him. Abiel replied, "I do not get bored, and I don't get tired, and John, you are my favorite right now. My next case will be my favorite. Also, even though I am just minutes away in earthly time from that happening, I will never forget you, John, and the life you have lived. You are not dead yet, so we must move on. Time waits for no man or angel, and I feel the grasp of time slipping away in this relationship. I have been with you always, but it seems like yesterday when you were born on that November day. We must not forget the reason we are here and stay focused on the task at hand." John became irritated at Abiel and shouted at him, "So is that what I am to you now, a task at hand, the moment my lungs take my last breath and I'm thrust into oblivion, you will be on to your next victim silently waiting for their final day. I know you have a job to do and it is a noble ordained job from the Lord Almighty, but in the matter of living and the human condition, that's my territory, and it will not be taken lightly."

"John, I feel your hurt from within, and I can feel the pain of a life once lived, but now it is in its final moments here in this earthly realm. It is true the words that you have spoken, but you do look through a glass darkly now, as in just a few of your minutes you will see face to face. So much more awaits you, and I'm so sorry that the end has come so soon. But in these days, as in all days, the end is never expected, even if you are on your last breath. I have had so many clients who knew they were dying but never expected it to be real. Just remember, you will not pass away from here alone. I will be there, and the angel of death now waits even as he slowly creeps towards us to carry you away. I have never gotten over why he creeps up on everyone like that, but it's his thing, and it comes with the whole Death Angel stigmata. You will now see things differently; you're not being shown the times you could have perished, but now it's the times you have lived. The times when you were closest to the Lord, and you didn't even know it; we must go now," Abiel spoke as they went into another dreamscape.

In the Night

"Night is a time of rigor, but also of mercy. There are truths which one can see only when it's dark."
Isaac Bashevis Singer

Johnny awoke in the middle of the night out of a sound sleep. His little head was still full of dreams as his mother and other siblings were quickly moving out of the house into the street. He couldn't remember ever leaving the house at an hour like this; it was so scary yet weird as he walked into the street to an awaiting crowd. He was excited but cold in the Southern California winter night. He could see his house across the street, and then next door at the Barkers' place, the roof of the garage was engulfed in flames as it blazed through the night sky. He had never seen a fire so large and majestic; even from across the street, he could feel the heat from the flames warming him up. "Why is the Barkers' garage burning, Mom?" He asked amongst the confusion, "I don't know, Honey, it must have been bad wiring or something. Maybe a can of gasoline caught fire." It was always bad wiring or smoking, but who would be up there at this time of night? Johnny was only 4 years old, but he knew that he was seeing something great and memorable. He hoped that the Barkers made it out, but who knew? Little Jerry Barker was a couple of years older than John, but they were friends, and at 4 years old, the neighborhood was very large, so he stayed close to home.

Fire has a funny way of drawing people in; it is devastating yet mysterious all at once. Since the beginning of humankind, fire has always been our friend and enemy. You could use it to cook and heat your house, but everything burns eventually; you just have to get it hot enough. They had to evacuate their home due to its proximity to the flames. Johnny hoped that the fire wouldn't attack his home and burn up his collection of cowboys and Indians figures that he loved to play with. He had a genuine Fort Apache play set that was his prized possession, and it would devastate him to see it turn to a pile of burnt plastic. They stood there, each caught up in their own thoughts and wonders. The fire was slowly extinguished, and they were all allowed to go back to their homes. Some were only there to watch and wonder, while others were there to witness something beyond their mortal life. Johnny went back to bed and fell asleep to the smell of wood smoke and dreams of camping. He often had vivid and powerful dreams even at this young age.

The morning came, and Johnny went to the kitchen to eat some cereal. He liked corn flakes but they never lasted around here, so Mom made him a poached egg and asked him about the fire, "Johnny were you scared last night when we had to leave the house while the Barkers garage burned?" she said, he replied "No Mommy I wasn't scared, it looked so beautiful and warm, I wanted to see more."

"But weren't you afraid of dying or getting burned?" she asked. "I wasn't afraid of dying or the fire because I knew that my other Mom and dad would look out for me." He told her. She had a shiver run down her spine as he said this. Just last week, he woke her up and asked where his real family was and why he was here with these strangers. It frightened her so much that she went to Father O' Reilly to get an answer. He told her that little children were much closer to God than we were, and they can still sense the great beyond since they have just come from there. Still, the look on Johnny's face said it all; he believed he came from somewhere else, and she was not his mother…

Abiel was asking John a question, but he was still in the dream or time warp as the angel spoke. Finally, as if he broke the surface of the water from a deep dive, he heard Abiel speak, "John, what do you think happened back then with the fire and your mother?" John thought about it for a minute then said "I think in some way that father O' Reilly was right about children being closer to God, I just never felt at home until years later when the familiarity set in and the mundane task of living day to day was a reality, then the world I thought I came from faded away with my hopes and dreams. "Abiel then asked him, "So what do you think of the afterlife now, John? Did all of your childhood dreams come true, and were you in fact right the whole time?" John knew the answer all along, as he had known it his whole life; the world we live in is just a facade that hides the inner workings of the universe from mortal eyes. Just a few times in a person's life are they allowed to see beyond the veil of reality and look into the unknown, and those times are rare. Most people never see the truth until it's too late. John was lucky, even though his life's blood was slipping from his body. He had always been lucky like that, and the wonders of this world never became dull or mundane to John.

"I guess, Abiel, that I've known it all along throughout my time on earth. I'm not a scholar or a wise man, but I do know things that cannot be explained by just anyone. I guess it took a heavenly host to bring it all into perspective. I know I was different growing up, but all that fades away when the rigors of life and puberty rear their ugly head. We all wish we could go back in time and change things. Even now, as I see time almost standing still, I am completely aware that it hasn't stopped or rolled backward. All humans sense the presence of death, even if it's not close enough to grab us; we still feel death's hand intertwined with life. Sometimes it is so common we see it on Television or in the streets and say poor bastard, or we just walk on by, hoping that somewhere in the cosmos, death is so busy he will fail to see our souls as we slip down the street. Am I scared? No, not really, you have helped me immensely in these final moments. Am I sad? Yes, I will miss my true love and all of my family. Such is the trade-off when we walk outside our front door, right? So, tell me, Abiel, why am I seeing this past fire now when I'm supposed to be seeing it when I almost died or became a statistic?" John said to Abiel. "That is true, my friend, but as I said before, this is the part of the show or tale, if you like, that shows you all of the times that Christ was there and you were a part of it, so pay close attention as it all unfolds," Abiel told him.

St Augustine's

"My concern is not whether God is on our side; my greatest concern is to be on God's side, for God is always right."
Abraham Lincoln

Johnny sat in the classroom staring out of the window in the first-grade class of St Augustine's church off of Pier Ave in Santa Monica. He could see the hill before him like a lazy dragon sitting in the sun. It was just a hill full of houses, but on the other side were the beach and the Santa Monica pier with all of its glory. "Johnny Pezdel, you pay attention in class and quit looking outside at nothing." Sister Julie said as she taught about the holy trinity and other things. Johnny didn't care about that or even about baby Jesus; he just wanted to go to the pier. Sister Julie told the class that today the award for the best story would be given out; Johnny paid no attention to her rhetoric as he dreamed of faraway lands and distant galaxies. Just then, a yardstick was slapped across his desk as Mother Superior appeared before him like a Ninja in black, scaring the wits out of poor Johnny. He paid attention now. "Class, the winner for the best short story is Johnny Pezdel. Will you come up here, accept your prize, and tell the class about your story called "Us and Them," please? Sister Julie asked.

Now he was really scared; he didn't like people, and he didn't like to be looked at. Johnny was a loner, and he loved to sit in the back, just being alone in his own little world. Slowly, he got up and headed to the front. Kids could be so cruel, even in the first grade; they sat and stared and made weird faces as he tried not to shake or sweat. Sister Julie gave him a golden crucifix made of plastic as the prize, then he had to address the mob. He told them about his story and how he was from another planet, far away from here, where there were real space aliens who liked him, and he was only wearing a mask on Earth to avoid detection. The children just laughed and made fun of him. He took his prize and went back to his seat in humiliation. After class, Sister Julie asked Johnny to stay for a moment. He would be late for recess, but he didn't have many friends out there anyway. He also liked Sister Julie; she was too nice to be a nun. She was very pretty from what he could see and kind. He sat down by her desk and asked why he was there. "I wanted to talk to you about your story, Johnny. It was very well written, and it showed me a great deal about your thoughts on God and Heaven. I know it was about distant worlds and space aliens, but that just shows me you are aware of a higher power in the universe and the existence of other possible worlds. Much like heaven, it also seems like a distant world. Don't you think?" she asked him as he stared out of the window.

He said, "It would seem likely, but I just thought this stuff up; it wasn't a real story, just make-believe. Why do you think it's a possible story to believe in?"

She looked at his young face and told him, "Johnny, life isn't always what you see. That's only half of the mystery; it's the things you don't see that make up our universe. Science is full of instances where cells and atoms make up all life and matter on the planet. You, at such a young age, have been given a gift to see beyond the veil of human understanding. Don't ever lose that ok?" he said. "Ok, I guess I will just keep being me then," as he left the room. John had forgotten all of this; he only remembered the golden cross and the kids being so cruel. He had forgotten Sister Julie and how kind a person she was. All of the rough times had worn away the good memories of his life; it was like a smooth rock on the beach that had once been a large jagged boulder. He didn't know where this fit into the whole dying narrative, but it must have because Abiel had taken him here. He was sure the angel had his reasons, and this did clarify the existence of our Lord in Johnny's young life.

On task

"That which we persist in doing becomes easier, not that the task itself has become easier, but that our ability to perform it has improved."

Ralph Waldo Emerson

The dashboard clock now read 3:18, as John stared out into the falling rain. The death angel was right in front of him as he slowly made his way to John; it was hard to remain on task with the sight of such a beautiful yet ominous angel in front of him. This was sure a strange night. He was sitting on the California beach about 12 hours ago, and now he was staring into the face of the angel of death. He knew fully that the angel would not leave empty-handed, and his life would not be spared. It was an odd yet comforting feeling as the blood poured from his veins, so did all of his cares and worries that this world had held for so long. The peace or torment of a dying person rivals no other feeling in life. To know that the end has finally come and death has set up camp at your front door is surreal.

Abiel spoke "John we are now on a different path then before, as I have said before, I took you down the memories in your mind to the times that the hand of God was upon you and I was with you even in the darkest hour, but now we converge on a different road less traveled to the times when you had the hand of god upon you and I was with you also, but the element of death and destruction is not present in these visions, only the moments that set you on the path that has lead you here. Not a path of pain and suffering but a path of retribution and enlightenment. We will visit a time when the work of the Lord was done in your life, and your steps were governed by his hand, with you always so willingly taking those steps. We will go to similar happier times and you will see the reason I am with you now in your final moments, all will become clear then my work will have been finished" John thought about this for a moment always thinking because Abiel could read his thoughts, "When the time comes will I be able to see your wings or do you have to wait for a bell to ring like on it's a Wonderful Life?" Laughing, the angel said, "I've seen that movie too, but I'm not Clarence, and the story doesn't end with you going home to Anna. You two will be reunited again someday at a different time and place, but not tonight. We have business to attend to. You will get to see my wings soon enough."

Paradise Lost

"Not all those who wander are lost."

J.R.R. Tolkien

Johnny had gone to church with his grandmother now and then, but today was different; she couldn't make it, so he went to St Luke's Catholic Church down the hill from his house. It was a beautiful spring day in Hawaii, as the trade winds seemed to push him toward the small church in the dirt field. His father had gotten a salesman job for a year, so this was his home for now. The air was strong with the smell of plumeria and pineapples. The nearest pineapple field was many miles away, but Johnny could smell them anyway. Johnny was running late, and he could hear the singing of the choir as they belted out another song that Johnny didn't know. He didn't really like to come here, but he thought it would put him on a better path in life. This was too much thinking for a ten-year-old boy who should have been outside playing.

He made it up the stairs and sat down in the back behind the Johnson kids. Trying not to get their attention because he didn't want Father Dominic giving him the evil eye, if that was possible for a man of God to do. So, he sat there for a while, sweating and thinking of all the other places he could be. He listened to the Priest as he told him he was a sinner and was going to hell if he didn't change his ways. He watched the people become entranced at the Father's words, almost like he was at one of those Baptist places. As this was going on, he felt weird and out of place; his body was really sweating, and he couldn't really breathe very well, as if he was going to pass out for lack of oxygen. Finally, he couldn't take it anymore, so he jumped up and ran out the door into the parking lot and up the hill. The further he got from the church, the better he felt.

When he got home, Grandma Pezdel was sitting on her rocking chair reading a book, "How did it go in Church today, Johnny?" She asked, although he could tell she already knew too much. He said, "It went ok I just started feeling sick, so I had to leave a little early." He knew that she knew something; she always did. Grandma Pezdel was a strange one sometimes; she looked just like any other grey-haired old lady, but inside those eyes of blue held a look of knowledge not known by most mortals. She had a "gift," so you might say, of talking to the dead. Whoever gave it to her couldn't have been too nice. It scared the hell out of Johnny, but he was mystified at times watching her go into a trance and talk to the dead like they were in the room. He could feel them around him as they told her of the great beyond or just to say hello. Johnny knew that he had some sort of ability, to say the least, but he kept it turned off for the most part. There would be no midnight visitors in Johnny's room if he could help it. But sometimes in his dreams, they would come and visit him, and he would have to tell them to leave because this was his dream, and they already had their chance in life. It seemed to work for the most part, but once in a while, he could feel a bad one try to commandeer his dream world. Johnny would not let them in and usually woke up startled and scared.

His grandmother had come from a long line of European descent, full of Germans, Irish folk, and gypsies; he sometimes could see their faces in his dreams. They were a mysterious folk who held tight to the old way and old-world beliefs. He knew he was one of them, but did his best to keep the old ways at bay. Sometimes he had bad dreams, and other times he would awake in the middle of the night, his little brother breathing in his sleep in the bed across from him; he could feel the presence of another soul or maybe something without a soul. Either way, he would pull the covers over his face and pray to the good Lord to take it away. Sometimes that worked, and then again it didn't. Johnny was bound to them as they were to him, always wanting answers that he did not know. He just thought this was his life, and he would forever be cursed with this "gift". In life, we cannot choose our genetic makeup as well as our spiritual makeup. We can only choose the path we go on and hope it takes us home someday.

He went outside and found some friends down by the playground. He forgot all about the church and the gift as he played in the Hawaiian sunshine with the trade winds blowing his hair. The cares of the world are so far away now in a boy's life lived so long ago. The look on Grandma's face said it all; he would not go back to that church or any other for a very long time. It wasn't that he didn't believe in God and Jesus; he just didn't believe in religion.

The Dawn

"There is only one day left, always starting over: it is given to us at dawn and taken away from us at dusk."
Jean-Paul Sartre

The EMTs and Firefighters were on scene now. As John looked outside into the night, he could see strange shapes that looked like people standing around his truck; the garbage truck had hit him on the driver's side and rammed his vehicle into a large power pole, wedging itself against the pole and truck. This was one of those wrecks that he had seen so many times and thought that the poor guy must surely be dead or dying. They would not get him out in time as his lifeblood seeped into the seat cushion and carpet below him. The only reason he was still here was the slowing down of time thing that Abiel had done. The people were frozen in time around him, and it was so slow that John could watch the individual raindrops travel down to the ground. It was so surreal yet frightening, like an out-of-body experience, but still attached somehow.

A few moments ago, this intersection was dark and deserted before all of this; now it was just another tragedy that happens all around the world every day. Except today it was happening to him. He could see the devil's minion in the shadows. His eyes glowed a brighter fiery red as if he knew that the time was short for John. Why would the devil care about a guy like him? Even though John had traveled through the days of his life to all the moments where the Lord was with him, he still didn't know why the devil cared if he lived or died. Yes, the whole balance of good and evil stuff was a sincere gesture on Abiel's part, but this night is old, and the dance is almost over. So, he dies, and the minion reports back to the devil. Then what's next? The devil sends him out to some other poor bastard about to depart this world to see if he has a chance to sway him in his final moments? That job sounds like it sucks.

"Abiel, why did we go back to the old church in Hawaii? I remember that church and feeling that way. It took a long time to believe in anything after that. My Parents gave up on God; Mom became a disciple of the New Age, and Dad became a Buddhist. That left me to fend for myself in a world where beliefs were as common as fast food restaurants; I was always left feeling empty inside. Like a part of me was missing. I remember the day I found the Lord again. It seems so long ago, but I will never forget it. I'm sure we will be going there soon, as you seem to have taken me to the proverbial hell and back." John asked.

Abiel knew the answer, but it was hard to put it on a human level. He tried, "John, that day was a turning point for you. A road less traveled in your family with your catholic upbringing and such. Both of your parents knew who God was, but they didn't know God; they tried to teach you kids, but you have to believe in something for it to be real in the eyes of children. You, of all of them, saw it first and turned away at a young age. It was more of a spiritual cleansing, if anything, because by ridding yourself of archaic beliefs, you finally found the true path, and that made all the difference. You see the souls outside as they frantically try to save your life. They look in on you as if you are a Hollywood movie being shown for the world to see. Tragedy is such an impersonal affair. You are displayed for the entire world to see, even unto death, as your body is laid in its final resting state. The morbidity of it never fails to astound me, humans and their rituals, since the dawn of time. Those same people out there will someday be in your shoes, as they, too, will taste the sting of death and the certainty of eternity. No one escapes the final moments, no matter how the circumstances or how quickly they pass. Whether it comes in the blink of an eye or a long, drawn-out illness, the final moments are usually the same. First disbelief, then the question "Why Me?" comes to mind, then denial, then the angel of death. Most times than not, I have no part in the final moments; today was different, and it's good to talk to you.

The day at the church represents a new beginning for you; it was just another day in a boy's life, but you know now how the story ends; all is not lost. I know you are thinking about that first time you met Anna, and you thought you saw a mighty Angel of the Lord behind her, did you, or didn't you? That is the question that I will answer. It is yes, and no, you saw a mighty Angel of the Lord behind Anna standing 10 feet tall in her kitchen, really, you only saw a glimpse of your own life laid out before you. Some people need a little prodding to go where they are supposed to go. That day, your mind was not so receptive to the moment, so I intervened. I wasn't the one that you saw, my old friend Marmaroth, who has been known to thwart fate and change the course of time. He was who you saw that day, but not in the moment; he was more like a hologram sent to awaken the sleeping giant inside you. It worked, and your path was forever changed for the best." John, looking puzzled, said, "You told me that the angels were not to interfere with another human's life or fate. Why that day, what was different?" Abiel told him, "Marmaroth did not alter your fate; more like he put you on the right track to continue your fate. Like a train that almost derails, his image was enough to pique your interest and let you choose your own way. It also helped when you fell in love at first sight; I had nothing to do with that. The human emotions of love and hate are powerful forces that we as angels cannot sway in either direction.

You thought that it was just another day in your life, but you also thought the same thing at the beach in Santa Monica when you were sitting looking at the ocean. How often in life is it the little things that make the greatest difference? We need to go now, there are many more things to see and places to go." Abiel told him as the moment faded away into the past.

The Teacher

JethroTull

The Teacher sat across the room, the center of a circle of chairs, studying the faces of her students. John was also studying her and the rest of the ragged bunch. He was only 14 years old, the youngest of the group, but in his mind, he thought he could have been the smartest person there. The Teacher was quite older than most in the group, giving the appearance that she was wise beyond her years. Wearing slacks and a tucked-in button shirt with her closely cropped hair, she could almost pass as a man. She was, in fact, a lesbian, but that was no surprise; everyone knew that about her. This was a class being taught by the reverend Lilith, who also ran the mental health center called "The Farm" in Santee, CA. There were no farm animals or crops, just a lot of people with a lot of issues. The Farm was started in the early 1970's to help the great number of hippies and New Age believers who had either done way too many drugs and had psychological problems, or those who just needed help. John's mom worked there as a receptionist and thought he might like to take a few college-level classes taught by Lilith. This class was about general semantics in daily life. At first, the course was boring, but John was a quick study and became interested in the class. It was an 8-week course, and this was week 4, so he was halfway there. Lilith always started the class with a prayer to the deity of her choice as the twenty or so students stood in a circle, chanting some mantra whose meaning only they knew, while they held each other's hands and made other sounds to appease the God they prayed to.

John stood there also so as not to make a scene, but deep inside his immortal soul, he knew that this was not the way. The class was taught for about 45 minutes, then Lilith would speak of the spiritual matters at hand. Even the leaders become lost at times, and this was one of those times. "Class, I want you to envision your inner self reaching deep inside and try to find the God that you are as a spiritual being. You are the center of the universe, and you have as much right to be here as the rocks and the trees. Your Godhead will guide you through these times of trouble as you seek enlightenment…" Lilith would preach to her flock as they sat glassy-eyed and dumbfounded at her wisdom, all except John, as he stared into her face and read between the lines as she spoke her words. She knew he was not absorbing the mantra, so she dismissed the class and told John to wait for a student-teacher conversation. The believers filed out in a single line, then shut the door behind them. Lilith looked at John and said, "So tell me, John, do you not believe in the teachings of the Universal Truth Church? These are ancient scriptures written long before Christ walked this planet. We have found the secret and want to share it with you and others. Do you wish to receive it?" John thought on his words before he spoke; he had dealt with Lilith before, and every word was an invitation to skew its meaning. John told her, "I have enjoyed the class and had a most pleasant stay, but truth be told, I don't think the religion aspect of it all is my cup of tea. I'm sure there are people here who need that sort of thing, but a religion that teaches we are God is not for me." She looked at him, kind of upset, but replied. "John, you are a bright young man who will no doubt go far if you get with the program. I see before you darkness and turmoil; you will always strive to meet the expectations placed upon you in your life, never really reaching your full potential. You will live your life always looking for what the status quo has to deal with you, never finding your true inner being. I feel sorry for you, and you had your chance to become an immortal. Do you still wish to receive it?" Lilith asked John as she studied him like a bug with an intense look on her face. John replied, "No, Lilith, I will pass on that offer and thank you for the words of encouragement," as he scurried out the door.

John left the room with the Teacher still sitting there. In his mind, he knew she was putting some dark spell upon him, and he wanted nothing to do with that. Outside, people were milling about in semi-trances, speaking of the profound knowledge that the Teacher held. They had the look of those about to lie down and be trampled underfoot. They could be called the walking dead. Whatever they were on, John didn't want any part of it. He knew she was trying to put some voodoo vision on his life; John knew his life was unwritten, and only God knew the outcome. His Mother, Father, sister, cousin, and anyone else he knew could have this place. He was fairly sane as far as he knew and had no need for a tune-up from the good Reverend/Teacher. God had given him a gift also of discernment and the knowledge that there were bad things in the spirit realm as well as good. He got a whiff of something in the air, and the musty mothball smell of lost antiquity and old religion. There is nothing new under the sun, as King Solomon once said. This was not the new age, just a new version of the same old crap that was being fed the masses for generations. It was just wrapped differently. He got on his bike and rode home the 4 miles to his house, trying to figure out what just happened.

Having plenty of time to dissect Lilith's words on the long ride home, he realized that no one could see his future, only God above, and anyone professing to that gift was either an angel or somebody on the road to hell. Lilith seemed hell-bent, so John just left it at that. He would return to the farm periodically, but it was never the same after that; a veil had been lifted for him that he could never be covered with it again.

"I see now why Lilith had been so weird toward me; she saw the light inside of me that I failed to see back then, she wanted to snuff it out before it got too bright. Too bad her schemes had failed, and now look at me awaiting execution." John said to Abiel. "It is not execution that you are waiting for, John, but absolution would be a better term. You have been on this path for so long now, and the end is just a passing through of a door, almost like the doors of perception that Jim Morrison had tried so hard to open; you, too, are at the gate, ready to walk through. Time is the constant here; it drifts and flows aimlessly like a mighty river, only to come back to its beginning. The things you learned in that class were temporal, but the knowledge you found from within was eternal. Lilith is in a place that you will not be going to, but rest assured, she made her choice. She believed her own doctrine and took many a poor soul with her. She is not in a good place.

John was beginning to see it all so much clearer; it was like a mighty ship that slowly crept through the fog until its true shape was seen, and he was in the fog but coming out of it now. John asked, "Is it the choice we make in this life that defines us, or is the life we choose that defines us?" Looking outside at the suspended raindrops and seeing the angel of death in front of his battered truck in full shape and form, John was good with all of it. He was feeling the peace that passes understanding, knowing that the Lord was by his side. Abiel spoke, "In answer to the time-asked question, I think you have the truth inside, but let's inspect the question again. It is a very profound question that all great people have asked themselves throughout history, but they didn't have their own guardian angel helping them get through it.

True, you were born into this world with free choice and will; everyone has it, but it is the most underappreciated thing in this world. The choice between life and death is sometimes clear, but the choices you make determine if you have life or death, and death is not always a physical thing; it could mean a spiritual death that you will not survive. The remaining days of a person's life would be half-lived without the Lord in their life and the promise of a better place. So, humankind has choices every day, but does the choice you make define you in life, or is it the life you choose that defines you? asked John. The answer is quite simple: you live your life and make your choices, and in the end, it all equals out. The life you lived and the choices you made define you; nobody else can do that for you.

I can listen to your thoughts, asking what if you didn't come this way. Or what if you stayed in California another day? And what if you never even made a choice to go to California and just stayed home in Tombstone, then would you be here in your time of dying? The answer is yes and no; you wouldn't be here in this truck on this intersection at this time, but you would be dead just the same, my friend. Your departure would happen as close to this time as possible, but not exactly. We do have contingencies for such matters. We have it all figured out up there after all, this isn't my first rodeo, John Pezdel." John took in the words Abiel had told him; the moment was all he had then, and he shall not pass this way again. He felt so thirsty and alone. John knew that even with his very own angel, the world could be so cruel. He remembered talking to his Father a couple of years ago when he found out his liver was failing. His Dad was 74 years old but still wanted to live another day. He would tell John he dreamed about living until he was 90 years old, like his Uncle Tom, but the reaper found him before that. He died shortly after that and was buried in a small cemetery in Reedley, California, in the central valley.

John now thought about his untimely passing and the conversation he had with Anna. If he went before her, he always knew deep down he would, but to keep the talk on a fair playing field, they played the what if I died first game. Anna wanted to be cremated and have her ashes sprinkled along the shoreline on a lake they used to vacation at in central

California. John had asked her why not the Pacific Ocean or even in a cemetery so the kids and grandkids could visit she said "John I want to be cremated and have my remains spread out along the shoreline at Pine Flat lake near Fresno, I always loved the times we went up there and I always remember when we first met and camped out in that pup tent long ago. Those seemed like some of the happiest times of my life, John, so that's what I want, where do you want to spend eternity beside heaven, of course?" John thought carefully and told her, "I have always loved Arizona since the early days on my Great Grandparents' ranch near Cibola Valley; I don't want to end up there, just here in Tombstone on Allen Street. I know what you are thinking: how do I do that? But all you have to do is wait until the monsoons start up on one Saturday night about 10:00 and just start at the Bird Cage and walk all the way down to Third Street, and I will be fine." She said, "You will just wash away during the rain storm, is that what you really want?"

"Yes, it is, and I don't care if I wash away; the thought being spread out there is that I will be around somewhere in Tombstone, and that's fine with me." He told her. He was thinking of this now because now was the time, and within a few days, he would be spread upon the streets of Tombstone. A smile appeared on his face because he knew that Anna would get the job done, and his earthly presence would be no more. When his kids and grandkids come to visit, they will walk the streets of Tombstone and remember him. Yes, there were many who went before him who walked those same streets, and some were famous for whatever reason, but that was what he wanted. Not too bad for a final goodbye.

As thoughts of being 14 again and seeing Lilith once more, even in a past life, John just wanted to move on from this dull charade of never-ending past lives. So, this is what they meant when they said you see your life flash before your eyes. This is way too slow for him. Knowing Abiel was listening to his mind, he shifted the conversation of thoughts to Abiel. "I know you're hearing this and everything else, so could we please just speed this up for the Love of God and all that's humane, Abiel?" John said in his mind. Abiel spoke, "John, would you speed up the birth of one of your children? Would you speed up the moment you first laid your eyes upon Anna and knew she was the one for you? Would you speed up the last moments for a dying man who was about to step into the ether of forever? No, you wouldn't so don't try that with me, they all get to this point in the end trying to make my job harder, but the truth of the matter is you are not expected until a certain time and the cosmos and eternity is measured not in time but events, and your event will play out as it should so let's move on my impatient one…"

Events

"There are no mistakes. The events we bring upon ourselves, no matter how unpleasant, are necessary in order to learn what we need to learn; whatever steps we take, they're necessary to reach the places we've chosen to go."

Richard Bach

John was sitting at home on a Friday night, pondering the news. Everyone had gone to the hospital in Fresno, waiting for the news about his grandfather, who lay in intensive care on death's door. John had known the feeling before in his own life, but now it was personal. Grandpa had a bad heart, and everyone knew this. He was the Patriarch of the family, and all who knew him loved him. He was only 58 years old, and he still had a lot of living to do. John had gone up to Fresno with Mom and Dad to donate blood, but the nurse told him he couldn't because his blood pressure was too low, and he would no doubt pass out. Arguing with her brought no relief, so he told his parents he was going home to check on his little brother. Joe, his brother, was out with some friends, so John was left alone in the quiet house that held too many secrets. Dad told everyone that there was an evil spirit living in the back bathroom, and normally that kind of stuff didn't bother John much, but right now he was a little uneasy. The old man would get drunk on bourbon and yell obscenities at the demon that lived in the bathroom. Once, he even lit off a couple of hundred firecrackers to banish the creature, and he even said he saw a large pheasant-like winged bird roll out of the bathroom and take off outside to parts unknown. He was proud of his exorcism.

He was thinking about Grandpa and all his stories that he told on the summer nights on the ranch. He would spin yarns about the Vikings being part of John's lineage and how he was a descendant of the Chickasaw tribe of Indians from Oklahoma. There were stories of his buddy Otto, who was a World War II fighter pilot who had shot down many Americans during the war, but that was a long time ago, and old wounds sometimes heal. He would always make you feel like you were the only person in the room, and all of his time and patience were being devoted to you. John wanted to be like that someday with his grandchildren. A man of virtue and patience is the best a man could be. The moon hung low on this winter night, and the air was quite chilly for a change, as if to say I'm back for another season, so get used to me. John enjoyed the winter months; summer was too hot up here, and spring was overrated, just a time for the trees to blossom and the snow melted in the highlands. Fall was nice, but winter held the most fun with bonfires and putting on your heavy coat to drink some beer at a nearby keg party or battle of the bands. Tonight held none of that, just a lonely vigil for John's only Grandfather.

His grandfather's name was Franklin, a tall, big man who seemed to tower over John when he would see him as a boy. He was a pilot, but not the military or commercial type, just a Cessna pilot who owned his own plane until the first heart attack 5 years ago. They all moved up north to the country, hoping for a better life and healthier living, but some people have their problems no matter where they go. As John looked across the barley field to his grandparents' house, he felt tears slowly making their way down his cheeks, not aware that he had been crying until now, he let out a sobbing cry that he hadn't done for the longest time. Like a summer rain bursting through the clouds to the parched earth, he cried the cry of the tired and lonely. He didn't want to lose his grandpa but felt helpless to do anything but cry. He looked up at the clear night sky into the cosmos, trying to find God. "I know you are up there," he said, "I know you can hear me also. I don't want much from you, and I haven't used up all of my hopeful prayers on childish things or earthly treasures. I know you are real, and I only want one thing from you, God, to save my Grandpa Franklin tonight and let him live out his years without pain and worry from a bad heart. Please answer this one prayer, Lord, and I will live up to your wishes for me." John spoke into the night to the stars and sky and the rising quarter moon in the east. His heart felt broken, and his soul felt lost to the night.

Many times, he had wanted to call out to God in the past, but he didn't want to bother him back then. Tonight was different. He wanted God to hear him and help him; he wanted the angels from high to come down here to earth and lift his grandfather up and out of the grasp of Death. This was such a tall order from such a young man of 16 years of age. He knew the truth about Jesus and all of the saints; he just didn't want to know them personally, and even now, on this night, pleading to the Lord, John was still a long way off from truly knowing the Lord in his life. But he was on the right path, a crossroads of sorts of the cosmic kind, where he must tread carefully because these steps he took on this night would take him on a road less traveled yet sought by many. Just then, he saw a falling star in the east and remembered the story of the birth of Jesus and said "Thank You" out loud to all of the unseen in his presence. He knew that something had changed and that the world and all its comings and goings and earthly events were shifting just a bit to accommodate the sparing of his grandfather's life. No one knew back then how many days his grandfather had been given, but John knew it was enough. Just then, John was startled from his thoughts as the phone rang. He answered it listening to his Mother's voice telling him that his Grandpa was having bypass surgery, but he looked good and should be alright. John hung up and walked out the porch door into the night. He looked up into the sky again and thanked the Lord on high for his miracle that night.

"He had 7,444 more days on this earth." Abiel told John as he looked into the night, "What are you talking about, Abiel?" John asked. "Your Grandfather lived another 7,444 days on this earth after that night you just saw. The prayers of the just and unjust are both heard by God, and he alone chooses to answer them. Not all prayers are answered as you would think. Some are answered in a different way, but still they are answered." He told John, "God doesn't always answer all prayers; it's a little more complicated than that." John asked him, "Why is it so complicated then? I would think that God would at least consider the prayer, then go from there. Am I right?" John said. Abiel knew the answer before the question was broached. All of the humans he has been guardian over sometimes ask the same thing; they all didn't know that he was their angel, but they all asked anyway. It is a basic human question about something that has no answer. Abiel tried to formulate his response so that at least John would leave this world knowing why God did what he did. "John, it's like this, you have kids, and when they were young, they always asked for this and that, although as an adult, you knew the requests were foolish and childish, but you still loved your kids and didn't want to deny them anything good in life. That's the way it is with God; he knows the desires of your heart, but also, he knows that the grass isn't always greener on the other side. God answers your prayers one way or another, and if it seems like he didn't answer them, then that is your answer. The Rolling Stones said it best, John: "You can't always get what you want; you get what you need…" Remember that one?" John remembered that one and a lot of other rock songs from his misspent youth. But what was the angel doing listening to rock and roll? It all must come with the territory, like doing research for a college paper.

"Abiel, what was the purpose of seeing my grandpa have another heart attack way back then, when he died from a heart attack eventually? Was it just for the time on earth, or deeper than that?" he asked. Abiel told him, "John, we were there on that night that you were praying, and I remember it well. I was there with you, and I felt your pain for the man you loved and didn't want to lose. The prayers you prayed did not fall on deaf ears; the Almighty himself heard them and granted your grandfather's life to be spared. Just like in the old times when God would smite his enemies, that day you saw was when he saved one of his chosen people. Also, you do remember the day that Franklin died? He went peacefully in his sleep with a glorious smile upon his face; he saw the face of God as he slipped into eternity. You will no doubt see the same thing as our friend outside comes slowly closer." As Abiel said, this John had forgotten about the death angel with all of the comings and goings through the sands of time, but now, as he gazed out into the night, the death angel was much closer than before. His angelic stature and brilliance had all but blocked John's view of anything else. He was magnificent in all of his splendor and beauty. Power and might just exuded from him as he slowly made his way toward the crumpled-up truck. John could see the determination and strength in his face and in his eyes, which held all of the souls that he had ferried away to the great beyond.

As if shaken out of his trance, John still wanted to know why he was seeing his grandpa and the old home he had lived in. "You went there because that was the point in your life that you moved closer to God and away from the things of this world. You unselfishly wanted to give of your own blood like the Savior Jesus Christ had done for you. Your prayers were of the heart with no motive except to save your grandfather. You performed the acts of kindness and servitude that are needed to enter the kingdom of heaven. You did this all with the heart of a child, which is the purest form of innocence. That, my friend, is why you went back, a moment once lost in time retrieved and shown to you in its truest form and simplicity. We are far from done, so stay with me as we travel down that road.

The Road

"If you don't know where you are going, any road will take you there."
Lewis Carroll

The weather was terrible that night as the wind howled and the snow fell. John looked outside into the blizzard and wondered how he ended up in this God-forsaken place. He was far from the warmth of Hawaii or the tomato fields of his youth. The warm, wet lake in the mountains near Orange Cove, near Visalia, or the deserts in Arizona, where he spent his summers as a boy. The snow was piling up, and the temperature dropped. This was not a night to be out in the elements as the wind chill dropped to -12 degrees. John had a dumb idea to have a few beers with two of his buddies from boot camp, whom he knew in San Diego. They had met up at the barracks earlier and started out to the Helm Club, the enlisted men's club on base. Any other night or place would have been better, but it was January 27, 1979, on a Saturday night at Great Lakes Naval Training Center, north of Chicago, Illinois. It was the worst winter in forty years, so they said, but they said that a lot out here.

Drinking their fill of alcohol like true sailors often do, they headed back to the barracks, just John and Reese. John never did like the cold; he didn't even like the fog or cool rains. This was beyond his normal range of comprehension for a winter. In California, he had gone to the mountains with his aunt and uncle. There had been only two inches of snow that day, and he was really cold then. This had to be a form of torture, and how could people live in this stuff? He asked himself. His friend Reese was about 5 yards ahead of him in the whiteout blizzard John was walking in. No worries if you just stayed on the path, you would make it back in one piece. John yelled to Reese, "Hold up, man, I gotta take a piss." So, he walked off the path and behind a snow bank, relieved himself, nothing like that after a few pictures of beer and some shots of Jack Daniels. John was feeling the effects of the alcohol, but was doing alright.

He turned to walk back to the path when something dark about 10 yards to his right caught his eye. He walked to the shape and realized it was a drunken sailor passed out from a hard night at the Helm Club, not worth losing your life over it, he thought as he bent down to wake up a shipmate. He turned the man over and tried to wake him up when he realized it was the third member of the drinking party, another boot camp friend named Tom Justice. Justice was a heavy drinker who liked to run his mouth a lot, the more drunk he got. He had gotten really drunk and was trying to fight every sailor in the club, so John and Reese told him they would take him back to the barracks to sober up. Being of unsound mind, he said he knew the way and left before they could stop him. There he lay in the falling snow, sleeping like a baby, oblivious of the knowledge that he would be dead in about three hours if John had not stopped.

John woke Tom up and pulled him to his feet, a little uneasy but managing to get Reese's attention, the two friends walked the other friend the 300 yards or so back to the barracks. Astonished by finding their friend, Reese said, "John, if you hadn't stopped to take a leak, he would be dead in the morning." Acknowledging the truth, John just agreed with him. He did feel lucky that night, looking into the falling snow. "What if it were me?" he thought, then dismissed the idea since he rarely got that drunk and had never passed out. The wind howled, and the snow fell as the three sailors made it back to the warmth and comfort of the naval barracks. Lying in bed, John wished he were back at home with his family and friends. He thought of a girl he once knew and wondered what she was up to. He thought about what possessed him to join the Navy and end up in this God-forsaken land. He thought about the warm summer nights in the Central Valley near Visalia, and lastly, as he fell into a deep sleep, he thought about Hawaii and the warm surf…

Home

"We are homesick most for the places we have never known."
Carson McCullers

"In the days and memories gone by, you will find the answers that you seek," Abiel told John as the rain fell slowly into the broken cab of what was once a truck, the smell of gasoline and gardenias filled the air, John couldn't see any flowers near but the desert had a way of bringing in smells from far off lands. "You don't really smell gardenias; they only exist in your mind, right now, as you slip into the nothingness and shed what was once all you knew of your mortal being, you smell flowers from your youth. The things in life that brought you the most joy are with you now, if only in your mind," Abiel told him. John knew that sometimes the smell of the departed souls or spirits would be present in a person's life. On several occasions, he had smelled the smell of old, nasty spirits as they wandered about; he would tell them they were not welcome here and to go away in peace. They would find no peace elsewhere, but they didn't want to stay once their intentions were known. He also could smell the good ones who have lost their way and wandered in and out of a person's consciousness. It was more a curse than a gift; he never could figure out why anyone would call that a "gift." It had brought on so much negativity and despair in his life. Only now that he knew Jesus as his Lord and savior did he finally find the peace he had always been looking for. Some people thought he was unhinged, but others knew he was true to his word because they had smelled the spirits also.

Tonight, it was different. The flowers got stronger as he looked out to see the angel of death coming ever closer. How slow could he be to just seem to hover in front of John? The gardenias were his grandmother's favorite, along with night-blooming jasmine. She had them growing in her yard when he was a boy, and they always reminded him of happier, simpler times. If it were that easy, he could just slip away to those days and start over. It was a game he played in his mind, and tonight was no different. He would think back to his past when it wasn't so great and imagine that if he could have changed just one thing, would it have made a difference? Most likely on the cosmic level, it wouldn't have changed a lot, but in John's life, it might have put him on another road than the one he was currently on, and that would have been alright with him.

He thought about that night in the snow many years ago and how that amounts to anything life-changing? "John, when you look at it from the surface, it was just another night; your friend Tom could have easily not woken up and passed into eternity that cold winter night. Your chance to stop to relieve yourself gave way to you discovering him and saving his life. Not everyone can save a life or even wants to try. You did the right thing and forgot about it the next day, as though you saved mortals all of the time. In reality, John, the life you saved went on to save many more, and so on, as you will never know. I'm telling you now that Tom Justice became a police officer for the City of Reno, Nevada, when he got out of the service in 1982. You might have forgotten that night, but he never did and never will. He served on the police force for twenty years, then retired. He still lives there with his family and grandchildren. His oldest son is named John after you. Any act of kindness or mercy that could be done in your life was done without regret or remorse. You have the heart of a warrior, and in God's army, you have served well. We went that night to show you your heart, and to also show you your soul." Abiel told him.

Angels

"The golden moments in the stream of life rush past us, and we see nothing but sand; the angels come to visit us, and we only know them when they are gone."
George Elliot

It was 1980, and Long Beach, California, was a busy town with the US Naval ship yard and all of the defense companies nearby; a lot was going on. John was in the barracks mopping away at the still clean floors once again. It had been his task for at least 4 weeks since he had a nasty motorcycle accident that left him limping and in a not very good state to be walking around a torn-up boiler room on the ship in the shipyards he was stationed on. He left the Great Lakes about seven months ago, hoping he would get on a ship going out to sea, that was what sailors did, but he ended up on a Tin Can in overhaul in Long Beach, so much for far and following seas. Lunch was coming up soon, so he put away his bucket and mop and was headed to the chow hall when he ran into a friend of his, Charley Valdez. Charley had been dating a young woman in Long Beach and was going to see her with a friend to have lunch; he asked if John wanted to come with them. With nothing else to do, he said yes and jumped into the car.

The woman Connie lived off Long Beach Boulevard, about five miles from the Naval Station. John was glad to get out of the barracks, at least for a little while. It was a typical Tuesday in Long Beach, it was March 13, 1980, and life was good for John. His leg was on the mend, and pretty soon he would be riding his motorcycle again. It was a short trip to the apartment as they pulled up out front. They went upstairs and went inside to see Connie. She was a tall blonde girl with glasses, and she looked too skinny for John's taste, but he wasn't the one dating her. They sat on the carpet and had a beer, watching General Hospital. Sandwiches were made and eaten when John was just about to get up, and the door to another bedroom opened, and he looked over to see who else was there. She walked out of that room and into his heart. She looked like a Blonde Goddess who just appeared on earth one day; her eyes were as blue as the ocean with just a hint of laughter behind them. She had on a pair of old Daisy Duke cut-off shorts and a white wife-beater tank top. John was in love, or whatever you would call it. He was staring at the woman for a second, then noticed something strange. He was looking up in a dim light, but enough to see the shape of a very large, tall Angel standing behind the woman. Only John could see the heavenly creature, and he looked past the woman and studied the figure in white. It stood over ten feet tall and commanded a look of strength and assuredness. The Angel looked back at John as if suddenly realizing he had been spotted, then disappeared into the dim light of the bedroom. Not believing what he had seen, John was filled with excitement and joy. He had just seen the most beautiful angel standing behind an earthly angel. He said to the woman, "Hello, my name is John, what is your name?" kind of in a slow manner. "My name is Anna, and I just came out of my room to see what all the noise was about. Glad to meet you, John." She told him as she went outside to check her laundry…

Abiel spoke then as the room faded away, and Tucson was once more John's reality. The scene before him unfolded as it should. "You just saw the happiest moment of your life but that's not why you saw it. You were brought back because, like in the Old Testament, you were one of the privileged few of humankind who had seen one of God's angels. Not unlike now, where you have actually been in conversation with me, one of God's special angels. You saw something that day that changed your life forever. All of the good and all of the bad that happened after that day were because of the path you took after meeting your wife and seeing her guardian angel, whom I do know personally and has spoken to me often about that day." John asked, "I thought you were supposed to watch over me when, if ever, did you find the time to talk to Anna's angel?"

"John, you guys have been married for over 30 years, don't you think it was a little crowded with two angels in the same house and your kids' angels and your grandkids' angels? We took turns watching the family, unless you guys were apart, then we were on task. I would fly to the island of Tonga or some deserted island in the South China Sea just to have some space. Anna's angel is called Marmaroth, who has been known to alter time and fate for those involved. He does not do this by violating the angel code, but more like a bending of the rules. We have been friends forever, I mean literally forever." Abiel said as he watched the night sky.

"That is all well and good, but once more, why was I there? I know there are millions of you guys flying around but why did I see this Marmaroth? He wasn't my angel so what's up?" John asked trying to get a glimpse of his last journey since it would be the last time he saw his wife even if it was in some time warp her appearance calmed him so much. Abiel spoke again saying "John my old friend I was there also talking to Marmaroth wondering why we were meeting there in that place. You can see angels, John you have all of your life. You just don't know most of the time that you actually saw one. That day it was unmistakable but most times they pass them self's off as almost human. The trick is to look really closely and that is where the lines start to blur. An angel can only mimic human form for a short period of earthly time. It isn't even a measurable amount of time but it's the energy required to maintain the form that determines how long the disguise will last. My record is about 8 minutes, almost like holding one's breath under water that is what it's like. You saw an angel in Hawaii that time that you thought it was a spirit trying to tell you something, it was an angel trying to tell you something, you just didn't listen. Since that day you have wondered if your life would have been different had you listened, no not really you would still be here dying.

We have no control over that, but I know what the message was about, and the angel was announcing the birth of your daughter that you didn't even know you wanted to have until you wanted to have her. God knows the desires of your heart, just as he can see you now in so much pain and despair. You sit there looking out into the darkness and seeing the death angel that grows ever so much larger. He is a beautiful angel, I agree, not like me, who only takes the image of the standard guardian angel. You only see what I want you to see because my true form is spirit and light. Your breathing has increased, and your heart rate beats much faster as the time comes for your departure. What troubles you besides all of this, dealing with death and ruin?" Abiel asked him. "Abiel, I know you have been with me since the beginning, maybe even more, and I feel you know me better than most, but at this moment, I'm having a hard time here in my time of dying. I know you slowed down time and made these last few moments for me bearable, but I just don't feel that I'm making the best of the time I have. I wish I could say goodbye to Anna and my family. I also wish when I left Tombstone on Friday afternoon that I really was able to kiss my wife and hug her for the last time and know it.

So much left undone and so much left unsaid, I only wish that we knew that tomorrow isn't promised, and when we wake up on a nice sunny morning, it could very well be our last. I get what we have been doing, and I smell the strange odor unlike I have ever smelled on this earth; I see things outside my torn-up truck that are not of this world, I'm talking to an angel, of course, I'm a little bit excited. This is my perception, and that does not make it all real, but to me it is, but I was hoping it wasn't the last thing I saw on this planet." John said to Abiel. "We seemed to have reached an impasse, my friend, and the distance we have traveled has passed into the moment, so we just have a couple of more things to see before the moment is here, so hang in there, John, and let's do this again…" Abiel spoke in a slow and soft voice as John heard him in a far-off tunnel, and his mind was struggling to keep focused.

Homeward Bound

"Home -- that blessed word, which opens to the human heart the most perfect glimpse of Heaven, and helps to carry it thither, as on an angel's wings."
Lydia M. Child

The bus was an old Bluebird school bus painted blue with children's handprints plastered all over it in different rainbow colors. It was old and worn out, but it still ran great as it ferried the children through the night. The kids called it the bible bus since a lot of ministry and bible lessons were taught in it from time to time. They were coming back from a youth rally at the church in Prescott near the foothills, driving down Williamson Valley Road, and the kids were glad to be getting home since the hour was late. John drove the bus sometimes for the kids' ministry and Anna's children's pastoral duties. It was a nice fall night, and the sky was starlit and black. The moon was rising in the east, giving off a beautiful, warm glow in the desert night. The road back to town was long and straight, and John had driven it many times. The voices of excited kids rang through the bus and felt soothing to John. He would never have chosen this route in life had it been up to him; church and God were a touchy subject growing up, and John did his best to run the other direction in life, hoping God would be too busy to find him. Funny how it works out, though, in life, when you think you have run far enough away from the truth, it usually is there when you stop running. Also, God is never too busy to help his own.

The drive back to town only took about 20 minutes, and this gave John time to reflect on the events of the past. Anna held children's church on Sunday mornings, and John helped her in any way possible. It was a labor of love and must be done with the purest of intentions. Children were precious cargo in the eyes of the Lord, and to be entrusted with such an honor as children's pastor was the highest of duties. He drove and thought of all the Sundays with their little eyes wide open, listening to the spoken word and watching Anna as she told them all of the stories in the bible. She was a visual teacher, which helped when some kids were only 5 years old. They loved to be there on Sunday mornings, and it was hard to get them to leave after the sermon was over. Anna would always make time for whoever stayed after to talk about their life and let them know that God was always there for them. John grew up a lot spiritually in that little classroom on those mornings. As he drove into the moonlit night with all of the stars in heaven before him, he felt a sense of peace that he had never felt before. He often read about it in the bible about the peace that passes understanding, but had never felt it in his own life until now, as he drove the bible bus down that lonely highway. Thoughts of joy and love and hope filled his head, and all of the things done for the Lord had proved to be not in vain. Through a child's eyes and heart, one can enter the kingdom of heaven, so that was what he was feeling on this grand night. The moment only lasted for a few seconds, but the feeling would stay with him for the rest of his days. "What are you thinking about? You look so happy," Anna asked him while the kids sang songs and played. John replied, "I was just thinking about the youth rally and how the kids had such a great time. How time seems to fly past us as we do this ministry for the kids."

It was true that the time was rapidly going by, and the world outside didn't seem to catch up. John looked ahead into the distant blackness of night and could see the road ahead illuminated by the bus's old headlights, dim but still somewhat able to see the desert beyond. They had been out here living in Arizona for almost 10 years now, and they both loved it here. All of the years spent somewhere else only led them to here and now at this point. This was the peace that passes understanding that he had read in Philippians 4:7

"And the peace of God, which passes all understanding, shall keep your hearts and minds through Christ Jesus." John had always wondered if that was obtainable in this life, but now, he knew. The feeling he had right now was better than any drug or drink or potion that could be found on this earth; he was feeling the true spirit of the Lord above, and that would not be taken away.

Family

"What greater thing is there for human souls than to feel that they are joined for life, to be with each other in silent, unspeakable memories?"
George Eliot

John could still feel the feeling of that night on the bible bus driving through the northern Arizona desert. The feeling of being touched by the hand of God while doing his will was the greatest of all things. He didn't want to lose this, but it was slipping away like the blood from his veins dripping into the carpet of time. He now knew that this was the moment of truth since there were no more roads to travel and no more places to be. Abiel sat solemn and quiet as he knew also that the time was at hand. "Are you going to ask me for any last request that I know you can't grant?" John said to the angel. Abiel replied, "No, John, I'm not going to do that because I truly can't reverse what has been done. We are at the crossroads, and now we must proceed down the chosen path. I will tell you that your cell phone is right next to your leg, and all you would have to do is hit the speed dial to call Anna. I don't think she will answer, but it's worth a try. The only problem is I have to set time back on its course, and you will feel all of the pain and agony that you felt earlier. Or I could just have the death angel take you now, what will you choose, John?" John knew Abiel wasn't joking. "You are a sly one, Abiel, so this is my last request if I want it. I can make the phone call and suffer the pain of all the damage my poor body has endured, or I can just slip silently into the great beyond without suffering. You know me too well, my friend."

John had Anna's number on speed dial, so it wouldn't be a great chore to just hit the number and talk to her. He looked at the dashboard clock that read 3:20, just 7 minutes into this ordeal, but it sure had taken so long to get here. Abiel had done well by slowing up the time and keeping the death angel at bay. John looked ahead and saw the angel right in front of him with an outstretched hand as if to greet him into the unknown. Not just yet, my friend, he looked over at the minion of Satan and saw his eyes glowing even brighter with the fires from hell as John's last moments were being played out. It was a fitting sight to see good and evil sharing such a timeless struggle. "No struggle here," he thought as he knew the outcome and what he had done for his part in the eternal play of life. John looked over at Abiel and said, "Ok, I'm ready. Abiel, put time back on track, my old friend."

In that moment that was just a moment several things happened. Abiel released his hold on slowing down the time that John had left. This, in turn, caused all of the pain previously felt to come back, but worse. John felt his legs that had been crushed by the large garbage truck that now sat on top of them, his left arm would not move, and he felt like it had been run through a wood chipper. His shirt was cold and wet with the blood that gushed from his neck, and he couldn't turn his head at all because his vertebrae were crushed from the immense force of the accident. He was lucky to be able to find the cell phone and pull it in front of his face to read the buttons. The phone was drenched in his blood as John wiped the face of it on his sleeve, where there seemed to be one spot that wasn't red. He sent the speed dial into motion as the phone rang in his ear, all this time trying to keep his eyes open as the pain of this final moment engulfed his tired body. The phone rang, and he could imagine Anna waking up in the night and hearing her voice, but what would he say? He didn't have the time to think about it as the phone went straight to voicemail with Anna's voice giving the intro. "Hello, you have reached Anna. I must be busy right now, so leave me your number, and I will make every attempt in the world to get back with you, or not. Have a nice day," then a long beep.

The condemned man sits on death row, and he stares out into the darkened space before him. The people stare in at him; some are angry, some are sad, and some are just there as witnesses to the end of a man's life. Whatever their motives, it's not their day to die. The man stares back and is asked, "Do you have any last words? "He ponders this thought for a second, then says "No," but this isn't a condemned man, no, this is the final few precious seconds in John Pezdel's life. He has to say something fast, and the sound of Anna's voice is so beautiful and missed. "Anna, this is John. I don't have much time, but I won't be here when you wake up. I just wanted to tell you that I've enjoyed every moment of our life together, and you are the only woman I have ever loved. I'm not alone right now. Abiel is here to get me through this, and there is hope after all this is done. Please remember me, as I will always remember and love you. He is right in front of me so I have to go now goodbye my Love…" then the message was over and John dropped the phone as all of the pain and hurt surrounded his every thought, just then Abiel slowed time for one last time and said to John "You have done well my Friend in this final hour, I will see Anna when you have gone and check up on her from time to time. Just go now, the death angel has his hand stretched out for you. Do not fear him; he has always been around you, but at a distance. Look into his face, and you will know him." With the pain gone and Abiel standing beside the death angel, now John could see Abiel's wings; they were as white as snow and huge heavenly angel wings like John had imagined. With a smile on his face, he grabbed the hand of the death angel and looked into his face.

He looked into the face of Jesus; he looked into the face of every good face he had ever seen in his short 49 years on earth. He saw every good person he had ever known, and now he truly knew that the death angel was not death itself but a culmination of every good thing that this world and the next had to offer. John's soul was pulled out of the wreckage and twisted metal, so full of pain, into eternity as his earthly body lay slumped over in the truck on a lonely intersection in Tucson, Arizona. The dashboard light read 3:21 as the firemen from Tucson Fire Station #10 had just arrived on the scene and began to use the Jaws of Life on the crumbled-up truck. In the darkness by a Palo Verde tree, the minion from hell slowly disappeared as the red glow in his eyes became dark once more.

Daybreak

"The breeze at dawn has secrets to tell you. Don't go back to sleep."
Rumi

The Whetstone Mountains were in front of her, and John was almost at the top of a large mountain; no matter how hard she ran, he was always out of reach. The sky looked dark and ominous as he made his way to the top. Anna felt a panic well up from inside as she climbed with the fury of a marathon runner. He stopped at a distance in front of her and waited with his back turned. She was almost there as John turned around and smiled at her with that beautiful smile he saved just for her. Just then, he turned and went over the top of the hill as the sky turned purple and red with the colors of the rainbow. She tried to get to that point but was stuck in the same spot…

Anna awoke again, dreaming the same dream, but this time it was different. John was in it, and she saw his face before he went over the edge of the mountain. She heard something in her sleep like a bell ringing, but put it off as part of the dream. The clock on the nightstand read 3:21, and sunrise would be coming soon; John would be home in an hour or so, then she would get up and make some coffee, as he told her about his trip in California. She could smell the strong odor of gardenia flowers as she lay in bed. Funny, she would smell them now since there wasn't a gardenia bush anywhere close to their house. Anna immediately thought of how John loves them because they reminded him of Grandma Pezdel. She was an odd one, John's grandmother. Anna only knew her for a short time when they got married, then she passed away a couple of years later. She lay there thinking about the beach and living by the shore in so many places. She thought of Long Beach and Hawaii, all the times she and John had spent with the kids living in so many places. That was such a long time it seemed, and Arizona was their home now. They were coming up on 20 years in this state, and she would never move away again. As the thoughts of these things and others overtook her, she once more drifted back to sleep.

A loud knock on the front door suddenly awoke Anna as she got up and went to see who it was. Opening the door, Deputy Marshal Brown stood in the morning light looking somber. "Hello, Anna, could I come in? I have something to tell you?" he said as she looked at him in a puzzled way. "Sure, Bob, come on in. What's going on? Did John have some car trouble? Did he get in a wreck?" Deputy Brown had known the Pezdel's for a few years and liked them; they were active in the community and well respected. He stared at Anna as she had a frightened look on her face. "He should have been home by now, Bob, it's 7:20 in the morning; I hope he didn't have car trouble." She said to him as they sat on the kitchen chairs. Bob was a deputy Marshal in the town of Tombstone for 22 years and rarely had to give news of this nature, but it was always hard, especially when they were your friends. He knew John and Anna well, so this was not a pleasant task by any means.

"Anna, there has been an accident involving John and a City of Tucson vehicle. He got off the I-10 around 3:00 this morning near Park

Ave to get gas and was struck by a city garbage truck. He did not survive the crash and, by all accounts, died quickly. I'm so sorry to have to tell you this, but he is in Tucson right now at the coroner's office; they want you to identify his body." He told her as the color suddenly drained from her face. Anna could barely hear what Bob was saying as she kept thinking about how she would have to identify his body. Poor John, she burst out in tears at the thought of his passing, and felt a sudden weight pressing down upon her of sorrow and grief. She just found out her best friend was gone in the twinkling of an eye while she slept warm and safe in her home. John was dying on some lonely road in Tucson. "Why, God, did you do this to him? He had so much more left to give and do in this world. He was such a good man and was loved by many. Didn't you have anyone else you could have taken instead?" She thought this and many more things as the Deputy gave more condolences and then left the home.

Heartbreak

"To love at all is to be vulnerable. Love anything and your heart will be wrung and possibly broken. If you want to make sure of keeping it intact, you must give it to no one, not even an animal. Wrap it carefully round with hobbies and little luxuries; avoid all entanglements.

Lock it up safe in the casket or coffin of your selfishness. But in that casket, safe, dark, motionless, airless, it will change. It will not be broken; it will become unbreakable, impenetrable, irredeemable. To love is to be vulnerable."

C.S. Lewis, "The Four Loves"

Anna sat on the couch in the living room, staring out at the Dragoon Mountains and weeping for her husband. They had been together for so long, and she never thought about a life without him; he was always in her mind whenever the talk of their future was discussed. Now, in the quiet old house in the middle of the southern Arizona desert, the world seemed like such a lonely place. This was not what they had planned, and this is not what she wanted. Anna never felt such despair and emptiness in her life. Even during times of separation, while John was in the Navy, they knew that someday they would be reunited again. Not this time, she only had the quiet old house and Elvis to comfort her. Elvis was John's dog that he had gotten at a yard sale in Benson one day. He was a sorry-looking thing with a curled-up lip, so John called him Elvis, and they were best buddies. Anna laughed and cried as she remembered the day John brought him home. He looked so pathetic and big, almost 130 pounds of coon hound and Rottweiler sitting on the floor. Now he was just a constant reminder of John; she would have to take care of him, and he would have to look after her. He used to tell her that the "King was still in the house" every time they let him in, then he would say "The King has left the building" each time he went outside. She knew it was kind of dumb, but John had a way of making people laugh when they needed it the most.

John was a dog lover from birth and told Anna stories of when he was a young boy, and he would bring home strays almost once a week until his mom and dad finally got him an old beagle that wasn't worth much. Still, John loved that dog and everyone that came after him; he should have been a veterinarian if things were different. But they never are different, she thought as John's memory and face were etched into her mind. He had a funny way of looking at life, wasn't afraid of anything, and didn't fear death like most folks. He just knew that the good Lord above had his back and would take him when he was ready. "I hope you didn't suffer my Love last night on the intersection. I hope you were thinking of me, and I would have given anything to be there with you, even my life for yours." She thought as the sun brightened up the town of Tombstone. He must have known that was his destiny; he always alluded to Anna that he wasn't going to die of a heart attack, diabetes, or any other ailment. How did he know?

It had only been about an hour since Deputy Brown had told her the news. She was going to get ready and head into Tucson to see the medical examiner at the morgue, where John was. She had to call the kids and let them know that their dad was gone; this was too much to think about on Monday morning after hearing the news. No news of death was good to hear, but it's worse when the person who died was your best friend. The smell of Gardena's still hung in the air, and Anna thought that maybe John was around, but she knew better; the dream she had told the story all too well. The fragrance was just coming from some passing soul who wanted to say hello. Anna told the spirit, "Ok, I know you're here, and I wish you a safe passage to where you're headed. If you see my husband, John Pezdel, on your way, tell him I love him so much." She doubted that the unseen spirit would see John, but it was worth a try. They came through this house like the wind. Every house and establishment in Tombstone had a haunted house angle, but their house was not really haunted, more like a hotel for wandering ghosts. They didn't stay long; they mostly came by to check out the owners and then moved on. Anna knew of several spirits that hung around the house. They would make themselves known on many occasions to let you know they were there.

She didn't know what to do right now except try to take in what the Deputy had said. Anna was supposed to go on that trip, except Elvis came down with a bad case of the dog influenza, so she stayed home and wished John well and told him to have fun. In her mind, she kept playing an image of him in the truck being hurt so badly with no one to help. Anna got up to get her cell phone to call the kids. She looked at the screen, and it said missed call "Husband" on the face. Her heart skipped a beat as she frantically went to retrieve the voicemail on the phone. The call came in at 3:20 this morning when Anna was asleep. She thought, "John, I wish I had heard you call so I could have spoken to you." Anna hit the voicemail button and listened.

"Anna, this is John. I don't have much time, but I won't be here when you wake up. I just wanted to tell you that I've enjoyed every moment of our life together, and you are the only woman I have ever loved. I'm not alone right now. Abiel is here to get me through this, and there is hope after all this is done. Please remember me, as I will always remember and love you. He is right in front of me, so I have to go now, goodbye my Love…"

The tears flowed freely like heavy rain as she played the message over and over just to hear his voice. Who was Abiel, and where did he come from? John was the only one in the car that night. The Deputy said that when the paramedics got there, they had to pry the roof and doors off to get John out. How could anyone else be there unless he was delirious? Too many questions and no answers, her mind was in a state of confusion as she looked up at the clock in the kitchen that had stopped at 3:21. She had just changed the batteries a week ago on that old thing. Now she knew what it meant that John had passed at 3:21 and sent this message to her. Still, she felt comforted with the call when he said he was not alone. Maybe an angel from the Lord was sent to comfort him in those last moments. That was a better explanation than him being out of his head. Anna called all of the children to let them know their father had passed away; it was very hard to relive the pain with each one of them. She had four kids, and each of them had kids, so John would be missed by many. They cried, and she cried some more as the ache in her heart grew bigger. How can one man mean so much to so many? She kept thinking about the phone call and why she didn't hear it ring during the night. Anna usually awoke at the slightest noise or rustle, but last night she felt like she was in a deep sleep, having dreams of John. Now she remembered the dream of her chasing John up that large mountain, and he finally turned around just in time before he went over the edge. It had to be God's way of telling her that he was with him now. It made perfect sense in the light of day, but in the night, dreaming that dream, she just didn't know.

The trip to Tucson took about an hour and a half, plenty of time to think of the future, what future could there be now that John is gone? Anna never imagined a life without him; they talked about what each other would do in this situation, but it was just talk that couples make when they deeply love each other. Now, the what if has become the what is, she remembered telling John if she left first, he should remarry and go on with his life. That thought seemed so foolish to her now, as she had just lost the only man in this world that she would be married to. John used to tell her he would just sell everything and move to Rocky Point in Mexico. It was a nice place to visit, but not live, Anna thought. She drove until she reached the County Morgue off the I-10. Dr. Mattson met her at the front desk and took her to see John. They entered a well-lit, cold examination room, and in front of her, John lay under a white sheet. Anna could not hold back the tears as the truth finally sank in that her husband had passed. "Mrs. Pezdel, you just have to take a quick look and confirm that this was John, just say yes or no," the Doctor told her. He pulled back the sheet, and Anna gazed down at what looked like her husband, but it was hard to tell; the trauma of the wreck and all of his injuries had given him a misshapen and battered look. She told him, "It looks like John, but it's hard to tell, he is so beat up and sad looking. He has a tattoo of his dog Elvis on his right arm. Check that." The medical examiner pulled back the sheet, and there was a picture of a coon hound Rottweiler on his right arm. Anna knew for sure it was him. The M.E. left the room for a moment to give Anna time with John. "Why, John, why did this happen? I just saw you on Friday, and everything was fine; how do I go on now without you? I am sorry, my love, that you had to go through this pain and suffering. I wish I could have been there with you. I would have taken your place." She told him as the tears rolled down onto John's lifeless body.

In that moment, she felt her future pass away; the dreams and hopes that they both shared were washed away like a sand castle on the beach. How could one man mean so much to one woman? She felt like cursing God, but remembered the tale about Job and the Devil. This was meant to be, and she knew it, but didn't have to like it. All those times she thought that John wasn't afraid of anything, she could now see why. He had a date with destiny, and it went as planned. Anna left the room and drove back home to her place of refuge in the town of Tombstone. They always said it would be their final resting place, and that was true for John, but now, at this time, Anna didn't really know anymore. She had a funeral to plan and people to see. The family will be here tonight, most of them, or by morning. There was so much to do, and all the time in the world to do it in. The phone message played over and over for a few times as she drove on the interstate. Questions kept going through her mind as she heard John's final message to her. "Who was Abiel, and where did he come from? Who was standing in front of John in those final seconds of life?" Anna kept wondering, but nobody had the answers except John. She knew he went home; he told her, and that was enough.

The Journey

"The road of life twists and turns, and no two directions are ever the same. Yet our lessons come from the journey, not the destination."
Don Williams, Jr.

The nights in Tombstone were a lot different than the daytime. The tourist and their families are gone or in the motels sleeping it off, the locals who dress as 1880 outlaws and womenfolk are mostly at home asleep. The only ones out at night were visitors and local friends having a good time. Anna walked past the Crystal Palace and glanced over at the wooden bench that she and John sat on many a night after having a beer or two. He used to tell her that if you listened hard enough, you could hear the sounds of days gone by when the cowboys and gunmen and miners roamed these streets. She never really heard anything except the music coming from inside the Palace. Right now, she could hear a local band singing "Copperhead Road" as she continued to walk toward the Birdcage Theatre. Looking up at the cloudy night sky, she could see the lightning flash in the south as a late monsoon storm was approaching. "That's just great, John, you didn't think this one out, did you?" she said as she got closer to her goal. Standing in front of the Birdcage holding her precious cargo were the ashes of her late husband. It had been about a month since the funeral and wake, John always wanted a good old-fashioned Irish wake, and Anna made sure it was the best. He made sure that Led Zeppelin's Kashmir was played at the wake. He really loved that song and a lot of other ones, too.

The kids had all left with their kids, as they had jobs and lives and mortgages to pay. Some wanted to stay, but Anna said that if she went, she would be all right. Standing there with the top of the urn off, she slowly walked down Allen Street and spread John's ashes a little at a time as she made her way to 3rd Street. She wept as she thought of him telling her to do this if he passed first. "That's great, John, but what if it rains?' she asked him on that long-ago day. "Well, if it rains, then that would be better, then I will be everywhere in Tombstone, even in the wash behind our house, so that will work if it does." He said back. Anna walked slowly and deliberately since this had been so important to him. Talking to him as if he were there, the ashes fell slowly to the ground to be mixed into the dirt and pavement, horse dung, and whatever else was left from that afternoon. She could feel some drops of rain on her head as she made her way to the American Legion near 2nd street. By the time she got there, it was pouring down rain, and all she could think of was John being washed throughout the Town just like he wanted.

The roar of thunder suddenly woke Anna as she sat on the bench in front of the American Legion Post 24. She was a bit startled and disoriented, but realized that she had just spread her husband's ashes along Allen Street and was waiting out the rain. The storm had passed, and she must have dozed for about 20 minutes until the sound of thunder awoke her. A feeling of mighty weight was lifted from her shoulders as she made her way home. John's final wishes were complete, and she could now let that part of him go. Someone is born every day, and someone also passes away. It was the great circle of life, yet it is seldom that the rest of the world knew them as sons, daughters, wives and husbands, brothers, sisters, and someone who once meant something to somebody. She tried to keep it together as she walked through the night. It was 5 minutes to the house, but on an early Sunday morning at 1:30 am, Tombstone was just another town in the middle of the Sonoran Desert. The wildlife was abundant with mule deer and javelina, which were nasty when confronted. She never feared any of those animals when John was with her. Hopefully, she has a guardian angel, she thought as the house grew closer. Inside, it was warm and quiet, so she rested on the recliner and tried to dry off.

Not knowing how long she had slept, Anna opened her eyes to see the shape of a young girl in front of her. Started and confused, she did not have any of the grandchildren staying tonight. She asked the girl who she was, "Who are you and why are you in my house?' she asked the dim figure before her. While not really speaking, Anna could hear her in her head. The girl answered, "Hello, my name is Lily, and I live here. I have been trying to get your attention for the longest time; I guess you can see and hear me now?" Anna knew then that the ghostly shape before her was the spirit of a young girl dressed in clothes from an era that was long past her memory. The clothing was possibly around the late 1800's. Anna and John shared certain abilities when it came to seeing the unseen and knowing when their presence was around. They did not think of it as a gift, but just another heightened sense beyond the normal five senses. He was able to sense an evil presence more readily than Anna, but she had the ability to talk to those not of this world.

Nobody really wants to commune with the dead. It's that simple, their world and ours should be on a different time and space continuum but that is not always the case. Tonight was no exception and although Anna had been here for over 10 years the only thing of supernatural nature has been the orbs that live in the basement and the occasional spirit that roams thru their house then leaves. None of them have ever said they lived here, where has this girl Lily been all of this time? Anna was not frightened just a little bit put off by the girl's response. Anna asked her, "What do you mean you live here? This is my house, and I live here. You need to find another place to haunt or reside, I'm not in the mood for visitor's little girl. Lily or whoever you call yourself. Go to the light or wherever you go but just not here" Anna looked over at the girl standing there as she wore a long dress that covered all of her body except her hands, her feet just sort of faded away into a smoky mist as the girl spoke to Anna, not in an actual voice but more like resonating in her head. "I have always been her you just didn't notice me until today, something is different and the man you lived with has moved on I see, He went with the angel to the other place, Abiel was with him until the end." Anna suddenly remembered that name Abiel and asked Lily who Abiel was? "He was the man's guardian angel who had been with him for all of his time on this earth. Everyone has one who is alive in your world, if your good or bad the angel is there watching and helping. I see yours standing behind you now as we speak." Anna turned around to catch a glimpse of this angel behind her but she saw nothing but the wall and a picture of Wyatt Earp. Anna asked "How do you know about John and this Abiel?" Lily explained "Abiel came here on the night your husband had passed away told us about him and where he had gone. He came to check up on you since he told John he would do that. The death angel took John home to be with the Lord." Anna was pleased to hear the confirmation even if it was from a ghost.

"How have you been here all these years and I haven't felt you or seen you until now?" Anna asked. Lily replied "We all live in the basement below your bedroom and its home for now, nobody ever bothers us and we stay together down there, your John used to come by and talk to us. He knew we were there but he just liked to wish us well and enjoy the house while we were here. I liked him." Anna tried to visualize John talking to the ghost in the basement and started to laugh softly. He always told her that the orbs down there were just spirits that hadn't moved on yet. "Who else is down with you Lily?" she said. Lily thought for a moment and told her "There is myself of course, and then there is Oly and Swan. I also have a friend whose name is Ned and occasionally there is Bartlett but he lives up on Skyline and only comes by when he passes this way. We have guest who come through now and then, just wandering spirits that have no home." Anna tried to imagine all of these spirits living in her house but couldn't grasp that there was that many. One or two is fine but four of them and an occasional roaming specter were a bit much. Still, she was intrigued at the arrival of Lily.

She asked Lily "So tell me Lily why you are an orb down there but a ghostly spirit up here? Why can't you just stay this way?" perplexed not knowing the ways of the departed. She knew that there were such things all of her life but no explanation was conceived until now. "True Anna we are just orbs most of the time and even then, we can't be seen. There is an exception to the rule we can be seen on photography or your movie picture machine but rarely. We maintain the least amount of energy to stay as orbs but we can, after much rest take on our original form so to speak when we passed from our time into our present state. The problem is we can only remain visible for about 7 to 8 minutes of earthly time." Anna then asked her "Why are you still here Lily if you died so long ago you should have passed on to heaven by now? What is it that keeps you on this earthly plane bound to the place you lived at?" Lily knew the answer vaguely but could never put a definite reason on it. She was just a nine-year-old girl when she died. "The only thing I can tell you is I feel unrest in my soul, I want to go home so badly and I can't find my parents at all. I feel abandoned without hope of ever seeing them again. I need to get back down below since I can't remain this way anymore. We will talk again" she told Anna as her ghostly form slowly faded away to nothing.

The Open Door

"Remember what Bilbo used to say: It's a dangerous business, Frodo, going out your door. You step onto the road, and if you don't keep your feet, there's no knowing where you might be swept off to."
J.R.R.Tolkien

It was now 3:00 in the morning early Sunday and Anna was so tired so she got up and made her way to an empty bed. Thinking of what had just happened she was amazed yet somewhat disturbed that these spirits had been here all along and she had no clue that they shared her home. John knew and had told he before about the people beneath their bedroom in the storage side of the basement but she thought he was kidding. Lying down in her warm bed she fell asleep quickly as a new dream came upon her like a wave on the beach.

Tombstone was still a roaring prospector's dream of a town in 1883 as Nellie Cashman worked her restaurant and boarding house on 131 south Fifth street right off Allen Street in one of the busiest towns in the west. She was well known for her generosity and compassion to her fellow man. The miners in the town loved her and called her "The Angel of Tombstone". Her sister Fanny had just passed away and she left behind her five children that Nellie took on as her own. They had no family except her so they just called her "Aunt Nelle". Nellie was of Irish descent and showed it often. She wasn't a large woman but commanded respect wherever she went. Tom Turner and his wife Irene stayed in one of the rooms with their only daughter Lily, who was 8 years old at the time. Lily was a happy girl living in the bustling western town of Tombstone. She loved to play with Nellie's adopted nephews and nieces. They were the Cunningham's and she liked Mike the best. He would fight whoever he wanted to but with Lily he was a very sweet young man. Nellie had raised them all to be respectful of others but to stand up for their selves. Tom Turner was a miner and he worked hard for his family. Life was hard for a man in Tombstone but harder if you had a family. Tom had done well for his troubles in Tombstone; he had a partial stake in the Victory mine east of town and was ready to buy a piece of land near the mine off of Fourth Street. It was an acre of hilly property but a flat spot was suitable for a small house that he would build for his Family. His wife Rebecca would work at the Russ house three days a week then help with the construction when she could. After six months of working the land, they had a small cabin built with a cement cistern to catch water for the animals. Lily loved the animals and she made up names for each of them; the horse was Jeffery. The two head of cattle were "This and That". The chickens were just numbered but still she knew each one personally.

Life was grand for the family and Lily explored every inch of town when the folks were busy. She didn't go out at night unless they were going to the Schieffelin Hall to see a show but otherwise between the Russ House, school, and chores and roaming the town she was a busy girl. It was the spring of '84 when Lily was helping her mom at the Russ House when it started to snow quite heavily on the streets of Tombstone. Rebecca told her "Lily you need to go home now before this storm gets worse while it's still light out. I have lots to do here with Nellie, so go straight home and I will be there in a few hours after I'm done here. Your Pa will be home for supper around 5:00 so he will be there with you. Be careful in that snow it's getting thick out there. "Lily knew the way home and had played in the snow before but this time it was really coming down. She went out the back way of the Russ house thru the Pioneer Livery then down Allen to Fourth Street. Her house was just down the road past Fulton Street. By now she could not see the road or many surroundings so she cut through the yard to get into the house.

Due to a cold front coming in from California the night before was bitterly cold. Temps dropped well below freezing and the surface of the cistern pond had frozen over. Nobody noticed this the next day so with the snow storm in full force Lily had no idea exactly where the top of the cistern was since the snow had covered everything. She walked across the surface of the frozen water tank until the ice cracked and gave way with her weight. Slipping below the surface and being trapped beneath the frozen ice she was just a young girl who got disorientated and could not find the way out it was so dark and cold she panicked and it took her life. She died that night in the cistern. When Tom came home, he couldn't find her so he searched the grounds for hours until he came across the cistern and her hat lay next to it. He found her beneath the ice and pulled her lifeless body from the watering hole. They had a memorial for her two days later and she was buried under a large mesquite tree on the other side of the house. The Turners owned three acres of land so a family plot was laid out when they bought the land.

Unfortunately, years later when the Turners finally passed away the plot was forgotten and they were put in the city owned cemetery off Allen Street.

Anna awoke in a panic; the dream she was having was so real that it was like she was there in it, but could do nothing to change the outcome for Lily. She looked at the clock, and it read 4:44. It was time to go back to sleep. What a weird night she had; she almost thought that Lily was in her imagination, but the cistern in her dream was the same one located in her backyard, full of dirt. She always wondered what that was out there, but now she knew. But it had to be a dream; she could not sleep now and made some coffee to help calm her. Not prone to remembering many dreams, Anna was surprised to have this one still fresh in her mind. It was like a movie playing over and over until you've had enough. Surely it wasn't real as she looked south and saw on the other side of the yard the stump of a huge tree that once grew there. It had been cut down years ago, but the tree stump was never removed, and it looked to be in the same spot Lily had been laid to rest. A chill ran down her back and arms as she saw the large stump in the early morning light. The time she dreamt about had to be over 125 years ago; how long had that tree lived before they cut it down, she wondered. As it grew lighter, her curiosity got the best of her, and she went to the base of the old tree with a shovel and started to dig. Anna thought about how foolish she must have looked digging around like this, but the dream was too real, and she had some time to kill. She dug in the front and found nothing, then both sides and to the rear until she was about to give up, and an idea came over her to get the digging bar that John always used and just shove it into the ground. After doing this many times, she hit something hard about three feet in front of the mesquite stump.

Her heart was racing as she slowly dug down to the object. It could be a rock, but after half an hour, she found an old headstone lying below the dirt. On it read, "Lily Turner, beloved daughter, 1875- 1884. Rest in Peace, Angel." Anna wept as she read the old, engraved letters on the small stone. To lose a child at such a young age was devastating. She now knew that Lily wanted her to find this place where she was buried, but she didn't know why, and she would find out soon. The poor girl never had a chance to become a woman and enjoy her life; she left this world too soon. Anna vowed to find out if her parents were still buried in the Tombstone cemetery.

Burial records from that time were scarce, but the city did a good job of listing all interments on the Tombstone Cemetery website. Anna found both Tom and Irene very easily. Driving over to the Cemetery on Allen Street, she felt excited and strange all at once. She never even heard of the Turners before yesterday, and today she was trying to solve a 130-year mystery. The old Cemetery was located on the west end of Allen Street, right before it turned into a dirt road. It was a good location set back from town with views of the mountains in all directions. Anna drove in and got out of the car to look around. The wind was blowing, and nobody was around, which gave off a lonely sort of feeling this morning. She had been this way with John, but they never stopped to look around. Too busy living, I guess. The road was lined with ponderosa pines that led to the back of the cemetery. There were over 1300 graves here, and she didn't know where the Tuckers were buried, so she started walking, just reading about the people who had been buried long ago. Some, like "Dutch Annie," who died in 1883 with no known birth year, were just a part of the history of the town of Tombstone. She read Henry Barber's tombstone and B.F Daniel, who died in 1881, then, as she took a turn past a large Monument marker, she read the name Turner on a dusty old gravestone. Tom Turner, Husband, Father, born 1850, died 1901. Next to his marker was Irene Turner, Wife, Mother, born 1853, Died 1907. She knew these had to be Lily's family. It had to have been since the dream was so vivid that she could still remember the details. The morning wind blew through the pines, giving off a whistling sound that just made this place that much lonelier.

Now she knew what had to be done for the young girl she had met. There is usually a reason for everything, but finding it was the hard part. Lily wanted her to see what she knew and where she was buried. It became all too clear that Lily wanted to go home and be with her parents in heaven. She must have been hanging around all of these years waiting for someone to find her remains and set her free. Anna made the preparations with the city officials to have Lily's remains buried alongside her mother and Father. The day came about 2 weeks later, on an early morning ceremony that was attended by several townsfolk who wanted one of their original inhabitants to finally rest in peace. With some words and some singing, Lily Turner was laid to rest.

Anna went home to her empty house and sat at the table having a cup of coffee. Looking down the hall, she could see Lily slowly gliding toward her with a smile on her face. Anna could hear her words in her head, "Thank you so much, Anna Pezdel, I will never forget you. I have been trying for ages for someone to find me out back beneath that old tree stump. I just wanted to be with my parents. You have helped me in a way that no one could, and I wish good things for you for all of your days. I have to go since I see him now coming to take me home. I told my friends about you, Anna, and they want to meet you, too. Please take good care of them. Goodbye." And just like that, she was gone in an instant, her ghostly shape fading in the morning light as if she had never been here at all. A lot of questions rolled around in Anna's head, but nobody was there to answer them. So that was the thing keeping Lily earthbound all of these years. The love of her parents and wanting to be buried by them was enough. Something must have happened all those years ago for the Turners to forget her on this property and get buried in the old cemetery. The past does not give up its secrets often, so this was enough for Anna.

The Visitor

"The ornament of a house is the friends who frequent it."
Ralph Waldo Emerson

The days went by in a steady fashion as life returned to Anna in Tombstone. She kept busy with work around the old house and some volunteer work at the local thrift store during the week. She liked working since it kept her mind from wandering too far from where it should be. Often, she thought of John and their life together; it was just too damn short, and she felt lost and alone at times. Elvis kept her company during the quiet moments, and he never failed to make her laugh. He was such a large, goofy animal, but she loved him just the same. The weather was changing, and fall was in the air. Anna loved the fall and winter months best out here. Summer was always her favorite, but that has changed like the seasons around her.

It was Sunday evening, and Anna sat on the couch watching some game show that was on while Elvis chewed on an old bone. She was dozing when she awoke to a strange sensation of being watched. Looking down the hallway towards the spare bedroom, she saw the shape of a ghostly woman slowly coming towards her. She was startled at first, then she remembered Lily telling her of the others who lived downstairs. The woman floated above the wooden floor slowly and with a purpose. She stood in front of Anna, not speaking, just looking at her for a minute. The temperature of the room felt a bit cooler as the woman stood in front of her. The smell of Lilac filled the air with an unnatural aroma. She was dressed in clothing of an era long gone now. Anna recognized the clothing from the women who dressed that way on Allen Street to look like women of the 1880s era. Her features were of a refined beauty that death only magnified as though she was preserved for all of time. Long flowing hair of white and pale translucent skin gave her a statuesque look as Anna just stared at her. Anna asked the specter, "So you must be Oly, the one Lily told me about. What can I do for you on this fine evening?" Oly just looked back for a moment she was not expecting the woman to see her or even talk to her but then said "I have not been able to find my friend and the others tell me she has gone on to the other side, I don't know how that happened but I was wandering for a while and when I came back, she was gone. Can you tell me what transpired?"

"I met the young girl a while back, after my husband John had passed away about two months ago. She knew him and told me things that I did not know about his journey to heaven and the one he was with when he died. We were able to finally put her remains next to her parents in the old cemetery on Allen Street then she was able to be released and go home. Can you tell me what keeps you here after all of these years? From the look on your face, I would say you have been in Tombstone for a very long time." Anna told her. Oly replied as though Anna could hear her in her thoughts, "My name is Olympia Simone Flanagan. I was only 26 years old at the time of my passing, but I knew what had happened. I really don't know why I'm still here, and I wish I could go where Lily went off to. Maybe we can talk again soon, but now I have to go, I'm late." And with that last word, she vanished into the evening air as Anna watched in amazement. "What would a ghost be late for?" she thought as she felt the room start to warm up a bit and the flowery smell diminished. Anna did not want to be the great redeemer for the lost souls of Tombstone; there could be hundreds, even thousands, of them floating around this town. She would just have to decline any involvement with this one and any other nightly visitor who wanted a free trip back home. "Why are they still here, and why can't they just go?" she thought again. Some answers are not so easily obtained.

That night was uneventful as the morning sun crept into the bedroom, Anna could not stop thinking about the strange events that had been happening since John had died. Was he able to communicate with these spiritual beings, but didn't tell her about it? They all seemed to know him and had good things to say about him, but what were they not telling her? The annual Territorial Days celebration was coming up, and usually John and she would be out helping the committee get ready for the event. This year, she would sit it out and just go downtown during the day to see the parade and soldiers reenacting those times. Anna remembered a line that Morgan Freeman would say in the movie "The Shawshank Redemption": "Get busy living or get busy dying..." She would choose the living part since there was way too much death and dying in her life right now. Looking in the bathroom mirror at her reflection, she seemed a little greyer and older since John had gone. Has she let herself go after all of these years of marriage with no man to look pretty for? She always cared about her appearance since she considered herself a striking woman in the twilight of her life. Now it just seemed so useless and mundane, the daily rituals of living. She still had people in her life who loved her, and they are the ones she cares about now.

All married couples at one time or another have the "What if" conversation, and it is usually the same all over the world. "What if I die first? What would you do?" That's the basic meat of it all. Both parties involved would like to know if the other would be alright if they passed prematurely. In most cases, this is never broached since either party dies at such an old age that the thought of getting another companion or spouse is not even considered. Anna and John had this conversation many times while drinking coffee on the back porch, looking at the Dragoon Mountains. They both conceded that the living person should get on with their life and find someone to spend their remaining time with. It all sounds good in theory or over a cup of coffee or a cold beer, but in the cold light of day, after the love of your life is gone, the mere thought of someone else is nonexistent. It's like losing everything you have ever owned in a massive house fire or tornado and not knowing where to start after the devastation. Sure, you will rebuild and buy new stuff, but the things lost will never be replaced, and the memories associated with them are gone with the wind. So, Anna did not entertain thoughts of finding a new mate; she just went about her day-to-day chores and duties associated with running an old house like this.

It had been over two weeks, and there was no sign of the new entity called Oly, and Anna did not want to see her again. "We don't always get what we want, we get what we need..." in the words of Mick Jagger. So, on this particular fall day, like most fall days, the weather wasn't much good for yard work, so Anna stayed inside and read a book about the fall of the Roman Empire and its correlation to modern times. What happens sometimes when you're reading, it gets a bit mundane, and soon your eyes are getting heavy? The book was kinda boring and a borderline conspiracy theory textbook manual, but John had read it before he died, and she wanted to see why he liked it so much. He used to say, "Just because you can't see them doesn't mean they aren't out to get you..." As she sat on the couch with eyelids growing so terribly heavy and feeling so tired, she closed them one last time, then out to never land she went.

Prosperity

"Fate often puts all the material for happiness and prosperity into a man's hands just to see how miserable he can make himself with them."

Don Marquis

Most of the respectable folk were off the streets or watching a show at the Schieffelin theatre tonight. The sound of music could be heard from one of the many bars on Allen Street as the woman walked toward the house on 2nd Street. She had only been in town for about 3 weeks now, and was just coming from San Francisco, then stopping off at Virginia City in Nevada. Virginia City was pretty much a ghost town when she rolled into it, as the mines were closed and most people had gone off to other boomtowns. A customer in the Bucket of Blood Saloon told her about Tombstone in the Arizona territory, so she headed that way. That was just a month and a half ago, and she was glad that she made the long trip. Standing on Allen Street looking north, she took it all in and smiled, not a bad sight to see if you like a good boomtown.

Her name was Olympia Simone Flanagan, and she was as Irish as a person could get; her mother, Susan Campbell, married her father, Shamus Magee Flanagan, 25 years ago in the city of Galway, nestled on the western coast of Ireland, on Galway Bay. The great potato famine hit Ireland around 1845, and many families immigrated to the United States then. Shamus stayed on as long as he could, then left with his wife for New York in 1852. She was born on April 13, 1857, on a cold fall morning in Five Points' district in lower Manhattan. Her family worked hard as factory workers and had little time to raise a family, but they made ends meet, and Oly was the fourth of seven children. With the start of the Civil War between the states, the workload only became more tedious and extreme for her parents. The children mostly raised themselves. Oly did her best to help around the house but at the age of 16 she left home and headed west. Not wanting anything to do with her life in New York, she made way for the West Coast and ended up in San Francisco in the summer of 1874. After working for a local seamstress in town near the wharves, she was talented and gifted in the trade, while being amazed at the sailors and miners who frequented downtown.

Oly was a good woman and did not give herself away like so many at that time but she loved the lifestyle of the miners and wanted desperately to go to where they came from and strike it rich in her own way. It was June 15, 1882, as Oly stepped off the Tucson stagecoach and surveyed her new home. Looking at her reflection in the window of a general store, she saw a beautiful Irish woman with red hair and green eyes looking back at her. She was excited with the hustle and bustle of the newly formed boomtown and had no problem finding a seamstress job with Mrs. Murphy down on 6th and Fremont in a little clothing shop. They catered to the miners in town as well as the local merchants and businesspeople. Everyone needed clothing and repairs to that clothing. Soon she was making good money and opened her own sewing shop closer to Allen Street near the Grand Hotel. One day, a man named James Locke came in for repairs and fell in love with young Oly

Flanagan. He was a miner at the Toughnut mine and worked long hours, but he was an honest man and cared deeply for Oly. Six months later, they were living together in a common law marriage, and not long after that, she delivered his first child, a girl named Sarah Jo Locke. Sarah was a joy and blessing to Oly as she took her to work and raised her up in the sewing store on 6th street. One day, about a year later, Oly came down with a severe case of diphtheria, and her health was rapidly declining. It was going around town as diseases usually do in a town so small with so many people. James had no choice but to remove Oly from the home and take her to a boarding house on 6th street so little Sarah would not become ill.

It was a cold day on March 10, 1884, when Oly was laid to rest in the Tombstone Cemetery on Allen Street. James and Sarah were there, as well as most people who knew him. She was loved by many in the town and never avoided a chance to help her fellow neighbors. In a month, she would have been 27 years old. After Oly got terribly ill, she never had the chance to say goodbye to James and Sarah since the illness was so contagious. She passed away, never knowing what became of her little girl. James and Sarah moved on from Tombstone since the loss of Oly was too much to bear, and new surroundings would be beneficial to all. Years later, the people of the town would see a ghostly shape of a young woman walking the streets of Tombstone looking for her lost child. Sometimes late at night, if you were out on the boardwalk on Allen Street, you could hear the wind rustling, and it sounded like "Sarah" in a low, ghostly voice.

Anna opened her eyes and looked around the room. The dream seemed so real, as though she was there in that time and place in old Tombstone. She now knew that Oly had died suddenly before her time and left behind a husband and a small baby girl. As a mother, Anna felt instantly drawn to Oly and her misfortunes brought on so long ago. Anna also found her own motherly instinct coming out since her own daughter was the same age as Oly when she died so long ago. Her daughter lived in Prescott, AZ, with her husband and three children. Oly had come to Tombstone like many who wanted to find a better life but were dealt a cruel hand by fate. Would she have died from a disease like that if she had never been here? Unlikely, but death would come eventually, like a thief in the night; it always does. Anna thought for a moment about her own mortality and what would become of her. She longed to be with John again, but it was against her beliefs to hasten her own demise with suicide. Surely God has a plan for her, and heaven can wait. Now she knew what kept Oly earthbound after death when others would have left by now. The love of a mother toward her child is the strongest bond on earth. Oly died of a disease but mostly of a broken heart. It all seemed so simple now, and Anna knew she had a part to play in all of it.

The afternoon was almost over as the sun began to set, and the shadows had grown longer. Anna thought back to when she was a young girl of about 7 or 8 years old. She had memories of strange dreams where people she didn't know who lived in places she had never seen would come to her in her sleep and show her their lives. Sometimes she would wake up scared and screaming, but most times it was like watching a movie and not being a part of it at all. Her mother would comfort her and tell her it would all be alright, and then Anna would fall back to sleep. From the porch of her house, she could see Boot Hill cemetery over the hill north of her. She could catch just a glimpse of it, but she knew it wasn't a good place to be. John always wanted to take her there after hours on a full moon, but she would have no part of that. A shiver ran down her back as she thought of that place at night; it couldn't be somewhere she would go to.

Anna had just eaten dinner and was watching some show on the History Channel when she saw Oly drifting down the hallway toward her. Anna felt no sense of fear, only a bit of excitement that she would come back to visit her now that she had seen her past life. The smell of lilac filled the air as the temperature dropped a few degrees slowly. Anna spoke to Oly with her thoughts, saying, "There you are, Oly. It's good to see you again. I now know what happened to you and why you have not moved on to the other side. You mourn the fact that you never knew what happened to your family after you passed on. Being a mother myself, it would be hard to leave. Also, I will look into the matter and get back with you in time. Tell me where you have been these past two weeks?" Oly stood in front of Anna radiant and beautiful and told her in a thick Irish accent "I have been traveling about and visiting some of my friends here in town. There has been news that Cowboy is up to his old tricks again, making things miserable for those who still remain. He is a sly one, I agree, and I have news that he walks amongst the town nightly looking for more lost souls to control. Last night I saw him standing on the hill looking down at your place for the longest time, just staring at the basement where my friends stay."

Anna felt a chill go down her spine thinking about this Cowboy person watching her home as she slept; she had Elvis and plenty of guns, so he would not be a problem. Oly said "I'm afraid the dog and guns won't help you Anna, Cowboy is not a person but a spirit that has only one purpose and that is to control the lost souls of this town and make them do his masters bidding. He is not to be trusted or approached; as long as you are here, he cannot come near you or your house due to the one who guards you day and night. Be assured that when you leave your property, he can come around anytime. You will know more soon, but for now, be on your guard. I will be back soon. I have to check on a few things, then we will talk again." And then she was gone in an instant, leaving Anna with a sad and uneasy feeling. Just the thought of such an evil spirit like Cowboy put her on edge. John was more adept at dealing with those types. He could tell when a person was demon-possessed, and even if something wicked came around, he would know. Just thinking about John, how she missed that man, and all of the moments just spent being with him. It was good that she knew love so well, but bittersweet that they were parted in this world. There is never enough love or time to go around, it seemed.

Trouble

"Crazy' is a term of art; 'Insane' is a term of law. Remember that, and you will save yourself a lot of trouble."
Hunter S. Thompson

These days, it was hard to keep her mind from wandering into unwanted territory. Anna sometimes doubted these little visits from the great beyond in the light of day, but right now, as the room was still cool with the passage of Oly to God only knows where, she felt alive and in touch with something greater than herself. It still didn't take away the thoughts of some crazy spirit lurking beyond her property line, waiting for his chance to strike. Elvis slept quietly at her feet as the cuckoo clock rang 10:00, time for bed. Anna told Elvis to come with her tonight as she grabbed the Colt .45 from the dresser drawer and stuck it under her pillow. It might not stop Cowboy, but there were other things in the night that it would take care of. Thinking it would take extra-long to fall asleep, she closed her eyes and was out for the night. A dream began to take fold of a different time and place…

Carlos Cruz Delgado sat upon his horse as Francisco Vasquez de Coronado's army slowly marched out of New Spain into the unknown. There were rumors of the seven cities of Cibola, but he had no use for gold or any other treasures. He took his reward from the misfortunes of others and delighted in their pain and suffering. He held a high rank in Coronado's army, and his fellow soldiers feared him. Carlos was the main interpreter for the army, and he had a purpose, and it was to question and torture the enemy until they talked or died. He never had any survivors after his sessions into madness. The captives always talked, but after that, they were of no use to him, and he didn't take prisoners. Right now, he was a bit uneasy as they made their way north into a land he had never seen before. The Indians that lived in these lands were well known to kill and torture their enemies, also. Carlos felt a kinship and admiration for these people; he also couldn't wait to capture some and see how long they would last. He would make it last as long as he could enjoy every minute of the ordeal.

Born the last of five sons, Carlos was a small child growing up as his four brothers picked on him daily and drove him to the brink of madness. At the age of 16, he left home and joined the Spanish army as an infantryman. Although small in stature, his fellow soldiers soon gained his respect as he fought viciously in battle. He volunteered for this mission into the unknown, knowing full well he might never return to New Spain or his homeland in Barcelona near the Mediterranean Sea. With a detachment of about 20 soldiers, they made their way north up the San Pedro River through the new land. Carlos felt more alone than he had ever been in his life. This was a beautiful land full of mystery and new things not seen in Spain or New Spain. It would be getting dark soon, and they must find a suitable campsite near the water and vegetation for the horses. It was a full moon as they finally stopped by what would be the town of Fairbanks sometime in the distant future. The land was flat by the river, and grass was abundant, so they set up camp as Carlos and his men took turns watching for the Indians that roamed this area, looking for intruders into their land.

Sometime in the early morning hours, Carlos awoke to the sound of nothing. He should have heard some of his men or at least the horses, but it was as though he was alone on the banks of the river. The fire was out as he made his way to where the guard would have been. There was no one to be found, and all of the gear and horses had vanished. Curled up in the roots of a large cottonwood tree, he must have been invisible to whoever had taken his entourage. With the coming of sunrise, he waited until sufficient light would illuminate the area. Upon scouting the camp, he found traces of footsteps of another kind; they looked like they were wearing slippers, but not shoes. Carlos knew these were the traces of the indigenous Apache tribes that roamed these lands. In the light of the morning, he found his men all dead and dumped upriver in a buffalo wallow over a ridge. Why hadn't he heard or seen a thing last night? Each soldier was mutilated badly and had their body parts removed in some gruesome fashion. Carlos began to wonder if he had met his match with this new discovery. Could it be that these Indians were more adept at torture and dismemberment than he was? The tracks of the horses led south, so that was where he would go.

Following the San Pedro River, he at least had water and a food source. His only weapons were his saber and a large hunting knife; these would do when he met up with the heathens. He had nothing but the clothes on his back, no provisions or maps to help him find his way, only the movement of the sun and the river flowing. Not knowing how far he had traveled, he rested in the shade of a large grove of cottonwoods. Sitting there for over an hour, he had dozed off, dreaming about his homeland and his family he had left behind. Suddenly, he awoke to the sound of horses coming this way in the water of the river. Hidden behind a clump of tall grass, he saw several riders coming toward him. They were the feared Apaches, and they were riding his soldiers' horses. Carlos could do nothing at the moment but watch them pass to the south in the direction he was heading. It would be nightfall soon, so he must find a place to hide from his enemy. Seeing a large outcrop of rocks above the river to the west, he went in that direction, looking for a cave or crevasse he could hide in for now. He found a shallow hole beneath a large boulder and went under to escape the watch of the roaming Indians.

The sound of Apaches talking woke Carlos from his sleep. They were really close, and they seemed to be looking for him. He must have been careless back there and left some sign that he escaped the massacre. Now would be a good time to get out of here, he thought as the searchers were drawing near. Slipping down the other side of the hole he was in, he found a small game trail and followed it out by the light of the full moon. Fear was something new to him as he felt it well up inside his chest. He used to be the one who made his victims afraid, but now he felt alone and isolated in a strange land. He would keep his head and wits about him and slowly leave this area for the safety of the nearest mountain range to the east of his position. Walking and crawling away in the night, he managed to make it out of the searching band of savages and proceeded to the hills before him; he should reach them by morning. The sun would be up in a few hours, and he had to find a place to hide. Reaching a valley with his on each side and a large range to the north, he stopped in what is now the future town of Tombstone. This being the year 1545, the terrain was slightly different, but the area was the same. He almost made it to the location of present Allen Street when the band of Apaches swooped down on him and knocked him unconscious. Blackness fell upon him as his legs buckled and his head poured red blood.

Not knowing how long he had been out, he opened his eyes to see his enemy face to face. They were adorned in animal hides with colored paint on their faces and arms. Yelling and screaming until he could take no more, a large Indian who looked like the Chief came over and pulled his head back while Carlos stared up into his dark eyes. Black and soulless they were as the Chief told his men something in his native tongue about the new intruders who must be stopped. Carlos was tied to the dirt with his arms and legs spread out. He could not escape, so he watched the show unfold. The braves would ride by at a gallop on the stolen horses and shoot at Carlos with their bow and arrows. At first, they missed by a long shot, then with each passing try, they got closer and closer until finally one arrow sank deep into Carlos's abdomen as he let out a terrible scream. Then one by one, they took turns riding and shooting him until there wasn't much to shoot at. With about 12 arrows buried deep within him, Carlos finally knew what it was like to be tortured to death. The pain too much for him as lie screaming for mercy and a sudden death and he could stand no more so the Chief took out his last arrow and planted it beneath his face deep into his throat, it paralyzed him from the impact then with just the few breathes left he in this world as he stared up at a beautiful desert sky into clouds of white while a cool breeze blew from the south. Then black nothing.

With eyes wide open, Carlos left this world hoping to meet his maker in some heavenly realm, but that would not be the case. He was greeted in a dark world by the Grim Reaper, who held a chain around the soul of Carlos as he tried to break free, but to no avail, as the reaper tightened his grip. He was left with only two choices: to go back to the land he left as a spirit working for the Evil One, reaping souls and creating an army of lost souls working for the dark lord, or be sent to hell and be tortured for all eternity until the end of days. In the wink of an eye, Carlos was right back on earth in the spirit realm, looking at his dead body in the sand as the Apaches mutilated what was left and took all of his earthly belongings. They then rode off into the west. The exact spot where Carlos was killed later became what is now known as Boot Hill in Tombstone, Arizona.

Spirits

"When the unclean spirit is gone out of a man, he walketh through dry places, seeking rest, and findeth none."
Matthew 12:43-KJV

Carlos roamed the desert land for many years, looking for the souls of the lost that roamed the earth like him. He would find one here and there, but for many years it was a futile quest. The ones he did find were sent out to villages and small towns to infest and disrupt the lives of those who lived there. The Indians knew too well that the forces of darkness were around and drove them back into the wasteland. For many years, this continued, and Carlos always returned to the place of his death, drawn to that area like a moth to a flame. He would find solace standing on the very soil where he lost his life. Then one day, quite inexplicitly, a lone traveler roamed the very grounds that he found hallowed. The man's name was Ed Schieffelin, and the rest is history. The town of Tombstone was booming, and the people came in droves to find their riches and fame. Some found it one way or the other, and the ones that found fame ended up buried here in Boot Hill.

The unsuspecting soul would go to heaven or hell, but for the few lost souls who were tied to the earth for whatever reason, then Carlos was there. He no longer went by the name of Carlos anymore, and for those who saw him for the first moment of death, he was greeted by a dark, ominous-looking man wearing a cowboy hat. When asked who he was, he just told them "Cowboy," and from that point on, they worked for him and the one who fanned the flames of Hell. Not knowing that they had a choice in the matter, they were shackled and chained to the will of Cowboy. They were sent throughout the town, causing havoc and unrest whenever they could. They were always bringing ill will and a foul odor wherever they traveled. When they were of no use to Cowboy anymore, then a couple of demons from hell would haul them away to the darkness and eternal damnation. Many souls would slip through the cracks and avoid the wrath of Cowboy, but they were few and well hidden. The power of God would shield them from his eyes, but he knew they were out there anyway.

As the light of the full moon shone down upon the old house on the hill, Cowboy's eyes burned with rage. Red and evil, his eyes gazed upon the house that was dark and silent. He stared at the basement where the souls that stayed there hid in darkness, away from his wrath and gaze. An evil servant of his named Jones said, "Should I go down there to make some trouble, Boss?" This only infuriated Cowboy more since he knew the power of the angel of the Lord who guarded the home and its property. But he wanted the ignorant fool of a spirit who worked for him to know the same, so he said: "Why yes, my servant Jones, go down there and pull those wretches from the security of their basement and bring them to me now." He knew full well what was going to happen, but Jones didn't, and that's all that mattered. The evil spirit slid down the hill silently and bathed in white as the full moon shone right through him. When he came upon the property line of the home, a flash of brilliant white light appeared, and the angel of the lord Marmaroth, who protected Anna as she slept, was suddenly standing before Jones. He raised his arms high and brought down the full might of God upon the lost soul. The spirit known as Jones was snuffed out and sent immediately to the depths of hell. This made Cowboy even more in a fit of rage as he stared at the guardian angel, and a slight chill ran down his evil back. He knew this would happen, but he had to be sure whether the angel was there or not. Cowboy did not want to tangle with such a mighty angel of the Lord without some form of backup.

Anna awoke suddenly from the dream about Cowboy. She had never known evil like that, but now she was sure that what Oly had said about him was true. If John were here, he would know what to do, but for some reason, this is all happening because he is not here; they never had problems before. Cowboy was from the dark side, searching for lost souls to take back with him to hell; he will never stop until he has met the quota that his evil master has set for him. She got up and looked out of the bedroom window in the direction of Boot Hill. The full moon shone brightly on the area north of her home as she tried to see if Cowboy was really there, as her dream had depicted. A faint dark shape of a man stood on the hill looking back at her home, and she felt like he was looking right at her. She could see the glow of small red eyes staring at her. Closing the blinds quickly, Anna's heart was racing from seeing the evil specter. She knew she was safe since her guardian angel kept watch, but that didn't make it any easier to sleep. The clock on the nightstand read 4:44, and she knew that number meant something good, but her memory was tired, and she wanted sleep badly. It would all have to wait until the morning.

Another beautiful day in Tombstone, Arizona, arrived as Anna got up in the morning. Today, Anna would help out her new friend, Oly, to see if the riddle could be explained. Lily was earthbound because she wanted to be buried beside her parents in the old Tombstone cemetery. Oly's problem was a little more subtle and harder to solve. Oly was a dignified and gentle soul that only wished to see her family again. Maybe Anna could track down her descendants and try to unite them here so that Oly could find eternal peace. Anna felt like a social worker for the dead now, and every day became more complex than before. Her only fear was that the spirit community would hear of her "talents" like in the movie "Ghost" and come to her night and day for help. One day at a time, and she could only do what was in her power to do. That was just a movie, and this was real life and death, so she must tread lightly. Anna had to start with the child Sarah, since she would have lived longer than James Locke, she assumed, but stranger things have happened. Was it Sarah Locke or Sarah Flanagan she wondered? The two were not officially married at the time of her passing; it was common back then to reside together without a proper marriage. Her mind kept going back to the evil spirit Cowboy, and why is he stalking her land and its occupants? Anna knew he was trying to sway the remaining basement dwellers to the dark side, but she didn't think it would happen since all of these years had gone by, and they were still down there. It's probably like when Elvis chases mice and lizards all day, even if he doesn't get them, he has to do it anyway. Elvis, being of pure coon hound descent, just can't help himself.

Anna started researching online about the Locke family after Oly had died. James Locke lived in Tombstone until 1886, when all of the mining had dried up, and the town looked like a ghost town. Sarah was just 3 years old at the time, so they headed up to Jerome in Yavapai County, east of Prescott. There was a copper boom going on the year before, and James was willing to leave Tombstone for a better life with his daughter. They lived on the side of Cleopatra Hill for the time that James worked at the United Verde mining company. James Locke met a woman named Audrey Murphy, and they joined in a common law marriage for about 6 years until June 13, 1896, when tragedy struck, and James was killed during a mineshaft collapse. He was a well-liked man in the community, and he left behind his new bride and child. Sarah and Audrey loved each other and were grieved at the loss of James. He was buried in a marked grave down the hill in the Jerome Hogback cemetery. With nothing much to keep them there in Jerome, they packed up and headed to San Diego, California, where Audrey Murphy had family.

Life in San Diego was pleasant, but Sarah missed her father and Mother. Audrey did her best to be a mother to her, but Sarah had a restless heart and left home at the age of 16, headed to the central valley near Visalia, California. She had read about this place in school and how they were going to turn the desert into an oasis for farming and crop growing. She loved animals, and growing things was a gift she had. Her first job was as a maid at the Palace Hotel downtown on Main Street.

She worked hard and eventually met her new husband, a man named Joseph Mitchell, who was a cook in the restaurant. Sarah was 18 years old and ready to settle down. The two eventually wed, and they purchased 25 acres north of town near a small Armenian settlement called Yettem. After that, it was just history. The Mitchells had 7 kids, who in turn gave them 23 grandchildren, who in turn had more kids, and eventually, a direct descendant of Oly Flanagan could be found still living on the original homestead, married and raising 5 children of her own. Her name is Sandra Roberts she was 25 years old, and Oly would have been her great, great, great, grandma. Further down in the southwest, unknown to Sandra, in the Town of Tombstone, AZ, the spirit of great, great, great-grandmother still roams the earth looking for her. Oly didn't know that she had any relatives left she just hoped she did after all of these years. It took Anna 6 weeks and a lot of research to find out about this family that lives just about 750 miles to the northwest. This was the easy part; the hard part is trying to get the two together for a meet and greet without seeming like a whack job to poor Sandra. Her work was just beginning.

Found

"If one tells the truth, one is sure sooner or later to be found out,"
Oscar Wilde.

Fall was here; you could feel it in the air. The sun set a little earlier each day, and there was a cool feeling in the air. It was, in fact, October now, and Anan had contacted Sandra Roberts about her long-lost relative. She did not disclose the whole story but told her that she was on the Tombstone historical society and had found one of her family members' gravestones, located in the old cemetery. It was true that Oly was buried there, but nobody really knew or cared nowadays. Sandra and her husband Joseph were due to arrive on Saturday at about 3:00, so Anna would take them to their hotel on Fremont Street and then see them the next day at her house. That would give them some time to see the town at night, then maybe get some breakfast in the morning. That was 3 days away, and much had to be done to make this work. Anna had spent her life helping the living, but now she was helping the dead. What a long, strange trip it's been. She had to get Oly here so she could explain the plan, but Oly was a free-roaming ghost who, in life and death, went wherever she felt pleased to. Anna did not have any way to summon her, so she went downstairs to the room where all of the spirits hang out.

It was a creepy room, and she rarely went down there for that reason. John didn't mind it, and he was the one who would store the garden tools and the things needed to maintain an old home like this. There weren't any lights in the room, so she propped the door open and went inside. Immediately, the temperature dropped about 20 degrees as she tried to get her eyes accustomed to the dim light. She knew that somebody or something was inside as she could feel their gaze of curiosity upon her. "I'm trying to find Oly. Could any of you help me?" she asked, knowing one in particular. Before her, a dim white shape was appearing as she stared into the semi-darkness. The shape of a man, perhaps in his late twenties, began to materialize in front of Anna's eyes. His features were well established, and he wore the clothes of a well-mannered person of an era long gone. The face was clear; he had a mustache and wore a bolo hat that the men wore in the booming heydays of Tombstone. He wasn't a cowboy; maybe he was from the eastern states. His form draped off into a misty, ghostly shape that dimmed to darkness. "Actually, I'm from the great city of Mobile, Alabama, and ended up here in this awful place. You need not be scared of me, I mean you no harm, so please tell me why you are here." He spoke to hear in voices that rang in her head instead of her ears.

Anna spoke to the man before her, "I'm so sorry to bother you down here, but I'm looking for Oly, and I have no way of finding her. Could you help me?" The man slowly looked at Anna, checking out her features and strange modern clothing; her tattoos were visible on her arms as the man stared in silence. He had never seen such markings on a woman, maybe on an Indian heathen or that guy he met in Borneo, but these markings were different, more of a storytelling nature. After a brief moment, he spoke, "Yes, I know where she is, and I can fetch her, but first, I'm intrigued by the strange markings you have on your arms. What is this, some form of religion or witchery? I will not help one who is league with Cowboy or his minions." Anna replied, "I am not in league with anyone except God Almighty, and these are called tattoos. A lot of people, male and female, have them in my time. It is a form of body painting that is non-removable. Please help me and get Oly for me. I need to talk to her. Also, who are you and what are you doing here?"

"My name is Swan, that's E.G. Swan to most, but I can tell more on another occasion when I return, my dear, so let me grab Oly, and I will talk to you later," he said as he slowly vanished into the darkness of the dank room. Anna left with haste, not wanting to encounter any new friend at this time.

Swan knew exactly where Oly would be; she was as predictable as the Arizona weather, and her favorite haunt was Big Nose Kate's Saloon on Allen Street. She loved to hear the music and see all of the people come in and out of the place. Oly had stayed here back when it was the Grand Hotel but the place had changed a lot since then. She knew Swamper when he worked as a handyman at the hotel. Word around the afterlife community in town says Swamper is working with Cowboy, but she knew better since she knew him when he was alive. He only works for himself. Down the spiral staircase, she floated as she came to Swamper's home below the surface streets and the hustle and bustle of Tombstone. At first, she couldn't see him, so she called his name. He came rising from the open shaft that led to the mines below, and like a reptile, he slithered to where she stood. Looking mean and nasty he stood before as if he would do her harm then said "Oly my love where have you been? I've missed you so much and have no time to seek you out since my work around here never ends." Then they gave each other a ghostly embrace and laughed without anyone in the basement shop noticing. Swamper's home had been turned into a gift shop, and at first, he didn't like it, but with the continued stream of tourists coming down here, he started to warm up to the prospect of haunting new souls. He was an old school ghost who believed his job was to wreak havoc and scare the living. There was nothing wrong with a little haunting now and then. He would grab the lady's skirt as they walked up the stairs, and sometimes, when it was late, and the crowd died down, he would drift around in the bar checking out the nightlife. Swamper looked the same in death as he did in life, a worn-out prospector with an eye for the ladies. He was nothing but kind to Oly since he knew her from the past when she was a living, breathing woman. He secretly had a crush on her, but she was a married woman, and Swamper had some virtue.

Swan floated through the door of Big Nose Kate's, then drifted down to where the two old friends were exchanging pleasantries. Once Swamper got a look at Swan, he turned back into his old mean self and gave him a piece of his mind, "What are you doing in my home, Swanny boy? I don't go hanging out in your cave of a basement where you like to reside." He told him. Swan said, "I'm here to find Oly and send her over to the house to see this Anna person; she is looking for you something fierce. If she is the one helping our friends to the other side, then could you put in a good word for me, Oly? I would love to go home and leave this place forever." Swamper loved Tombstone and all of its nonliving inhabitants, good or bad; he didn't choose sides. He just didn't like Cowboy and the way he tricks the newly departed into servitude to the evil one. He told Swan, "You sound like a little schoolgirl, Swanny boy, with your northern accent and your educated words. Why do you always have to ruin it for me and take my girl away? She would rather stay here and have some fun, that's why you came here, isn't it, dear?" Oly replied "I did come to see you, but it's more of a goodbye. Anna is my friend, and she's working on a way to get me home away from this place, but I have been here for such a long time, and that time is drawing to a close, and I feel it getting closer each day. I do call both of you my friends, and I will miss you, too. Perhaps I will see Swan up in heaven someday? I know you, Swamper, would prefer this over heaven any day, but just remember that all good things come to an end, and this, too, will fade away to dust, so just have an exit strategy for when that day comes. By the way, boys, the war between the states has been over for about 150 years or so. Let's try to be friends, ok?" With that, she vanished into the dim light of the subterranean abode of Swamper. Swan, not wanting to be left with the old codger, followed suit into the thin air. Swamper stood there mad as usual, then glided up the spiral stairs to find a young, pretty thing to bother.

The twilight was descending on the town as the two old friends decided to take a walk down Allen Street back to the house. It wasn't the same as when they lived here, but both knew that time was short and this little walk may be their last. They stopped in front of the OK Corral, then Swan told Oly, "I've been up and down these streets a million times, and a lot of those times were with you. I sure wish I had the chance to know you back then, but it wasn't meant to be. I know your Anna was the one who led Lily home to her family. I really didn't have much family when I was a breathing soul, but now that I think about it, I would love to see you with yours up yonder past St. Peter's gate. I'm just asking for you to have Anna help me since I have never known why I stayed in this place while others went to the great beyond, some good and some bad, but they got to leave anyhow. Could you do that for me, old friend?" She was looking at his face and heard his words. In the spirit world, they don't see each other as a white misty specter; they see the other ghost as they looked in life. Oly studied Swan's face and saw the face of an old friend she had known for all of these years. A friend who was there for her in the darkest moments, he was there the moment she woke up dead in the boarding house she was at. She thought he was an angel until she looked over and saw her own guardian angel slowly fading to nothingness by the door. His work was done, and Oly was stuck between two worlds. They have been friends since that day.

A memory came to Oly just then; she had been present when Swan was killed on the streets of Tombstone. No wonder he was there when she passed away; they shared some kind of bond that was stronger than death itself. For a moment, she was there at that moment on that night so long ago. Oly had just left Mrs. Murphy's tailor shop as the sun had set already. Crossing an alley, she heard a couple of men yelling, "Swan, you no good thief, we know you took our money like a thief in the night.

That game was rigged, and we are going to get our forty dollars back…" Just then, two shots rang out, and then the sound of footsteps running away from her. She was a bit scared and wanted to run home, but then heard a man moaning in pain. Cautiously, she walked over to the hurt man lying in the dirt. His face was staring up at the sky as he muttered a few last words. Oly held his hand as he died in the alley that night in Tombstone, Arizona Territory, with no one but her to comfort him. A crowd began to form, and someone knew the man; his name was E.G. Swan, and he was a gambler from back east. "I remember that night when you came to me as I lay dying, not 100 yards from here in that alley across the street. I looked up into the face of a red-haired angel with beautiful green eyes and knew I was going to heaven. I waited and waited while you left, and the crowd died down. Then they carried my body to Doc's office and laid me on a board. Still, I waited for the gates of heaven above to open wide and bring me home. I'm still here Oly and I don't know why. I wasn't the best of people back then, and I don't think I deserved to be shot in the back and left for dead in a Tombstone alley, but we don't always get what we deserve, do we?" he told her as they continued down 4th street to their home in the basement.

Oly listened and thought back on why Swan could be stuck here like her. Could he have to pay back for the wrong things he had done in life? Maybe he's here because he didn't have anyone to go home to when he passed. Either way, she would have Anna work on this one because the sky was growing dark, and her time here would be short. She suddenly felt uneasy and afraid as the thought of being out here on a night like this could bring about undesirable spirits. Just then, up ahead in front of them stood a dark figure with a cowboy hat on, blocking their way to the house. Cowboy was waiting for them, and he wasn't moving as they drew closer. As they drew near, more shadowy figures could be seen behind him as if they were just waiting for Oly and Swan. "Don't be afraid, Oly, I won't let that spawn of Satan hurt you in the least. Stick with me, and we will get out of this." He told her as they got within a few feet of Cowboy. In the spirit world, the spirits don't see each other as we would see them; it's more like an old image of what they looked like when they were still alive. Cowboy could be seen as a dark-skinned Spaniard wearing a black cowboy hat and black clothes. The others were dressed in various outfits, but none of them looked remotely friendly.

Cowboy spoke as the two walked up to him. "So, what brings you two wretches out on a wonderfully black night like this? You two love birds would be hiding under your covers in your beds right now, afraid of the boogeyman or someone like me would come to snatch up your pathetic souls and have you work for me." Not wanting to hear his ranting and raving, Swan spoke up, "Cowboy, you don't scare us. We all know your story and how the Apaches killed you up on Boot Hill way back when. I think they did a good job; you were lousy as a human and worse as a spirit who goes around telling the others that you are the king of Tombstone. So, get out of the way before another angel appears and sends your scorched carcass of a soul down to hell where you belong." Vanity was always a big influence in Cowboys' life and even in the afterlife, but Swan had hit a nerve, and his eyes glowed even more red and fiery as he thought of something to say, but it was too late as Oly and Swan pushed through his little barricade of lost souls and continued home. "Don't try to leave Tombstone Oly I have my minions keeping an eye on you and that Anna woman and it would be tragic if anything happened to her." He told her as she walked up the hill to her house. Looking back, Oly gave him a parting reply, "Go ahead, Cowboy, give me your best shot, and don't let that angel of the Lord that follows her night and day give you any problems. Your boy Jones didn't last too long, and by the way, to all of you minion followers, your master Cowboy knew that Jones would be snuffed out that night. I saw it when he purposely sent poor Jonesy into the path of the angel, so think about that next time you come around my place."

They faded into the darkness, and it didn't go as planned. Cowboy wanted to be seen as an overpowering dark force that had the power to make those two tremble with fear, but it didn't go as planned. He looked at his assembled group of lost souls and barked out orders, "What are you fools waiting for? Go forth and terrorize this town as you must do each and every night, go now before I lay you to waste." They hastily vanished to their assigned haunting locations; it wasn't much terrorizing, more like an occasional bump in the night, but they went through the motions anyway just to try and make Cowboy a little more bearable. With the motley crew gone and on their familiar haunts, Cowboy stood on the hill overlooking the Pezdel home. It was dark except for a light in the living room where Anna was awake. The hatred blazed in the Cowboys' eyes as he couldn't look away from that place.

He would deal with those two annoying spirits when he had a better chance. Best to catch them separated, then he could do a better job of capturing them. There were ways to catch and torture a free spirit, but you just had to do it at the right time. All things in the right time, and he had plenty of that.

Cowboy let it be known that he was the first to roam these hills that were now the Town of Tombstone. He shed his lifeblood that day when those heathens took his life, but in a way, they did him a favor. In Coronado's army, he was just the interrogator, but now everywhere his eyes could see was his domain to conquer and divide as his master had taught him. Yes, his master was Satan, and he made an occasional trip down this way every 100 years or so, and he was due to come here one of these days. Cowboy did not want to disappoint him if he happened by. One never knows. He had to find a way into the house where this woman, Anna, lived, even though she would occasionally leave the premises. He could not get inside because there was some sort of spell or magical potion that kept him at bay. The times that he has tried, he felt violently ill, and his spirit body felt like it was fading away. The evil minions that he has sent into the house have never returned. So, into the night, he slipped unseen and unnoticed in a Town where so many had passed through in life and in death.

Reunion

"Every parting gives a foretaste of death, every reunion a hint of the resurrection."

Arthur Schopenhauer

Three days had passed when Anna awoke with no sign of Oly. Today was the day that Sandra Roberts and her husband, Joseph, arrived in Tombstone to meet her at 1:00 this afternoon. Anna was filled with dread and anticipation as time drew near, hoping that Mr. Swan would have come through with his part in all of this. She took a shower, then got dressed. Entering the parlor, she saw Oly sitting in her recliner, looking at her with that ghostly, far-off gaze. Emotionless and well-behaved, she started to talk to Anna, "Anna, my friend, I hear you have been seeking me. Whatever could I possibly do for you this fine morning?" Sitting there and using her Irish brogue, looking so calm. Anna could actually hear the brogue in her mind, thick and colorful, as her grandmother would sound like after a couple of Irish Coffees in the morning. "Well, I was looking for you, then I found your friend Swan in the basement, and he went searching for you about 2 or 3 days ago. How big is Tombstone if you can't find one little ghost among the living? Pardon my little ghost statement, not sure what you call yourselves these days. The reason I have been looking for you is that someone will be coming by the house to talk to me about you in a few hours. I don't know if you can tell the time where you are, but please be here in this room when they show up. It will be a man and a woman, so just come by and kinda stay well hidden from them." Anna told her as Oly had a perplexed look on her face. She spoke to Anna again, "Anna, I will stay out of sight, although you and John have been the only living persons that have ever seen me. I know my presence will go unnoticed, I assure you. We don't have a concept of time in the traditional earthly way; we just spend our days and nights in one continuous movement, never grasping how much time has passed. For you, the living time is such a precious commodity, but for the dead, we just don't bother since eternity is forever. So just do not worry, and I will sense their presence and remain out of sight." Then she vanished into thin air, leaving the smell of Lilac behind.

As arranged at 1:00 that afternoon, Sandra and Joseph stood at Anna's door ringing the bell. Anna opened the door and stared at the young woman before her. She had hair of red and eyes so green they looked like emeralds. Sandra introduced herself and her husband, Joseph, who then came into the house. She was amazed at the craftsmanship and love that the house possessed. It was done in an old Victorian style that many Western homes were made in. They sat down on the couch, and Sandra said, "I'm so glad to finally meet you. I love that fragrance that you have around the house. What is it? I remember my grandmother wearing a perfume like that long ago." Anna was about to say that she didn't have any fragrance out, but then noticed Oly standing in a dark corner staring at Sandra as if she was in a trance. Anna told them, "It's the scent of lilac, and I use it often around here." Just then, Anna could hear the voice of Oly in her head saying, "Anna, you didn't tell me my great, great, great granddaughter would be here today. She looks so beautiful, and I can see the face of Sarah in hers. She can smell my perfume, and she keeps looking over here at me as if she could sense me or something." Anna could not respond to Oly and talk to Sandra at the same time, so she just sort of ignored Oly and told Sarah about finding Oly's grave and tracing her history.

They talked for hours until it was time to go to the cemetery and show them where Oly had been buried. Looking down at the old headstone, Sarah wept for the woman who had been given such a short life on earth and left behind a young daughter. As the tears fell and the wind blew, Sandra spoke to Anna, "She's here, isn't she? I can still smell the lilac, and we are not at your house. Also, I feel as though someone else is near right now." Anna said, "Yes, she is here, and she wanted to meet you and know that her life had meaning and substance. You are living proof that her daughter, Sarah, did well in life and lived for many years, creating a life and family long ago. She is standing right next to you and would like to give you a hug if possible?" Sandra told Anna, "Yes, I would love a hug from her and maybe a kiss for good luck." So Oly wrapped her ghostly arms around her family and wept as she held tight to Sandra. Sandra could feel the warm energy that Oly gave off and the beautiful scent of Lilac as she slowly faded from this world. Sandra asked, "She's gone, isn't she? I mean, she's really gone to heaven now? I can feel her warmth fading up into the great beyond. I love you, Grandma Oly, and may you rest in peace with the Lord."

Anna saw the whole event before her eyes, and she felt the love that each had for the other as Oly's spirit slowly faded away and left this place where she had spent so many years waiting for this day. Anna could feel the tears of joy flow down her face as she thought of John and how he left this world, probably feeling the same way. So much joy and love could be felt by all of them as they slowly made their way back to the house. Looking back at the cemetery with the wind blowing through the pines and the sun slowly setting, it all seemed so surreal. Anna felt overjoyed but exhausted at the same time. She had been through a lot in these last few months, but inside, she knew that more was yet to come. The Mitchells said their goodbyes as they left Tombstone and headed back to California. Anna felt happy and sad at the same time as she already missed having Oly around. It seemed ridiculous to an outsider, maybe, to think that one could miss a ghost, but Oly had that effect on the living and dead. Now she would be safe from the cowboy and all of his evil schemes. He would have to find another lost soul to fill his quota with.

A Broken Heart

"I think you are wrong to want a heart. It makes most people unhappy.
If you only knew it, you are in luck not to have a heart."
L. Frank Baum, The Wonderful Wizard of Oz

John's birthday had come and passed as Anna tried to pull out of the spiral of a broken heart. She had never felt this pain before, and in time she had thought that the wounds would heal and she would at least be able to live a somewhat normal existence. Now looking at the falling snow and a herd of mule deer seeking shelter under a tree near where the body of Lily once lay, Anna could only become more depressed and isolated. Her children had come by to visit and try to help the situation, but they have lives, jobs, and kids of their own, so they went back to their homes to continue the daily grind. It was good to see them, but Anna always hated to say goodbye to anyone, and the thought of never being able to say goodbye to John only made her worse. She didn't drink too much, maybe an occasional shot of tequila, but tonight was not a good time to start that. She missed Oly, even though they didn't get too close; she just loved her for what she did in her short life and the legacy she had left behind. Maybe someday, when she is long gone, her offspring will remember her and smile.

Elvis was sprawled out in front of the wood-burning stove as the snow piled up outside. It was going to be a cold one in the old Town tonight, but that won't stop the tourists who frequent this Town, rain or shine; also, it was a Friday night, so the bars will be full. Anna thought about the wild nights they had going to town on a Saturday night and hitting the Crystal Palace or Doc Holliday's for a cold one and some music. They would stay out until about 1:00 am, then walk home to their house on the hill. If they happened to pass down 2nd street and walk by the Buford house late at night, Anna would get a little creeped out with the weird lights in the attic and all of the strange occurrences that had happened over the years. John would hold her tight as they walked home and tell her it was going to be ok. She thought about those times and felt the sorrow set deeper into her soul. Heartbreak and loss of love are sometimes worse than death. As the cold set in and the fire grew low, Anna shivered from the night air. Just then, sitting on the couch, she felt a rush of warmth cover her body from head to toe as it engulfed her and made her lightheaded. It was not an awful sensation, more like being in a warm bath, floating away. Just then, she snapped out of it and saw Swan sitting across from her in the recliner, looking dapper and well-groomed as always. "Swan, you scared the dickens out of me. Let me know you are here and quit making me feel like I'm in a Jacuzzi, alright?" She told him in that mental way they have of talking to one another. He replied with a smile on his face, "Yes, Miss Anna, I mean you no harm. I am just making my nightly rounds of the premises, and don't see that no good Cowboy around or his miscreants. I guess the cold keeps them underground in that graveyard. I miss seeing Oly around here, and I know she's in a better place and all, but my affection for her has grown after all of these years. She still is a married woman, and I would not take any advances toward her since I am a gentleman."

Anna pondered his conversation, then told him, "Swan, she hasn't been married for over 130 years, and you do know that the marriage vow says till death do us part. I still fancy myself married to John, but in my heart, I know that the bonds of matrimony do not survive the sting of death. We tend to view things in a forever context, but nothing is forever, you know. I appreciate your nightly security checks over this property, but as you can see by the angel in the room, I am well protected." Swan looked behind Anna and stared at the huge angel that stood in vigilance over her. He knew that in life he had one too, but that cord was severed when those two scoundrels put two bullets in his back. He often wondered why he didn't pass on to the other side, but looking back, it was more likely a good thing he stayed here. His short life on this earth was spent hustling and gambling away his time and money. In his heart, he was a good man, but his deeds on earth said otherwise. He probably deserved the death he got and often waited for the Devil himself to take him down to Hades. Oly and this place saved him from going to the dark side; Cowboy had worked on him for decades to join his band of demons and misfits' souls. Swan did not want to go there and held out for a better deal, always the gambler even unto death. "Miss Anna, I will take my leave, but it's getting a little quiet downstairs with just Ned and me. We are the only ones left. That drifter Bartlett comes by once in a blue moon, but otherwise, we are just the two of us. You really should meet Ned one of these days. He is a bit shy, but he is a great fellow once you know him. I will see you later, dear," he told her as he vanished into the night.

How strange her life was these days; it seemed that she talked more to the dead than the living. She will be like them one day, and by then, she wishes that her soul would be taken up above and there would be no need to commune with the living. Meeting Oly's family was a joy and a blessing. Sandra called the other day and thanked Anna again for finally putting a face to her grandmother, long past. This old house was feeling less like a home more and more each day, with John gone and all of his pictures and memories that were made here. Anna was entertaining the thought of selling and moving on. They had always been drifters at heart, and the time spent in Arizona was the best they ever had together. How bittersweet the feeling of knowing this was the place they would become separated. Looking at John's smiling face in the pictures on the wall brought back memories of a happier time and place. They were supposed to grow old together here, and eventually one would pass before the other, but that was to be years from now. God had a funny way of doing things in life and in death. Outside, it got colder and drearier as the snow piled up in the driveway and the silence of the storm blocked out most sounds that you would normally hear on a Friday night in Tombstone. She didn't know how to help Swan since he had no family and no reason to be left behind; she was sure that the reason would be clear sometime soon. As the fire crackled in the stove and the snow fell steadily outside, Anna was lulled into a deep sleep.

E.g., Swan stepped off the stagecoach that had arrived from Tucson this afternoon. Looking around at the busy scenery that unfolded on a typical day in the new boomtown called Tombstone, he had a feeling of excitement as he saw all of the saloons and gambling halls on Allen Street. Being a man of sophistication and good manners, he had been steadily making his way west since that little scrape in Wichita a month earlier. He had nearly lost his life when he was caught manipulating the cards at a Faro game in the Buffalo Lodge Saloon. He was an honest man at heart, but his skill in cards was unmatched by most common players. Now and then, a player of skill and talent will come along and try to outsmart him, but those times were far and few. Mostly drunk miners or cowhands were upset about losing their money to him. He had left home at an early age of 14 and traveled the highways and byways of the great frontier. Originally from Mobile, Alabama, his Daddy fought for the South in the Civil War and lost his life in the battle of Gettysburg, serving under Robert E. Lee. At Cemetery Ridge on July 2, 1863, his Daddy E.A. Swan was killed by a bullet fired by a Union soldier. E.G. Swan was only 11 years old on that terrible day in July. He never really had much family; his mother passed away when he was 8 years old from dropsy. With nothing to lose, he headed west at 14 and never looked back.

As he stared up and down the street at the casual life of a boom town, he felt happy and sad at the same time. With no one to share his newfound home, he was resigned to find a room at the Grand Hotel and clean up for dinner that evening. The days passed uneventfully, and he went to the local tailor around the corner from the hotel. Inside, he saw the most beautiful of Irish maidens, and her name was Oly Flanagan. Before long, she was courting some miner, so Swan just moved on to the bargirls and street hustlers. There was never a dull moment in Tombstone. Days and nights rolled by like the wind, and the day came when Swan felt that his luck was changing, and San Diego sounded like a good place to go. He would try his luck at the poker table in the Oriental. He was good at poker, so tonight he would get up enough money to hitch the next stage out of here to San Diego and try his luck at the bars and clubs downtown. A lot of sailors and prospectors rolled through there, and he knew the weather was much nicer.

It was a crowded night in the Oriental tonight; the cowboys were in town raising hell with the Earp brothers, which was just enough distraction for Swan to make a bundle then call it quits. Everything was going fine until a couple of ranch hands from the Circle Seven came in and started playing. Swan had a funny feeling about those boys and tried hard to keep the game on the up and up, but by sheer dumb luck, he was winning each hand until he had enough money to leave Tombstone behind. He got up and walked out into the night with the music playing and the stars out, and he felt so alive. Turning to look behind him, he saw the two ranch hands following him down the street, so he headed towards 4th street by the tailor shop to escape down the alley to his room. Too late, those boys must have run because they were right behind him. The tall fellow with the black hat said, "Swan, you no good thief, we know you took our money like a thief in the night. That game was rigged, and we are gonna get our forty dollars back…" he then pulled out a 44-cal. Revolver as Swan turned to run away and shot him in the back twice. The noises rang out loud and clear in the quiet of the night as the gunman ran away into the dark. Swan lay there dying, looking up at the night sky, sad that he never got to see the ocean or have children or even do anything decent in this life. A woman ran up as he was slowly passing, and he looked into the face of an angel named Oly Flanagan with her red hair hanging low and green eyes sparkling with life. He whispered something only she could hear, "Oly I will see you again" as the darkness crept in and his life bled away into the Tombstone dirt.

As they took his dead body away, Swan felt sad but detached as he became a spirit. He was not in heaven but stuck on earth for some reason. He looked down Allen Street, and a figure in black approached him wearing a cowboy hat. He said, "Swan, you are dead now, and this is my town, I'm Cowboy, and you will work for my master and me." Swan looked past the figure, then saw a host of dark souls standing behind Cowboy, awaiting some orders from the great beyond. Knowing he didn't want to work for that evil bastard, Swan turned north and fled toward his hotel room since he knew it would be empty tonight. He lost the crowd of ghouls and settled in to think about his options. Not knowing why, he wasn't in heaven, or hell, he slipped out of town and headed towards Bisbee to the south. That would be a great place to hole up for a while. Bisbee was an active boomtown that specialized in mining copper. They had the bars and gamblers so that Swan would feel like he was at home. The only problem was his newfound state of being dead, with no one to talk to. One night while strolling the streets of Brewery Gulch, he spotted a young ranch hand staring at him from across the road. He thought the man was alive until he walked up and realized that he was a spirit also. He walked up to him and asked: "I noticed that you seem to be staring at me, do you actually see me, and are you dead like me, also I presume?"

"Yes, I have been killed by those no-account Cowboys who bushwhacked me down by the border, but if you're needing some company, then we can hang out for a while," Bartlett replied.

They became good friends and traveled together for company. He called himself Bartlett and had been a ranch hand for years down by the Mexican border until one day he was bushwhacked by that bunch that called themselves the Cowboys, and they shot him dead, then took his horse; he managed to take one with him, but that guy went straight to hell. Swan and Bartlett were different, but they shared the same love for the southwest and the mining towns. They eventually met up with Oly and ended up staying on in Tombstone in various homes and businesses until they found the place they called home on 4th Street. Bartlett was a wandering soul who came by now and then but always returned to the wilderness and uninhabited regions. Swan could not figure out how or why he was still in the spirit form on earth, but he knew it had something to do with his past behavior and selfish ways.

A person could spend their whole life wondering why this or that happened the way it did, but for those without a body in the spirit realm, they had an eternity unless something changes, and when Swan met Anna that day, he felt a bit of excitement and hope that had been gone for a long time.In life and in death, sometimes it is the things you hold on to that keep you from letting go. Swan wasn't held earthbound for his family or any ill that he had caused; he was here because he couldn't let go of something as simple as a bag of gold. He had been collecting the loot for a few years from the winnings from his gambling. The night he was shot, he was trying to win traveling money so he wouldn't have to spend his "Retirement" fund. The bag held various amounts of gold coins of about $2000, which was a lot back then. Today, from the weight alone, it would be worth over $320,000. Swan had buried the gold in the cemetery off of Allen Street in a grave marked Levy Mark. It was buried about two feet deep, so nobody would think of digging it up.

For years, the gold kept Swan obsessed with how to get it, even though he was a ghost. The allure of gold has destroyed many a good man. After he had joined forces with Oly and the gang, he quit thinking of it, and now it was just sitting in a shallow hole in a shallow grave. He rarely thought of it now, but it still had a hold on him. Somehow that curse must be broken.

Desire

"There are two tragedies in life. One is not to get one's heart's desire.
The other is to get it."
George Bernard Shaw

Anna awoke with a weird sensation of knowing the truth for the first time. The clock read 0237 am, and she was still in the living room with Elvis at her feet, snoring away as old dogs do. She figured out why Swan was still here and how he was unable to do anything about it during his long stay in the spirit world. He realized it one day and let it go, focusing on helping his friends and keeping that evil Cowboy at bay. True, the lust for money and gold has a negative pull on one's spirit, but Swan had managed to accept his fate and make the best of it. It's never too late to do the right thing until you can't. He could not change the past, and the future is uncertain, but Swan knew that he would help when he could and suffer the consequences. The snow had finally stopped, and Anna put another log on the fire to warm up the room a little. Making her way to the bedroom, she passed the large mirror in the hallway and took a long look at herself. It had been a really long time since she had really stopped to see her reflection, but tonight, she saw the woman that she had become. She looked tired and worn with a hint of grey slowly making its way through her hair. She never thought of herself as a beauty, but John always told her how pretty she was and how lucky he was. Letting out a laugh now as she thought of him tonight, she mentally vowed to take better care of herself and try to live up to what her husband once saw. The world still existed outside her door, and she was a part of the grand scheme of things. Tonight, she would sleep without dreams if she could help it, no more ghostly adventures tonight, just a good old-fashioned slumber. Looking over at the dresser, she saw a bottle of Hornitos that had been the last bottle that she and John had before he left. Picking it up and pouring a shot felt right. She wasn't sure if the bottle should have been saved for prosperity, but John would have had a drink on her behalf. It tasted good and brought a warm feeling to her insides. Tonight, she would have no dreams.

The thing about living in Tombstone was that even if it snowed hard like last night, in the morning it usually melted when the sun came up. Today was no different as Anna made her way once more to the town cemetery to look for Mr. Mark. There was a listing online of all who were buried there, and a Levy Mark was not on the list. She made it there after breakfast at the Longhorn, and the sun was bright and warming up the grounds. Today, she came prepared with a shovel and a metal detector that John used to hunt for gold. She would try her luck at finding Mr. Mark among the dead and buried. The wind blew cold from the east as the snow could be seen in the foothills. She never tired of seeing the pines rustling in the wind with a lonely sound. This was such a pretty area to live in, and the weather was nice most of the time. After searching for hours, she was about to give up when she noticed an old stone marker by the fence with the name of Mark Levy written on it in faint words. The date of burial was May 5, 1881, which is before Swan had come to Tombstone. Could this be the gravesite that she saw in her dream? It could have been purposely told to her backward by Swan, with his hopes of her not finding it. The power of gold does strange things, even in death; his spirit seeks riches.

The ground was hard when she tried the shovel in the dirt. Using the metal detector, she was getting a loud noise coming from the middle of the grave. It could be gold or maybe some old buried junk from years gone by. Looking around so as not to make a scene, the last thing she wanted was for someone to see her digging up a grave or even looking like she was doing just that. No one was in sight on this chilly morning, so Anna commenced to desecrate the gravesite in search of lost treasure. While she dug, she thought about what would happen if she did find it. Surely, she couldn't keep it since the only way to break the curse would be to use it for some good in this world. With no known living relatives to Swan's name, so to speak, it would be hard to convince anyone that the money came from a ghost that sort of haunted her lovely home. That was too much drama and unwanted attention. She would figure all that out later if she found it.

While all of this was going through her head, the shovel hit something hard and metallic, not a rock or old junk, just a metallic sound that comes from gold hitting gold. Anna's heart raced as she took another look around the cemetery. With no one in sight yet, she furiously dug harder. She could see the remnants of an old leather pouch that housed the gold. Carefully pulling out all of the contents, Anna managed to get it all out of the gravesite and into a white plastic cleaning bucket. Her pace quickened as she jumped into her car and drove the mile to her home. No sooner had she walked in the door and locked it than E.G. Swan was standing in front of her, looking kind of crazy and confused. Anna was a bit frightened since she had never seen him like this. The power of the gold brought out long-forgotten feelings of greed, power, and lust for money. Swan was not himself and told Anna, "Anna, could you please get it out of here so I won't have to know it's back? I have done so well not having it, and now I'm almost back to the man I once was, and it scares me so." His eyes were wide, and his face distorted to the point where Anna could hardly recognize him. "Yes, I will remove it from the house and store it in the garage away from you until we can figure out who to give it to." She said, but the thought of giving away his precious gold made him worse. Anna told him, "It will be alright, Swan, we will work this out." Then she went outside and stored the gold in the garage freezer. As the gold coins slowly froze, the effect on Swan diminished to a dull sensation that he was able to overcome. "Thank you, Anna. I can no longer feel its pull on me; I want to get rid of it as soon as possible." He told her.

"Swan, I have some work to do on the computer, so you can find your way back to your little hideout downstairs, and I will call for you when I have figured this out," Anna said as Swan disappeared into the morning sunlight. She knew he didn't have a clue as to what a computer was, but he went anyway, too much excitement, and also, he can only retain a ghostly image for a short time, then they get winded and crawl back to their ghost hotel. She remembered talking to him about children one time, and he wished he had led a better life and raised a few of his own. Maybe this money could be donated to some children's cause for the purpose of helping out some needy souls. They say that not all that glitters is gold, but she did have gold, and it would be hard to explain where over $300,000 dollars of gold coins came from. She could see she had dug it up in her yard, but Anna did not want the publicity. Tomorrow she would call a family friend who is also a Tax lawyer to help her figure it out, many hands make light work was what her grandma used to say.

Swan was in the basement trying to make sense of how his treasure ended up here, of all places. The boy, Ned, was beside him, asking him questions. "Swan, where is everyone going, and are they coming back? I miss Lily and Oly so much. They have been so kind to me for all of these years. Why are you acting so strange, also?" he told him. Swan stopped for a second and thought about all that had been going on with Lily leaving, then Oly, and nobody telling poor Ned where or how they left. He still thinks they are just out traveling and will be returning home someday. The mystery of the gold can wait; he had to help his friend understand. "Ned, my good friend, we have been friends here forever, and I would not tell you anything that would harm that friendship, but Lily and Oly are gone now. They went home to heaven and their families. You remember heaven when you were a living child, and the preacher would tell you that if you were good, then that's where you would go when you died. Do you understand now?" he asked Ned. Ned replied, "I remember grownups talking about heaven, but why did it take them so long to get there, and we are good folks, so why aren't we up there also? I'm just a kid; I should have been in heaven the moment I died from that cholera back in 1903. What's the problem, Swan? You're still here, too."

Swan knew the boy was smart, maybe too smart, but he had a right to know what was going on. He told Ned, "Ned, you're right about all of that. Anna is upstairs helping us out. She was the one who helped the girls get home, and she's going to help us also. I trust her and remember that man John, who used to come down here and talk to us? Well, that was her husband, and he died a while back and went to heaven also. Anna will help us just watch and see. You don't have to be afraid of her at all." This seemed to satisfy Ned, so he quit asking questions and resumed his orb state of slumber. Like this, he could still think and act if he had to, but like a bear in a cave hibernating, he used very little spiritual energy and was able to remain alert. Upstairs, Anna was making plans to talk to Mr. Henderson tomorrow to work out a plan where the gold could be donated anonymously to a worthy organization. She had no desire to keep the money since it seemed like the only avenue available to help Swan return to heaven. She wondered who would greet him at the pearly gates since he had little family, but he still had his friends from downstairs, and they really loved him. They would be there to greet him into the kingdom.

The next day, Anna met with Ron Henderson in his office in downtown Tucson. She was on the 7th floor of a high-rise downtown off Stone Avenue. She looked outside onto the street and watched the people below, so busy in their daily grind as they went to and fro from their jobs to their homes, then back again. It seemed like such a long time ago when she and John were in the same cycle of endless work and dreams that were put off for the future. It was funny how it all seemed so surreal and petty now. She was liberated from a treadmill life and now looked forward to whatever lies ahead. "Mrs. Pezdel, Mr. Henderson will see you now." The woman at the desk called to her. Anna walked into Ron's office and gave him a hug, then sat down. They had known Ron for many years, and he seemed like family. His familiar face was a welcome sight to Anna as she gazed about the office, seeing pictures of John and her with Ron down in Rocky Point during Bike Week two years ago. He asked her, "Anna, how have you been? Haven't I seen you since the funeral? I'm hoping that all is well and that I can be of some assistance to you." She proceeded to tell him about the gold and left out the whole dead Swan and graveyard story. She said that it was an heirloom from her grandfather and that she wanted to donate it to some local children's charity without them knowing that she was the donor.

After much talk and debate, they came up with a plan to donate it to an organization in town that helped the children of parents who were incarcerated for various crimes. These children were being raised by the state or by relatives of those in prison. Ron had to know, so he asked her, "It is a noble sentiment to donate such a large sum of money, but you could just keep it and be taken care of for a long time. Are you sure that this is what you want?"

"Yes, it is Ron, I really don't need it, and I have plenty of money from the insurance John left and the settlement I received from the city for the wrongful death. I just want to do something for someone else, and this seemed like the best way to accomplish that. I'm not sure of the specifics, so you might walk me through that part. Otherwise, let's get this done soon." She told him as she stared out the large window facing the city park on Stone Avenue. Ron explained it to her right then and there. "First thing, I have a client who will buy all of the gold you have and give you cash in return. It's so much easier to make a large contribution if the currency is in dollar bills and not $20 gold coins. Next, we open an account in a fictitious name to cover the money transfer to the charity of your choice. This much money is never taken seriously as an anonymous donation. There is always some government agency that wants to make sure it isn't some drug money or terrorist funding of some sort. If and when they try to find out who you are, they hit a brick wall in the name of some company out of Wisconsin that is an LLC in another person's name. They can't go anywhere else. I will start this ball rolling today if you can get me the money."

Anna opened up the large bag that looked like a purse and dumped out the gold coins on the office carpet. There were over 20 pounds of gold sitting there as Ron stared at the small fortune on his floor. He had never seen that much gold before that wasn't behind a thick plastic wall or locked up in a vault. It had a weird pull on him, almost like he wanted to just scoop it up and head off to Mexico. Anna kept saying "Ron, Ron" for about 5 times until he looked over at her and realized her lips were moving, but he couldn't hear because of the roar in his ears. "I'm sorry, Anna, I just never have seen anything like this. I will write you a receipt and get this over to my client's business now. I'm feeling kind of weird and flushed right now. Don't know what it is, but it should pass." He told her as they gathered up the coins and put them in a small briefcase. Ron gave her a receipt, and she left the office, glad to be rid of the coins that had been buried in a Tombstone grave for over 125 years. Anna knew what was happening to Ron as he stared at the lost treasure from the swan. It was pulling on him to take it and run away with the coins. It didn't have the same effect on Anna; it just made her feel weak and sick when she was close to it. "It won't be long now until Swan is released from the hold that the gold has had on him for all of these years. She knew it would go fast once the gold was converted to currency and then donated to the children's foundation.

Lost

*Never regret anything you have done with a sincere affection; nothing is lost that is born of the heart. "**Basil Rathbone**"*

It had been over a week when she heard from Ron about the donation to the Children's Foundation. He told Anna that the check had been hand-delivered and the funds would be in their account in the morning. She was in great spirits as she ran down to the basement to tell Swan the news. Opening up the old door and stepping inside, she got that old, creepy, spooky feeling from the darkness that crept toward her. "Swan, are you here? I need to talk to you," she asked the darkness, hoping he would hear her.

At first, no sound penetrated the blackness, but then a small child's voice answered back. "He isn't here, Mrs. Pezdel went into town to see the Swamper, then visit Oly's grave. He hasn't been himself lately; I was afraid that Cowboy did something bad to him. Could you find him and bring him home? I don't have anyone else down here to stay with me, and I'm scared. Please help me." The tiny voice said from the dark depths of the stone room with the dirt floor. Anna didn't know of anyone else being down here; she thought Swan was the last of them, and her work would be done.

The voice of the small boy pulled at her heart as she felt the loneliness that must have engulfed him. She asked, "Who are you? And what are you doing down here in the basement?" He said, "My name is Ned, and I've been living here with the rest of the gang for a very long

241

time. Please find my friend and bring him home." Anna spoke "Ok Ned I will head into town and find Swan and bring him home to you, so don't be afraid, no one is going to hurt you, this house and property is protected by Gods mighty angels' day and night so you just sit and relax, or whatever you guys do down here and I will be right back." With that, she closed the door and started walking into town.

Winter was here as Anna felt the cold north breeze upon her face. She wanted to walk since it only took about 5 minutes to reach Allen Street from her house. She had the strange feeling that someone was watching her as she made her way to town. Once she turned around suddenly to see who was behind her, but only caught a glimpse of a shadowy substance disappearing into the thick brush along the road. She could feel his eyes staring at her, and she knew that it was that evil Cowboy creeping behind her. "I know you are there, Cowboy, so just come on out and show yourself, you're not very good at sneaking around." She told him halfheartedly, not thinking he would show up in daylight. Just then, the shadowy figure slid slowly to where she was, but he stopped short for fear of the guardian angel that protected Anna. He materialized in front of her, a dark soul with red glowing eyes and wearing dark clothes that looked like those from the 1880s. He was wearing his famous Cowboy hat upon his grinning skull. The smell coming off of him was wretched as Anna took a step back from the stench. He smelled like rotten meat and sulfur mixed together.

"Don't you have anything else to do besides stalk me while I walk into town? You better watch out, or I will lose this angel who watches over me, and he will send you back to Hell in pieces." She told Cowboy as he stared past her, looking at the guardian angel who stood over 10 feet tall behind her. He knew full well that the angel had no power to hurt him unless he sensed danger from Cowboy. He said to Anna, "I see the accursed creature always following you around like a little lost puppy. He won't touch me if I do you no harm. I just wanted to see where you are heading on this fine winter day in my town. "That's too tough to die." You have been very busy, my dear, as of late, and my boss has noticed the activity going on up here. We don't need any more of your mischief, stirring things up, and sending souls up instead of down. This is not looking good on my permanent record. If one more soul goes to heaven instead of Hell, then I have my orders, and all hell will break loose for you in that shack you call home. I have demons that can take out your angel friend, so you have been warned. As of today, no more activity or else." Then he disappeared as quickly as he arrived.

"That was strange," she thought as she kept going toward Allen Street to Swamper's house. Upon arriving at Big Nose Kate's, Anna ordered an ice-cold draft beer and sat at the bar looking around for Swan or Swamper. She knew they would be downstairs because legend has it that he lived down there and protected his fortune, which he had buried long ago. As far as Anna knew, there could be a million dollars in gold and silver stuck in some mine shaft, but she wasn't here for that. Time was quickly drawing near, and Anna desperately needed to tell Swan what was going on.

After finishing the beer, she walked down the spiral staircase that led to the gift store. It was once the Swampers' bedroom, and he had spent many a night down here when this used to be the Grand Hotel. Looking toward his bed in the corner, she saw him sitting on it, looking at her. He became puzzled as she came right up to him and started talking as if she could see him. "Don't be afraid, Swamper. I can see you sitting there in your little cave room. I just need to know if you have seen Swan, and can you tell me where he went?" she asked the apparition before her. She looked over her shoulder to see the woman at the cashier counter staring at her. After a moment, he replied, "I'm surprised, little Missy, that a living being can see and talk to me. I've had a few in the past who saw me, then ran out the door screaming. You don't seem like that type of person. I will answer your question if you answer one of mine, ok?" She thought about it, then told him, "Yes, that would be fine, so you ask first."

The old Swamper asked her, "I was wondering what happened to Oly? I haven't seen her around, and I don't feel her anymore. She was really starting to grow on me after all of these years. Could you help with that?" he asked her. Anna knew where she went, but Swamper might not like her response. She told him anyway. "Yes, Mr. Swamper, I do know where she has gone, and she will not be coming back this way again. She went to heaven above and is with her family as we speak. How about you? Do you have anyone you care about besides your fortune?" she asked him as he thought about the question.

After a long pause, he told her, "I did care about this woman once back in '65 when I was prospecting out in Prescott during the gold rush. It was the middle of winter, and I hadn't had much luck panning Lynx Creek, so I came into town and went into the first saloon I could find. There, sitting at the piano, was the most beautiful creature on God's green earth. I was at a loss for words. Her name was Emily Buchannan, and she had the bluest eyes I ever saw. I fell in love, and we messed around a bit, but the gold kept calling me on down the road, so I left her in the spring of '66 and never went back. I think about her from time to time, but I know she's up there, and it gives me a kind of peace. I will never leave this hole in the ground. I have come to that conclusion, but if you could help ole Swanny get home or at least away from that Cowboy, then I would be obliged."

Anna took a long look at the spirit called Swamper, just an old miner who lost his mind looking for his treasure. She saw before her an old prospector with a long white beard and shabby miners' clothes, with a floppy western hat. He looked like every crazy old coot she had seen on television or in some old movie. She said her goodbyes, then went out onto Allen Street to find Swan. He would surely be at the cemetery now, visiting Oly's gravesite and paying his respects.

She decided to drive to the old cemetery in her car since the day was getting long and the shadows began to creep in from the setting sun. The cold breeze blew hard from the south as the pines whistled and the trees shook. Winter was here to stay as Anna walked toward Oly's grave, looking for Swan. It was hard to see a ghost during daylight hours in actual daylight, but the incoming shadows cast darkness upon Olly's grave, making Swan quite visible to Anna. She called his name, and at first, he didn't notice her arrival, but after a moment with Anna next to him, he turned and spoke to her. "Well, I'll be, fancy seeing you out here, Miss Anna. I know why you are here; I felt it this morning, kind of like a shift in the universe. The planets aligning and all that nonsense, I can feel it in my soul, the feeling of losing oneself but gaining the kingdom of heaven. I never did have much in this world, but when you found that money of mine and gave it to those poor children, I think that's when I found hope. I don't know why you do it, Mrs. Pezdel, why you help all of us lost souls. We are beyond redemption, but you seem to find the very thing that makes us human again. I know the end is near, but I also know that I will see you again in the next life up above. For so long, I have been stuck in this place with nowhere to go and no place to call my home. Your house has been great for our little bunch, and before it was built, we lived near here in a shack that belonged to Lily's folks. She has always called this place home, even though they tore her house down to make way for your house back in '55. We ghosts don't feel time like you living ones do. For us, it's just one long day that never seems to end."

She felt proud to have known him, and the words he spoke rang true within her soul. She knew that one day it would pass away and a new world would be reborn. Anna looked long at Swan and noticed that he was growing paler and translucent. She could see right through him now and knew that time was short. "Swan, thank you for all you have done and for the kind words you have spoken. It seems like these days I have more friends dead than alive, but that's not such a bad thing; we all end up there eventually. You have been a good friend, and I wish you Godspeed on your journey. I will miss you, and don't worry about Ned, I will get him home somehow."

With that, Swan slowly faded into the daylight with the shadows of night creeping slowly toward Anna and Oly's grave. Anna went home to an empty house once more, knowing full well she would have to address the "Cowboy" problem if she was to remain here in Tombstone for the rest of her days. "Why can't it all be normal like when John was alive, and we wouldn't have to talk to dead people?" She thought to herself as the night closed in.

Youth

"So wise so young, they say, do never live long."
William Shakespeare

Ned knew that Swan was gone; he could feel it now with the wind howling outside and the sounds of the night so lonely and loud. He was just a timid lad who left this world before his time was due. He loved having Lily around. She was so smart and fun. They would often play together on the property, just being kids forever. She was gone now, and that Pezdel woman kept taking all of his friends away. He only had Bartlett as a friend, and you never knew when he would come by. Ned looked outside to the west toward Boot Hill, and a shiver ran down his ghostly spine. He could sense an evil presence out there roaming these lands. It must be Cowboy and his minions from hell. They would possibly try to take him away from here now since all of his friends have gone. Tonight would be a good time to visit the widow Pezdel and maybe sleep in her pantry or closet. Ned did not want to awaken her because she had been through a lot these last few months. Everybody loved John; he was special and would talk to the gang in the basement when he was around. They all could feel his passing from this world. The angel Abiel had been by on occasion to check on the misses and see the ones who lived below the house. He was such a nice angel, and he told us that changes were coming soon, so be ready.

The house was dark and quiet as Ned roamed the rooms looking for a safe place to dwell. He liked Anna's large walk-in closet because he could get lost among the hanging clothes. Ned could smell the different scents from the various items. He imagined being a kid again and going too far off places and just having fun. The living could sometimes smell the dead, but it worked both ways. Ned could smell an evil person from far off because they reeked on a spiritual level, and the demon spirit within them could not hide its true smell. He would be safe in here, away from the outside. Ned could also see the large guardian angel that stood guard while Anna slept. Nothing alive or dead would get past such a magnificent being. The angel stared at Ned with a slight curiosity, then he went back to being a statue and guarding his human. Ned had a guardian angel while he was alive. He saw the angel leave the day he died in Tombstone as a young boy. Thinking that the angel was making a path towards heaven for him, he was surprised to find himself still on this earth, but in a spirit's form. He never knew why he couldn't leave, but he knew that somehow the woman asleep in the other room would help him find his way home. She had to. Ned could not go on living like this with no one around to talk to him and help him get through this stuff.

Down she went deeper and deeper down the rabbit hole until everything she knew or thought of was gone. Her mind was blank until she saw him. The young boy, Ned, whom Anna had met in her basement, was standing on Allen Street looking alive and well. He was 9 years old and had just gotten off the stagecoach with his parents. They had left Chicago, Illinois, on March 30, 1903, bound for Tombstone, Arizona. Today was May 5, 1903, and it was a long, dreadful ride. Ned loved it since he was still a young boy. His mother, Beatrice Henry, wanted to stay in the great city of Chicago, but Mr. James Henry had other plans. He had gotten hired by the Town of Tombstone to be the new Utilities Manager and was offered a large sum of money for his trouble. The small family saw many sights on the journey. They had taken a train, river boat, covered wagon, and stagecoach to make it thus far. Ned Henry was a wise boy for his age, and the sight of an actual western town filled his imagination with wonder and awe. He studied every person and animal on the street. He was not in the windy city anymore. They met up with the town Mayor and got situated in a house off Skyline Drive up on the hill.

Looking out of the large picture window, Ned could see the whole town below him. It reminded him of a far-off land where he was the king in his castle, surveying his kingdom. The town looked small from here. Since the mines closed, it was hard to keep things going. The local businesses were barely making it, but there were still the necessities of life to be bought each day. James Henry had a busy schedule, and Beatrice made sure Ned was dressed and fed before going off to work as a baker on 7th Street. She worked at the Bee's Nest restaurant, which served mostly town folk and miners who were still working some of the claims. Hoping to get rich like their former miners before them, they still worked the dirt, hoping to hit a rich vein of silver or gold. The streets looked like a ghost town most of the time, but the Henrys got by and had food and shelter to show for it. On most days, Ned would go down the hill to Mrs. Johnston's house off of Toughnut Street to stay with his friend Milton, who was about his age. They had met a few weeks before and were going to start school soon, just a few more weeks of summer, then another school year to go.

Ned's mother had left already, and he was going out the door until he saw something shimmering on the hill down from his house. "It could be something valuable or some sort of treasure." He thought as he made his way down to the area that he saw the thing that sparked his interest. Carefully making his way through the tall brush and rocks, he came upon what looked like an old cover to some abandoned mine. The bleached wood was old and worn from lying in the Arizona sun for ages. The shaft was just another abandoned mine shaft that littered the countryside since mostly all of the big claims were shut down. Ned pulled the big wooden door to the side as he peered into the blackness below. He began to get scared and started trembling with the large door to his side. Trying to push it away, he only managed to lose his footing and fall down into the dark pit with the large door resting over the hole. His fate was sealed as he fell down the shaft that was over 200 feet deep. He hit the ground with a dull thud, then rolled dead under a large shelf of rock. The mines of Tombstone had taken many a life, and today was no different.

Ned looked up into the darkness and was afraid. He didn't know what had happened because it went so quickly, but now, he stood up and looked around. A sliver of light from above illuminated his crumbled-up little body as the spirit of Ned just stared at himself. Alone and scared, he cried out for help, but no one came. His parents came home that day looking for their son, but never found him. They searched the countryside and sent out work for all who would help locate their lost boy.

The community rallied and looked for one week with no luck. Someone had even pulled back the large wooden door of the mine shaft, but Ned's little body was hidden below under the rock shelf. Ned did not leave the hole for the longest time until one day a fellow named Bartlett came by and got him out of there. Bartlett was dead like Ned, and he took him to his friend's place down the hill; there he met Lily and the gang, who took him in and made him part of their family. Not knowing how much time had passed, Ned looked for his parents, but they had left for Chicago a couple of months after Ned had passed. He often roamed the town looking for them, but never found them. After too much of this, he just decided to stay at Lily's home with her and the others.

Anna awoke in the night, breathing hard and sweating. She felt like she had run a marathon, but then the dream or vision came back to her with all of the feelings of loneliness and dread filling her up. She now knew what became of Ned and how he ended up in Tombstone. Anna felt so sad and weary for the boy as she played back the story in her mind. He must have been in that mine shaft for a very long time without ever seeing his parents again. No human or ghost deserved that kind of experience. He must have gone out of his mind trying to escape that tomb. With all of his friends gone now, he must really be feeling lost and abandoned. With that thought, she drifted off to a dreamless sleep.

November had come and gone, and Christmas loomed in the distance. Anna used to love celebrating Christmas with her family, but this will be the first year without waking up on Christmas morning with John by her side. He had missed a few while in the Navy, but after he got out, he was always there to celebrate with his family. Nobody knows the hardship that being in the military can bring unless they have been down that road. The military sacrifices more than their time; they also lose their lives, families, and their freedom when deployed. It's a hard road to travel, but for the few who have been there, it is worth it. It was early Tuesday morning as Anna looked out of her living room window into the grey, dreary Tombstone landscape. The Dragoon Mountains were barely visible due to the morning mist that hung low over the valley below. The temperature was in the mid-30s as Anna thought about poor little Ned down below. She wanted to help him so bad, but she had no idea how to do that. His old, bleached-out bones were still down at the bottom of that mine shaft unless somehow someone had discovered them already, but that was a slim chance. She would have to enlist his help in this matter.

Liberation

The true value of a human being can be found in the degree to which he has attained liberation from the self.
"Albert Einstein"

She always hated to come down here; the basement would be so cold and damp this time of year. Ned probably didn't care since he was a spirit and they liked it that way, but still, his friends were gone. Anna opened up the old wooden door and searched out the darkness for a sign of Ned. "Ned, are you in here? It's Anna from upstairs, we met a while back. I want to talk to you if you're here." She said nothing in particular. She was feeling a bit strange talking to ghosts like they were real humans, but then again, they were real humans at one time or another. No one answered her request, so she was just about to close the door when she heard a little voice in her head, "Please wait, I'm here, and I want to talk." He said to her just before the lights grew dim. "Ok, Ned met me upstairs in the parlor so we can have a chat," she told him as she shut the door to that cold, freezing tomb of a basement. Then, up the path, she hurried to get out of the cold and drizzle that felt like rain but more of a mist. Inside, it was so warm and cozy as Anna put another log in the wood-burning stove and sat down waiting for Ned. Ned arrived a moment later, standing at the foot of the couch, floating in the air, looking so lost and forlorn. "Hello, Ned, do you guys ever sit down for a while to take the weight off your ghost feet? I've never seen any of you do anything but stare at me and talk to me in my mind. It must really be a drag being dead and so expressionless." She told him as he stared at her

"Anna, we don't sit; we just float here like I'm doing, trying to save up our energy, or else we will just fade from your view. We are not even what you see in front of you; it's just the last thing we remember about our former selves, so it's comforting to us to project this to you and each other. Please tell me you have a plan. Without my friends, I'm not sure I can stay here much longer." He told her as he hovered over the coffee table. Sensing his urgency, she knew that time was short for him, so she told him her plan. "Ned, I know what happened to you and why you're still in Tombstone when you should be gone. You fell down that mineshaft and were never found. Your mom and dad left, never knowing what happened to you. If you help me locate the mineshaft, I can get your body removed and buried in the cemetery so you can rest in peace. That's what happened to Lily; now she's home with her parents. Can you help me?" He took it in for a moment, then spoke: "I can help you do that; it's not far from here. If we go to my old house, I can retrace my steps to the mineshaft; it's been so long since I've been up there." Anna told him, "Meet me at the house on the hill, and I will help you. Give me a few minutes to get there." Getting dressed in warm clothing, Anna drove to Skyline Drive, where Ned had once lived. The home he had lived in was said to be haunted by a woman and her daughter who had been murdered one night. This happened shortly after Ned disappeared, and they were standing on the porch when Anna drove up.

It was startling to see two ghosts waiting for her when she got there. They didn't know she could see them, so she stepped on the porch and asked them who they were and why they were waiting out there. Not knowing that any human could see them, the two vanished into thin air. "That seems to happen a lot these days," Anna said to herself. Ned arrived a moment later and asked her, "What did you do to scare the Olsen family off so quickly?" She answered, "I only asked them what they were doing on the porch." That was enough to scare the ghosts who were scaring everyone else out of their house. "Never mind, follow me. I see the mineshaft down the hill to the right." He told her. Anna couldn't see anything but desert brush and wild cactus. Getting closer, Ned told her to be careful since the wooden door was really old now and would not hold the weight. She threw a rock at the door, and it made a hollow sound. Carefully pulling back the door, Anna shone the powerful light into the darkness. It was a deep shaft, and little Ned didn't have a chance when he tumbled down this hole. A foul smell rose from the darkness of death and decay from a forgotten era. "Ned, go down and see if you're still at the bottom. I have to know you're still there to be able to get you buried at the town cemetery." She said to him.

Not wanting to go down to that dreadful place where he lost his life and all of his hope in this world.

"It's alright, Ned, I'm up here waiting for you. You won't be there long, and I won't leave you here alone like before. Just do this quickly and come back to me, ok?" she told him as he glanced down the dark shaft. He just went down in a flash as Anna watched him disappear.

Down at the bottom, it must have been about two hundred feet down, Ned saw the remains of his little body in a pile of dust with the same clothes he had on when he tumbled to his death long ago. He felt the sadness return for just a second when he thought about how he was down here for a long time until Bartlett came by and saved him. The thought of Bartlett and Anna gave him hope, so he dashed out of there as fast as light to the top. He said to Anna, "Yes, Anna, I'm still down there, just a pile of bones and old clothes. It doesn't bother me anymore. I'm ready to leave this place now." Anna said, "Slow down there, partner. We still have to get the city to pull you out of there and bury you properly. No one should be left down there as long as you have. I will do that for you; in the meantime, you just need to chill out in your basement for a few days. Can you do that?"

"Could I stay upstairs with you? I will be quiet and out of sight. I just don't want to be alone. I've been seeing Cowboy around getting closer to your house night after night. I think he's going to try something soon. Bartlett is coming by in a few days to meet you. He has some good news for you to hear." Ned told her as they went back to the old house. Looking at Ned, Anna told him, "That will be fine if you hang around upstairs with me for a while. I could use some company."

Anna did not want to go to the city and report that she had found a pile of children's bones at the bottom of a mine shaft. It had been a couple of days, and Ned was growing antsy, floating around the house, being so morose about his fate. Anna knew people in town who could help her in this area. Her first choice was an old hermit named Bruce who lived off Middlemarch Road outside of the town limits. She and John had known Bruce for years; he was a walking Wikipedia when it came to Tombstone History. He had a couple of blogs online and mostly chatted about mining and Tombstone history. She would talk to him and tell him a distorted form of truth about Ned and his remains. Bruce could then say he found the bones while prospecting the area. It all sounded so easy, but in life, most things aren't that simple.

The following day, Anna met with Bruce outside the Bird Cage theatre in town. She pointed out the area that Ned had fallen into, which was only about 300 yards from where they stood. Bruce knew that she and John had some abilities to commune with the dead; he just didn't know how much. She told him about the dream and how this kid, Ned, had fallen down a mineshaft in 1903. It all sounded so weird, but Bruce loved it like that. This wasn't tourist season in Tombstone, so the streets were mostly bare today. They both headed up towards the mine shaft with Bruce carrying a large backpack. When they got to the rim of the dark hole, Bruce took out a portable camera on a long cord connected to his laptop. The cord was over 300 feet long, so it should work. He dropped the small camera slowly down the shaft while the laptop recorded it all on a zip drive. They were at approximately 220 feet when they came to the bottom of the mineshaft. Panning the camera in a circular motion, a small pile of human remains was resting in a corner about 10 feet away. "The boy must have fallen and then rolled under that rock formation about 10 feet away. Back in 1903, it would have been impossible to see him unless they went down the mine shaft. They wouldn't have done that since there are about 35 shafts within a 1000-foot radius of where we are. I'll get with the City Marshals department. and see if they can send a rescue crew down there to retrieve the body, I would do it, but it's a crime scene right now, sorry." He told Anna. They walked back to their vehicles; Anna told Bruce, " Thank you, " and then they both went home. He would keep her notified of any new progress.

At home, Ned was pacing back and forth when Anna got there. She told him "Ned if you don't quit doing that, I'm going have you exercised from this house by a catholic priest." Not really being serious, but Ned was a very serious ghost, and he took it all to heart. "Are you a magician, and what is meant by calling for this catholic priest?" he asked. She now realized she was dealing with a child spirit and felt bad telling him "I'm sorry I said that it's just that you have to slow down and relax. It will work out in good time and you will soon be united with your family. That's what you really want right?" he replied "More than anything in the world or universe I want to be with my family and friends. I miss them all so much. I don't know how long I've been here, but things are different now, and the world is a lot faster than I remember. I feel a great sadness upon us now, and it is pushing me down in a heavy way. I used to feel safe down below in my dark room with my friends, but they are all gone, and I just want to leave." Anna knew how he felt; her world had changed so much since John had left. Who could have imagined that one person could mean so much to another? "You should be going home soon, Ned. Just hang in there." She told him as he faded into the nothing.

Bruce had news the next morning that the Marshals had pulled up Ned's little bones and taken him to the county medical examiner. It won't be long, and Ned will be laid to rest in the cemetery down the street. Bruce told her that they found an old silver bracelet around his wrist that had the words "Ned Henry" engraved into it. It won't be long for them to do a name search and turn up his disappearance from the area in 1903. That's good news for Ned because it will expedite his burial and departure from this world. A week later, after the medical examiner figured it all out, Ned's remains were buried in the Tombstone cemetery on Allen Street. Anna was there for the modest ceremony as Ned's small casket was lowered into the earth. She could see him standing by a pine tree with a smile on his face, watching the event unfold. They managed to look into each other's eyes as Ned said the words "Thank you, Anna, and goodbye" as he slowly faded away from this earth for the last time. With another great sadness in her heart, she felt that even the dead people were too much to bear when they left. Somehow, she knew that her task was complete in this town, even though the much-awaited arrival of Bartlett was still looming. Anna would have to do some traveling after the new year to get away and see her family in California.

It was Christmas day in Tombstone, and a light feathering of snow blanketed the cold ground outside. Elvis lay at Anna's feet as the fire burned slowly in the wood stove. Some of the kids would be here in about an hour for the weekend, then the house would be empty once more. Her oldest daughter and her husband arrived with the two girls in tow. They exchanged presents and asked how she was doing. Anna was fine, just a little tired from the entire psychic occurrences over these past few months. Nobody would have believed her anyway, since the "gift" seemed to have passed by her oldest daughter and other children. Anna sat watching her granddaughter playing with her toys and wondered if she would be the one who was able to see and hear things not of this world. Time will tell. They stayed a couple of days, and all was well. There were no visitations from the other side, or bumps in the night, not even a glimpse of Cowboy lurking outside.

Just then the phone rand and she answered it "Hello Anna this s Marty Burrows Johns cousin sorry I haven't been InTouch since Angela and I have been up in Prescott taking care of some family business, I hope you are doing well down there and we miss you terribly, I hope you are in good spirits," Anna told him "Thank you Marty john has always spoken highly of you and has loved you very dearly, enjoy your stay in Prescott and give Angela my love,"

The Traveler

*"I travel not to go anywhere, but to go. I travel for travel's sake. The
great affair is to move."*
Robert Louis Stevenson

New Year's Eve came and went, and with it came the big build-up
for another year of hope and life yet lived. Anna spent it at the American
Legion on Allen Street with some old friends. It was a long tradition for
John and her as the minutes ticked down to seconds, and they would
kiss each other like young high school sweethearts, long and loving,
while they just felt great about another year together. This time was
different as the ball slowly dropped and all of the Legionaries waited
with anticipation. Anna wished she were somewhere else. Too late, the
time had come with all of the celebration and noise that accompanied a
great New Year's Eve party. This was the first time since John was in
the Navy that they weren't together on New Year's Eve. But she did
have hope, being a Christian, she always knew that heaven waited after
this life, but the events of the past year just solidified it all into faith that
all is well with the world and with her heart. She was getting tired and
told everyone goodbye as she walked the short half mile home. Anna
only had one shot of tequila all night. Outside, the sky was a beautiful
sight as all of the stars shone just for her on her path home. Not wanting
to walk by the Buford house due to her long-held suspicion that it was
haunted was now a reality. She knew that something lurked in that house
at night and stirred in the early morning hours, looking for a living soul

to scare. She wasn't afraid anymore as she saw the dark attic with only one dim light shining, giving it an eerie glow. Turning back toward the road, she saw Cowboy at the top of the hill grinning like a dead Jack o' Lantern in the pale moonlight. She let out a laugh as his eyes shone with a fiery red from her amusement. Knowing that her guardian angel was present, she ran up to him so fast he barely had time to vanish into the night. He must have still been near because she heard his wicked voice in her head. "Don't think that little prank scared me, Missy. I see all of your tenants are gone except that vagrant Bartlett. If and when he ever comes back, tell him I'm waiting. Ha Ha-ha." Then he was gone.

She thought to herself while walking home, "So he knows they all have left, and Bartlett is the only one left, or their little ghost family. I guess he watches my place constantly; he must be obsessed with my spirit friends. That is one sick demon spirit." She got home with no incident and made a cup of hot cocoa while Elvis watched her intently. A moment later, he was staring down the hall, growling at some unseen entity. Anna felt the air shift in the room, and she knew someone or something was coming down the darkened hallway. "I know you're there, so come on out and show yourself." She told the unseen guest. A form of a man began to materialize, walking toward her. He was just a wispy white ghostly form until he stopped in front of her and Elvis and began to take form. Anna didn't have that hair standing up on the back of her neck, so she knew the visitor was not there to harm her. She also knew that her angel was close by and no harm would come to her. The figure began to form as a man, dressed in late 1800's western garments.

He looked like a young man of about 23 or 24 years old, wearing a large cowboy hat and a long-sleeved button-down shirt. He had on an old, worn pair of chaps and a six-shooter tied to his side. Most ghosts didn't have much for feet since they sort of just got all wispy and fuzzy down there, but the man had on a pair of worn cowboy boots.

As if in a trance, Anna just stared at the stranger in her living room. The apparition then spoke to her, saying, "Ma'am, I don't mind you looking at me, but you look like you've seen a ghost. Let me introduce myself to you. My name is Bartlett, and all of my friends spoke highly of you before they all took off yonder to those pearly gates. Rest assured, I do not want that from you. I'm here on a mission, and I won't stop till it's over." Snapping out of her gaze, Anna told him, "I'm sorry, Bartlett, it's been a long, strange year, and you're the first thing I see on the New Year, besides that evil Cowboy I just saw. Glad to finally meet you, sir." Upon hearing the Cowboys' name mentioned, Bartlett got a stern look on his face and asked her, "When and where did you see that scoundrel, Ma'am?" She said, "Just down the hill about 20 minutes ago. He was waiting for me to come by, and he said to tell you he would be waiting. He was extremely at ease around my angel and me, so I think he is planning something soon." Bartlett looked over Anna's shoulder at the large guardian angel standing in the corner. That was enough to scare any creature of the night, but Cowboy wasn't afraid too much. Bartlett was thinking of why Cowboy was causing so much grief; he must want to take Bartlett down to his home called hell and get him acquainted with his devil friend. He also missed the boat on getting four friends to go. He must be steaming inside. Bartlett has known Cowboy for as long as he has been dead, way back when he met Swan down in Bisbee. He has wanted to send him back to hell since then.

"I have a plan that will most likely involve you and that large heavenly brute behind you. It will be difficult since Cowboy is a cautious fellow. He only does things that will help his game. He has been in league with the devil for over 500 years, and his main goal as a human was to torture and kill as many people as he could find. He hasn't changed much since the old days." Bartlett told Anna while she listened with a sense of wonderment and interest. She had never met a ghost or person with so much determination to rid the world of something so evil. She was glad he was on her side; had Cowboy been able to turn Bartlett to the dark side, then things would have been really bad around here. Suddenly becoming very tired, she was almost dozing in front of Bartlett, so she was going to have to call it a night. "Tell me, Mr. Bartlett, is that your first or last name?" she asked him. "No, Ma'am, that's not even my real name; they've been calling me that for so long as I can remember, since I love to eat those Bartlett pears. My real name is Lester Higgins, but I never did like being called that, so you can just call me Bartlett, and we will be alright. Get some sleep now, and I have to do some reconnoitering down by that Boot Hill." And just like that, he vanished into the night, leaving nothing but the smell of old leather, horses, and maybe the smell of pears. Anna smiled as he let his thoughts wander about how each one of the dearly departed had some kind of smell associated with them. I guess they just are attached to it like that, she thought as she got up and went to bed. Elvis followed behind wagging his tail as he did when he was happy.

Anna was asleep before her head hit the pillow; she fell into a deep dream that started down by the Mexican border on a ranch called the Square D. Bartlett was trying to break a wild painted horse that was just not having any of that. He was an experienced cowhand at the age of 24 and was a master in roping, cow punching, and also a great shot with a rifle or pistol. He was raised to fear the Lord and be nice to people whenever possible. With a name like Lester Higgins, he knew that life was going to be rough, so at the age of 13, his best friend Tommy Landers told him one day, "Damn Lester, you eat more pears than a Billy goat, you love those Bartlett ones, I'm calling you that from now on." And so, the name stuck, and he became just plain old Bartlett, except by his folks, who were the only ones who called him Lester. He was finishing up rope breaking the paint when the foreman told him to ride down by the San Pedro and round up whatever cattle he could find. The water was good down there, and there was lots of shade for the cattle to graze under. The problem was its close proximity to Mexico, only about 2 miles.

Bartlett rode down south to the point in the river where the foreman said the cattle would be. It was almost high noon, and the weather in late August was a bit warm. Bartlett found all of the stock after about 20 minutes and started them back to the ranch; there were 8 steers total until one decided to break off to the east in the nearby canyons. Bartlett left the other steers by the river and took after the wild renegade steer.

He almost had him deep in the rough hills when a bunch of the local gang called the Cowboys rode out in front of him with their guns raised to his head. "Off the horse, slick and drop that six-shooter from your holster slowly, or I will gut shoot you as you sit, then I will shoot your horse," said the meanest looking of the bunch. Bartlett could get two, maybe three of them, but not six; that was too many. Maybe they will just rob him and let him go. Looking past the group of thugs, Bartlett could see some of the Square D cattle getting their brands altered for sale in Mexico. Just then, he knew he wasn't getting out of here alive, so he drew quickly and got the leader in the chest, then he fired off and winged the guy next to him. A second later, they all began to let loose as Bartlett felt the slugs enter his chest, arm, and neck. He knew he was a goner as the sky grew dark and he fell with a thud onto the sandy wash.

He could see the leader of the gang dead beside him, and the other guy was crying like a baby. That was all he saw on this earth as his eyes glazed over, and all sight was extinguished. He died of his wounds quickly and found himself looking strangely at his own dead body below him. Waiting to go to the pearly gates, he looked over at the dead Cowboy as his soul stepped out of his body, and a host of dark evil demons grabbed him and pulled him into hell as he screamed the whole time. Not wanting to be the next one, he started walking out of there and found himself in Bisbee, wondering what had happened. A few months later, he came upon Swan standing on a corner in Brewery Gulch. They traveled together for a while until Swan told him about the woman he saw as he lay dying in Tombstone. He wanted to at least pay her a visit for being with him when he took his last breath. They arrived in Tombstone in the evening, and Swan took Bartlett to her residence. He couldn't find her there, so they followed her husband to the boarding room she was staying in because of her illness. Upon walking into the room, Oly was talking to her husband James, then she turned and looked at the two spirits as they stood behind him. "What are you guys doing here? I remember you, Swan, from that night in the alley. How come I can see you now even though you're dead?" she asked the strangers. Swan replied "Oly you can see us because you are on your last few moments in this world. Say goodbye to your husband because you're not coming back."

After hearing what Swan had said, Oly knew in her heart of hearts that this would be the end. There would be no more living on this planet. Her days were numbered. Oly knew he was right; she could feel her life force leaving her body even as they spoke. She said her goodbyes to James and watched the room go from light to dark, then black. She thought she had gone down to Hades until Swan yelled "Oly we are over here come join us." He was standing by the door wanting to leave. Looking back at her grieving husband, Oly left the room and her life behind. They walked the streets and back streets of Tombstone looking for a safe place to go. Cowboy still roamed the town with his band of ghouls, looking for unsuspecting spirits to join his cause against the powers of goodness. They were walking down 4th Street when they saw Lily playing outside her home. Oly knew her from when she used to come by the store to talk and play with Sarah. Oly spoke up to her "Hello

Lily, do you remember me Oly? When would you come to the sewing store and visit us? What are you doing out here?" She seemed startled at first because nobody ever talked to her after she fell into the cistern that night. She thought her parents were mad at her since they left town without her. Lily said, "I remember you, Oly, and your girl, Sarah. How come you can see me and talk to me? Nobody does anymore."

"Well, Lily, we have all died, and we no longer have our bodies; we just think we do. I can see you, and you can see me. These are my friends, Mr. E.G. Swan and Mr. Bartlett. They are good people, and we were wondering if you would like us to live with you for a while? We could stay in the root cellar so we don't disturb anyone." Lily seemed really excited to have someone to talk to. Her parents were gone, and the old house was empty now, so she invited them in. Before Bartlett went inside, he looked west to Boot Hill and could see the dark shape of Cowboy watching them as they went inside. So much for being nonchalant, he thought as they all went into their new home.

Elvis was having a bad dream and stirring in his sleep. Anna woke up suddenly from the noise, then looked at the clock on the end table. It read 3:21. Anna knew this was when the firemen came upon the scene of John's wreck, and he had just passed on. Knowing now that the dream she just had was not really a dream but more like watching the past being shown before her, yes. Being incapable of doing anything but watch, she now knew why Bartlett didn't want to go. He was killed away from Tombstone in a lonely canyon 20 miles south of here. His body was most likely eaten by scavengers, and he was left to roam the land with a restless spirit. He was part of the family of ghosts that lived beneath her, but also, he was a free-roaming spirit who made his own rules and didn't stay in one place too long. She could see it all so clearly; they were all friends living here, keeping an eye on each other and just staying away from Cowboy and his gang. She also knew that Bartlett wasn't here for her to help him; he was here to get rid of Cowboy once and for all. He had alluded to her that he would need her help soon to rid this town of that monster. She hoped he would tell her his plans soon, since she had a trip planned to go see the ocean and her family in Santa Cruz, California. She and John would go there with the kids sometimes and stay at a little motel a block from the boardwalk. They would ride those carny rides and try to win prizes from the games. Anna could see the time she was on the merry-go-round with one of the kids, and she grabbed the brass ring from the pole as she went around. John thought that was so cool of her, so they kept it after all these years. Looking over at a hook on the wall was the brass ring she had grabbed long ago.

She would do this last thing for Bartlett, then take a little break from all of this madness. Outside, the wind blew as Elvis made snoring noises at the foot of her bed. How lucky she was to have a guard dog and a guardian angel protecting her right now. Smiling about that, she slipped off to sleep. Thinking as she was dozing, how this was going to be a great year.

Retribution

"Though the mills of God grind slowly, yet they grind exceedingly small: Though with patience He stands waiting, with exactness grinds He all."

Henry Wadsworth Longfellow

It had been three days, and still no word from Bartlett. Anna had scheduled her trip on the 7th of January, so time was wasting. She would take this time before her trip to get everything in order at the house. She planned to be gone for a month, so Elvis would stay at a friend's house on 2nd street, about a block from here. They had chickens and ducks for him to chase around so he wouldn't get bored. The moon will be full tonight, so that will add to the craziness that has persisted for these last months. Putting on her jacket, Anna went outside to the garden to water all of the plants. It was midmorning, and the temperature was heating up a little bit. All of her flowers were gone until spring, and the Mesquite trees were looking bare without any leaves. Still, she had to give them a drink or two now and then. Looking over to Boot Hill, Anna could see visitors milling about, reading the grave markers in the morning light. If only they knew what she knew about that place, they wouldn't be there for long. She and John had been over to Boot Hill about a year ago before all of this went down, and even then, she felt a bit creepy not knowing that the presence of Cowboy was permeating from the ground and surrounding graves. They didn't stay long because of some unseen force or entity that caused her to feel that way, so she has never gone back.

Sitting on a bench in the shade was Bartlett, who was watching her as she watered. Surprised upon seeing his appearance in her garden, she asked him if there was any good news yet. He replied, "Ma'am, I can only surmise that tonight would be an excellent night to perform our disappearing act on old Cowboy. He will be especially busy tonight, being it's a full moon and all. We can catch him off guard at the back of Boot Hill around midnight tonight. My sources say he goes there each night at that time to meditate on doing evil, if that's even possible? Now I know what you're thinking: how will he not see the big guy behind you as we just walk in and send him straight to hell? I have a plan, and we will do this tonight so you won't have to ever see that no-good scoundrel again." She thought about what he said and told him, "I think you have it all figured out, I will see you tonight upstairs in the parlor around 10; 00 or so." And with that said, Bartlett faded into the morning light just a wispy, smoky thing that got less and less noticeable until he was no more. Shutting off the hose and calling Elvis, she headed inside to prepare for the final battle with Cowboy and whoever he might bring along. How she will ever hide the angel at her side was beyond her thinking right now. Bartlett will have a plan; he seems to be well informed on this type of thing.

Inside, she sat in the parlor and opened up her bible; it immediately opened on Ephesians 6:11, "Put on the whole armor of God, that ye may be able to stand against the wiles of the Devil. For we wrestle not against flesh and blood, but against principalities, against powers, against the rulers of the darkness of this world, against spiritual wickedness in high places." Anna was excited by the scriptures that she had just read. God was telling her to be prayed up and wear the armor of God and the shield of faith, which will protect her from the evil one. She knew that Bartlett had a plan to hide the sight of herself and her angel until it would be too late. She would just have to have faith that this will work. There was still much to be done around here. This was a large old house that needed maintenance and care. She could only do so much until she had to call the local handyman for help. She called Marty Borrows, who was the best in town; he also happened to be John's cousin from his mother's side of the family. He said he could be right over.

Marty Borrows had been living in Tombstone for as long as he could remember. His father lived here most of his life until he joined the Navy. His mother was also raised in the area. And when they passed on, he naturally inherited their old home on some acreage of Middlemarch Road. He spent many days and nights fixing up the old homestead. After he finished the project, he found out that he was a very good handyman and repair person, so he started his own business. Word gets around in a small town like Tombstone, and before he knew it, he had more work than time. He hired some help from the high school and was able to keep the schedule rolling and help out the community. The only problem was the dreams he had every night. He would wake up in the morning and feel like he hadn't slept. The work he did during the day was what kept him normal to a degree.

Marty showed up at Anna's door at about 4:30 that afternoon. She gave him a big hug, then showed him the area along the roof fascia that needed repair and painting. He asked, "How have you been getting along, Anna, these days without John? I sure do miss him a lot. I miss him so much, boy, did we have some times together growing up, and it's been great since you two moved to Tombstone." Anna felt blessed that Marty liked John so much. He would help him on projects if he couldn't get help elsewhere. They were close cousins, and Anna knew that it tore Marty up to lose John. "Thank you for asking, Marty. I'm doing ok and keeping busy. I have good and bad days, but I just keep going until it gets better again. I know how close John was to you, and we always thought highly of you, even though the years have separated you a lot. I'll be gone for a while on the 7th, so you can work on the house after I leave." She told him. He left, and Anna had some time to kill before Bartlett returned. She was a little apprehensive about going against Cowboy on his turf, and if they failed, then Cowboy would be relentless in trying to destroy her. This had to work or else. After some chores and dinner, Anna fell asleep watching television as she fell into a restless dream.

In her dream, she was at the cemetery with Bartlett, and they were ready to confront Cowboy. The full moon peaked through the clouds as it illuminated Boot Hill and all of the graves. Cowboy noticed them from across the cemetery and was coming at them fast while he laughed an evil laugh with his red eyes glowing and his grin lit up by the light of the moon. He looked like an evil pumpkin ready to devour them. As he got closer, Bartlett yelled "Now" to the guardian angel that was nearby. But he didn't show himself, and Cowboy got closer while the graves started to open and the undead climbed out. Anna tried to run, but something was grabbing her leg as she looked down to see a bony hand clasped tight on her foot. Fear and anxiety held her firmly in that spot as Cowboy was inches from her face, laughing hysterically and reaching for her.

"That was some dream, Ma'am. You can wake up and feel comfort in knowing you are protected," Bartlett told her as she shook off the nightmare. Anna said, "He wasn't there, I didn't see him, and my guardian angel was gone. I was alone with you, and Cowboy had me." Bartlett reassured her, "He's right behind you, and he is a big one. I think he knows what we are up to tonight, so let's go over it and get it right the first time." The two of them talked and talked until all of the details were worked out and each had their own job to do. "Let's go now, Ma'am, so we can get the jump on those vermin," Bartlett said as they made their way to Boot Hill.

If the plan was to work, then they had to get in their places before midnight. Bartlett knew of a gardener's shed close to where Cowboy would be tonight. Anna just had to get there and wait until midnight without detection by Cowboy or his crew. Even though she knew that the angel was with her and Bartlett was around, she still felt alone. The full moon broke through the clouds as she climbed over the fence that led to the graveyard. This was the scariest thing she had ever done, and the thought of seeing Cowboy out here was terrifying. She could hear

Bartlett in her head, "Ma'am, you're doing fine, just a few steps more, and you and your angel can hide out in that shed until I confront Cowboy, then you know the rest. It was an old wooden shed that smelled like rodents and wet dog. Anna could imagine rattlesnakes and black widows crawling all over her. "Keep it together, girl," she told herself. She just breathed slowly and listened for Bartlett to call her out.

Anna was barely awake when she heard voices outside by the shed. Cowboy was there with some of his minions as he confronted Bartlett. "What is a slimy, sniveling man-boy doing in my graveyard tonight? Answer me, Barty Boy, before I send you to Hell in a hand basket." I'm here to join your gang, Cowboy. All of my friends are gone, and I want to raise hell and torment the living. How about it? Can I join?" he asked Cowboy, trying to sound convincing. In his mind, Bartlett was playing out the scene before him like a Hollywood movie. He just had to find the right time to finish the job. Cowboy wasn't stupid, and he always felt that there was a trap even if there wasn't. He looked around and walked behind Bartlett, staring into the desert, looking for a trap. Feeling at ease, he said, "Why yes, Barty Boy, you can join us, but you have to pass a little initiation if you want to be one of us. First things first, you have to go down to that house you were living in, and when that woman goes to bed, you just start a little fire and burn it all down. Can you do that? If so, then what are you waiting for?" Anna could hear the conversation between the two of them, and she was filled with rage when Cowboy told him to burn down her house with her in it. She knew

Bartlett was working up to the final showdown, but how that would happen was a mystery.

They spoke back and forth about the duties of working for Cowboy and how Bartlett would be on the last rung when it came to being a servant of the Devil. When Bartlett agreed on the terms, he told Cowboy, "Alright, Cowboy, you have my word that I will be your humble evil servant. Also, I will leave now and go burn down the widow woman's house with her, so you can be there when she passes and pull her down to hell. Do we have a deal?" Cowboy's eyes glowed so bright red that Boot Hill was basking in a red ember from his hate. "We have a deal, Barty, so let's shake on it, then you get to work for me forever, ha ha ha," he told him as he reached for Bartlett's hand. Bartlett knew that he had to shake his hand because that was the only time that Cowboy could not escape. He couldn't vanish when he saw the angel since the spirit rules clearly state that if one entity has a grip on the other entity, then they are bound on earth until they release their grip. Cowboy grabbed Bartlett's hand to hold him down while his boys worked him over. Bartlett knew this might happen, but he had to chance it. When the two enemies grabbed each other's hands, Bartlett let out a yell to Anna, "Now, Anna, now is the time."

So many things happened in that moment, when Bartlett yelled to Anna, it made Cowboy turn his head to look at the wood shed; the door flew open as Anna jumped out with her guardian angel behind her, towering over the scene below. Cowboy was trying to struggle and get loose from the grip Bartlett had on him, but it was not happening. The angel of God reached out and grabbed Cowboy and all who were around him in a second, then sent them screaming to hell. It all happened so quickly, and Anna was able to see her angel doing the Lord's work for just an instant. He was bathed in bright light from above, and the roar of heavenly trumpets filled the air as those lost souls were cast out of this world and into the eternal fire and damnation that awaited them. A second later, it was over, and the smell of sulfur hung in the air. Anna was amazed and astonished at how fast it all went down, then nothing but quiet and a full moon. "Let's get out of here, Bartlett. We did our job. Thank you for all of your help." She told him as she turned to see his face. A bright light from above surrounded Bartlett as he stood there smiling and happy. "I'm not going to make it back to the house tonight, Anna; you have been so kind and wonderful to us all. I will see you again, I know it," as he slowly faded away from this world into the next. Like a dream, it was over so fast, and Bartlett was gone. Boot Hill didn't seem so terrifying with Cowboy gone. Still, it wasn't her favorite place, so she headed home to put Elvis to bed. Walking back to the house, Anna thought of all that had happened and what had just transpired before her eyes. She was one of the few in history who had witnessed the ultimate power of God and the eternal struggle of good over evil. It had taken a lot out of her, and she just wanted to rest. Tomorrow is another day unless she dies tonight, and right now, she really doesn't care either way.

Her house was a welcome sight as Elvis greeted her at the door. He seemed a bit agitated and was acting weird. He didn't want to go into the bedroom. "That's strange." She thought that since he loved to sleep at the foot of her bed. Anna walked into the dark room and turned on a light on the end table. She immediately smelled a pungent odor of garden flowers filling the room. Turning around, she was surprised and frightened to see a ghostly shape hovering in the corner of her closet. "What are you doing here? Leave now, this is God's house, and you are not welcome here." She told the apparition as it slowly materialized before her eyes. It was a beautiful woman of about 28 years of age wearing expensive clothing from the late 1800s. She looked elegant and well-mannered in dress and attitude. She had on a flowing dress with a matching hat. "I am not here to hurt you, Anna. My name is Lea, and I have just stopped by as a favor to Bartlett, my good friend. I know he has passed to the other side, and he asked me to visit you in the event he did not return this evening. We were friends from long ago, and I used to travel with him on his trips out of Tombstone. He never really felt like he belonged here; he just stayed around for the rest of us. I will miss him dearly. What I came by to tell you, Anna, is that now that your basement is empty, there is some talk about town for some new tenants. I just came by to let you know that what you thought was over on the whole helping the afterlife is really just beginning.

I hear them every day talking on Allen St about making it home or just getting out of here. Your name comes up a lot these days, and I'm so proud to have met you. If you want my opinion about this whole ordeal, it would be for you to find another place to reside in another state that is not so close to Tombstone. You still have time to get your affairs in order and perhaps sell this old place. It's just food for thought, my dear. Happy trails and may God bless whatever road you take." She slowly faded into the night, just another visitor from the other side. Anna took it all to heart; she was feeling different about this town and could probably leave it all in her rearview mirror someday. Maybe the time had come to look at her options.

Seclusion

"If you don't know where you're going, any road will take you there."
Lewis Carroll

It was mid-June, and the boardwalk was packed with locals and tourists alike. Anna sat on her porch at her newly rented home on Cliff Drive in Santa Cruz, California. She never wanted to move back here, but the events that drove her here were like an open wound that tried to heal itself but would just start bleeding on the next day. Time heals all things, so she would try that approach. Anna could see the beach and the surf rolling in as it pounded the shore. The San Lorenzo River flowed to the sea in front of her two-bedroom, one-bath home. Everything worked out great for her in selling her house and moving to Santa Cruz. She loved this town and the way it made her feel.

That was a whole other life ago, and now she could find some peace and tranquility for herself. Looking at the beach before her seemed like a picture in a gallery, sort of too good to be true. She had always loved it here, but Arizona had been her home for almost 20 years. Elvis was asleep on the porch, dreaming whatever dogs dream when life is good. Maybe she would go down to the boardwalk in a little while, just to check it out. A day like this had to be enjoyed. The sun was slowly creeping its way west for another gorgeous sunset. She never grew tired of seeing those, no matter what city she was in. It was something she picked up from John, since he always stopped what he was doing to enjoy the moment. He taught her a lot, and she returned the favor. Now, looking back, she could see the big picture and the reason for a lot of what had happened. Time does heal all things.

Anna got up and told Elvis to come inside the house. He walked through the front door and stopped in his tracks. Staring ahead into the small living room without moving, he was fixated on the couch. Just then, the room was filled with the scent of Gardenias in bloom, and there before Anna was Lea sitting on her sofa, smiling and looking so sophisticated in her old-world charm. Anna was a little put off seeing Lea so casually sitting on her sofa, looking so great, even if she was a ghost. Anna asked her, "Lea, I didn't expect to see you again. I thought Tombstone was your favorite haunt. What brings you to my home, and how did you find me?" Lea smiled sadly. "Anna, my dear, it wasn't hard to find you. I just went through your address book before you left town. I'm sorry to be here, but it's for a good reason."

This was too much to take in as Anna sat across from Lea, staring at her like she had seen a ghost. She asked her, "Lea, tell me why you're here. I thought I had left all of that back in Tombstone. I'm waiting for an answer, please." Lea was never one to be hurried by anyone, much less this living soul across from her, but she did love Anna, so she told her what was coming for her. "Anna, my love, I thought you and Bartlett had rid Tombstone of the evilest creature in existence, and by the way, Cowboy was dragged to Hell, would seem the problem was solved. But like all things, it only got worse. The big guy down below was so upset that he sent a posse of Hell's worst to bring you to him by all means possible. I'm sorry to break it to you, but the devil put a bounty on your soul, and I think even Johnny Ringo is trying to find you. If I could find you, they can also, so tread lightly in Santa Cruz and stay away from the boardwalk at night. They say that's when they all come out. I have to run, dear, but I will check on you soon." With that said, Lea vanished from sight, leaving the faint smell of Gardenias in the air.

Anna was sort of in a daze until Elvis barked at a cat in the front yard. Snapping out of it, she was trying to make sense of all of that trending news. Her thoughts went back to Tombstone and how she could never go back there again. She was sad, but she vowed to start a new life, and Santa Cruz would probably not be her last home. Out her front windows, the waves were rolling in on the shore as seagulls flew and children played on the waterside. Such a calming view, but behind all of that lurked a world so dark the sun can never shine on it. She thought it was done, but now she went into a new mindset as the thought of Hell's posse looking for little ole Anna. It was almost quite comical except that she knew how things were. It would be time to close that door forever and let the dark live in the dark, and the light live in the light.

The End